# Advance Praise Jagged Edge:

"McCullough did it again with Jagged Edge! Hooked after reading the first novel in the On Edge of Now series, the new sequel may be my favorite, so far. Coupled with his ability to weave an intriguing, engaging plot, McCullough created another group of memorable characters I'll remember long after turning the final page. Great read... can't wait to find out what peril awaits the Travelers!"

—DENTON CRAIG

"Book V is full of action, and exciting plot twists and turns! McCullough's vivid imagination balances fine attention to detail as the characters are once more placed in extraordinary circumstances, but equipped with the tools to succeed. With logical explanations, the reader is permitted to suspend disbelief, and the author delivers a story on multiple levels, always with the underlying message of hope!"

—ROBERT CLARK

"Once again, McCullough masterfully moves our heroes into another version of Earth with suspense, and surprising twists and turns in the plot—a real page turner! As with each book in the series, I look forward to McCullough's weaving the Travelers into completely new environments while retaining the essence of the underlying theme. I can hardly wait for the final book! It isn't surprising McCullough's books are receiving award after award!"

—ARIANA BRACKENBURY

"Jagged Edge is just that—the book keeps you on the jagged edge for the whole story. Brian transports you into the Traveler's current world, changing how he tells the story, and it's totally different from the first four books. Another book of Brian's I couldn't put down, I'm happy I could read this story on the long weekend so I wouldn't be pulled away for something silly—like work.

Thank you for this experience, Brian!!"

—SHANE POTTS


"I've been fortunate to be a test reader for each of Brian's books—it's not the same old, same old. Jagged Edge will take you on a wonderful adventure, and it's an adventure you don't want to miss! What really gets me is McCullough is an award-winning author—not even a year since he published his first book!

—BARRETT E. MCKINNON, AUTHOR
the Manufactured Messiah


"First, I'm not a science fiction reader—but, after a friend recommended McCullough's books, I'm hooked! I read each book through Book V (she loaned me her test-reader copy), and I find myself looking forward to the Book VI launch date. Even though I know it will be the end of the series, I'm hoping McCullough keeps writing—what a talent!

—L.A. Ilsley

BOOKS BY BRIAN MCCULLOUGH

*On the Edge of Now: Book I—The Departure*

*On the Edge of Now: Book II—No Man's Land*

*On the Edge of Now: Book III—Redemption*

*On the Edge of Now: Book IV—Fulcrum*

# ON THE EDGE OF NOW

# ON THE EDGE OF NOW

Brian McCullough

McCullough Media

**Copyright** © 2015 by Brian McCullough
*On the Edge of Now: Book V—Jagged Edge*
First Edition, Paperback – published 2016
Published by McCullough Media

ISBN: 978-1537217826

ISBN: 1537217828

All rights reserved. You may not transmit in any form or by any means, electronic or mechanical, including photocopying, recording, or by any information storage and retrieval system, any part of this publication without the written permission of the author, except where permitted by law.

*Printed in the United States of America*

# DEDICATION

To Yvonne for your love, friendship, and support.

# Prologue

Many species don't get along.

Some hunt for survival—for others, it's simply a territorial issue. With mankind, we domesticate other species as a food source. Then, there's the case of hunting another species for sport.

Should aliens treat us differently?

# Chapter One

Dragging badly after a ten minute flat-out run, Claire had to call a halt. Considering it was only weeks since her serious abdominal injury during a battle on a version of Earth two times removed, she did a reasonable job of keeping up with her companions. Devin was the first to notice her dropping back, calling ahead to Rose and Tag whose long-legged strides were putting considerable distance between them and what they just witnessed.

He gently placed his hand on her back. "Hey—I think it's time for a break . . ."

Claire nodded. "Great," she mumbled. "Unfortunately, I don't have a choice—obviously, I'm not completely healed yet."

Tag and Rose circled back, Rose getting on one knee to get a better look at her friend's face. They knew each other for so long, Rose took her best friend's physical strength for granted—it tore her apart to see such limits. "How are you doing?"

Claire clenched her teeth. "Just peachy, thanks—if I can get this stabbing pain in my side to stop, everything would be grand. Except for the little fact we just landed on a slave world with butt ugly alien overlords apparently in control."

Rose agreed. "It does pose a wee problem. However, let's get you taken care of first—then we can figure out what to do . . ."

"Whatever it is, it better be damned good because what I saw scares the hell out of me!" Claire slowly straightened, finally standing upright.

Everyone recognized her discomfort, so Tag waited before asking his question. "Can you carry on if we slow down? I'd like to put more distance between us and those things . . ." He thought for a moment. "Why don't Devin and I take a side to help you?"

Claire nodded.

As it turned out, Tag's idea was a good one. With their help, Claire managed to keep a reasonable pace and, after another hour and a half, it was time for a break.

"Okay—let's rest," Tag suggested, "then we'll keep going for a couple of hours. We need to burrow deep into the jungle so we're hard to find."

It was obvious from his comment the other Travelers weren't the only ones shaken by what they witnessed . . .

## On the Edge of Now: Book V—Jagged Edge

****

By late afternoon, they located a decent spot a couple of hundred yards from the trail, setting up camp in a small clearing surrounded by boulders and vegetation—unless they were loud or started a fire, finding them would be difficult. The real plus was a decent-sized stream was only a ten-minute walk, and it appeared clear enough to chance using it as drinking water.

Each Traveler kept busy with mundane tasks so they wouldn't have to talk about what they saw—clearly, it took awhile to process. Finally, Claire broached the subject. "Okay—my assessment of what's going on here is humans are slaves, and whatever the hell those big walking Lizards are, they rule . . ."

"I agree," Rose commented. "That's what it looked like—but what about the rest of the world?" Both girls were grim as they considered the possibilities.

"Another alternative," Rose added, "would be the people we saw were criminals, and they were in some sort of prison work camp."

"If so, why were they torturing one of them with that prod thing? And, it looked to me like it wasn't the first time—the humans were skittish as soon as they saw it." Claire paused, disgusted. "What kind of prison tortures its inmates?"

"Apparently, an alien prison," Devin offered. "I still think it's more of a slave situation, but I can't tell you why. It just seems that way . . ."

"Either way, it sucks. There's no way we should be anywhere near this . . ."

"If this is everywhere," Tag added, "we may have difficulty avoiding it. The criteria for survival may be how extensive this jungle is—and, here's another thing to think about . . . do those beasts come in here for any reason?"

Rose glanced at him. "Say we can stay in here and manage to avoid them—what about food sources? The supplies we brought might hold us for a week—tops. Then we need to hunt and gather, and this environment is different than the forests of the primitive world we were on. It depends largely on what this jungle can provide—if not enough, we'll have no choice but to venture out."

Everyone fell silent.

"Why don't we get something to eat," Tag finally suggested, "and settle in for the night? No fires until we scope out the situation—let's not do anything to attract unwanted attention. We can scout the area in the morning to determine if there's anything constituting a risk to us in the immediate area . . ."

****

By the time they ate, cleaned up, and tended to other housekeeping duties, it was dark—although it may not have been so outside the tree canopy. As they moved through their chores, there was little in the way of idle chatter even between the couples. Tension stemming from the day's surprises sucked the energy out of them, and each finally lay in darkness wondering what other nasty surprises may be in store for them.

*Just once, why can't we land on a different version of Earth where the inhabitants are friendly and welcoming—where nothing is actively trying to kill, control, or enslave us?*

It was Claire's last thought before drifting into a dreamless sleep . . .

\*\*\*\*

Rose's disturbing dreams involving oversized Lizards and screaming people were unsettling, and Tag reached over several times during the night to reassure her. Finally, she woke slowly as filtered sunlight bathed her face in diffused light after hours of tortured sleep. As she came to and opened her eyes, she found herself staring at the subject of her dreams—or, so it seemed. A Lizard stood immediately in front of her face, filling her field of vision and scaring the hell out of her. But Rose's startled movement spooked it, and she watched it scurry to safety. *That was weird*, she thought as she tried to focus on her surroundings.

Tag and the others were still asleep—the previous evening they decided to forgo having one of them stand guard overnight—it seemed they were burrowed into a remote location, and each was exhausted.

Rose scootched from under Tag's arm, careful not to disturb him. But, as if on cue, Tag awakened as he normally did, suddenly alert. "Hey, gorgeous . . ."

She smiled, looking down at him. "Hey, yourself . . ." In that moment, she realized how deeply she loved him.

"Are you okay now?"

"Yeah, I'm okay—just bad dreams."

"Good—you had a rough night." He gracefully rolled into a standing position. "Stay right there—I have to find a tree . . ."

Minutes later, both were digging through their packs sorting out what could be on the breakfast menu, their noise waking Claire and Devin.

As Devin headed into the trees to commune with nature, he called over his shoulder to Tag and Rose. "I'll have my eggs over easy with a side order of bacon—crisp—and OJ on the side."

"Dreamer," Tag muttered.

Rose just laughed.

"What I wouldn't give to order that, and have someone bring it with coffee—plenty of coffee," Claire chimed in as she managed to get to her feet.

"Hey—maybe the Lizard people dig coffee! We can

check it out . . ." Tag grinned at Claire as she wandered into the forest on a mission of her own, sticking her tongue out at him as she disappeared from view.

"Were you giving me attitude, or simply doing a Lizard imitation?"

He grinned at her response from the bushes. "Idiot!"

"If it were an imitation, you need to know it wasn't a very good one . . ."

"Tag!"

He looked at Rose. "Too much?"

"Yes! Especially when you know Claire isn't the brightest ray of sunshine first thing in the morning . . ."

"I never could figure out why some people are grumpy when they get up. They just had the whole night to get well-rested, ready to meet the challenges of a new day."

"That may be, but I'd leave her alone for a while until she wakes completely—otherwise, this jungle might not be big enough for you to hide in . . ."

"Good point . . ."

## Chapter Two

Once she got over the funding issue, it was clear sailing as the acquisition of suitable space as well as a few upgrades were done in an amazingly short time. Her dream of opening her own art gallery was about to be realized.

Jackie stood from across the street, taking it all in. The only thing missing was the sign—she ordered it weeks ago, and the company promised delivery in two weeks. In the mean time, she jury-rigged a temporary one which would do the job—although, it could be more aesthetically pleasing.

*All of this is happening because of Kyle,* she thought as she admired the front of her gallery. Kyle insisted on helping her to the point where it became a real issue between them—she refused to take money from a boyfriend who had been in the picture for less than six months. True, their relationship grew exponentially during that time as she helped with his search for Tag—however, she still didn't feel right using his money for her dream.

Now? She was engaged to a bright, gorgeous man, and she owned an art gallery, fulfilling her dream. There was only one thing missing . . .

Tag.

\*\*\*\*

Munching on dried meat, nuts, and berries, the Travelers decided to tackle the important question of what to do next. Without stating it, no one wanted to go back the way they came.

Claire decided to offer her opinion and concerns first. "I keep having flashbacks of the poor man getting zapped by the cattle prod thing from the Lizard creature. At least, that's what I think it was . . ."

Rose shuddered. "It was ghastly . . ."

"So—what do we do to avoid them," Devin asked.

"We know where some of them are," Tag commented. "Now we have to scout to figure out what's going on here—I think stick to the jungle, but investigate the perimeters."

"What happens if they're in all directions—as in owning the planet?"

"Then I guess we'll have to learn to live as jungle creatures. If—and, that's a big if—they're everywhere, they must have superior weapons as well as considerable numbers. Depending, of course, on the starting human population . . ."

Rose glanced at him. "Why would the Lizard things come here?"

"It could be for resources—or, to create a slave market. Maybe the humans are for sport, or used to show everyone the Lizard people have power over other worlds. Who knows?"

Claire nodded. "Was it a conquest? I wonder if there are resistance pockets left over?"

"The problem is we don't have any idea at what stage of development the human population was at the time of the attack. How advanced was their weaponry?"

Devin posed additional questions. "How did they get here? By portal? Maybe they had a time travel operation like Callie did in the last world. Or, did they arrive in a good old-fashioned spaceship?"

"All good questions, but what's more important is how widespread they are, and their numbers . . ."

Claire shook her head. "Geez, I hope there are some free humans left—if not, this could be a very bleak place in which to live . . ."

Tag took the lead. "Okay—what do we know about

them, so far?"

"They're huge, easily half again the size of a normal human male—and, they're bipedal as well as obviously intelligent," Devin offered. "Or, they wouldn't have gotten this far. They're reptilian looking with green and brown coloring and wart-like bulges protruding from their skin. They appear to communicate with each other—although that's not a big surprise." He paused for a moment. "And, they seem to be mean sons of bitches. Did I miss anything?"

"Not much. Ladies?"

Rose shook her head.

Claire hesitated, recalling the encounter. "We saw maybe two hundred humans—but, only three of the Lizard guys. However, our view was limited and brief—it makes me wonder if they're supremely confident, and they only need a few to guard many. Or, are their numbers limited? Obviously, the fewer of them is better for us . . ."

"I know we had only a brief look at them," Tag agreed, "but other than some machinery used in whatever they're constructing, I didn't see any form of transport—nor have we seen anything flying overhead. Granted, the jungle canopy covers much of the sky view, but, if something is flying around this area, we'll most likely hear it . . ."

Devin looked at him with pronounced doubt. "I don't know what that means—they must have higher technology to win out. Not only that, how did they get here? It doesn't make sense unless we missed whatever transport they do have . . ."

As everyone processed the questions, it was infinitely clear there were currently more questions than answers.

Tag broke the silence. "The next thing to consider is their weapons—what do they carry? We only saw the prod thing—is it basically the same as ours, or more advanced? We have assault rifles, pistols, and a few explosives that Callie gave us. What if they have defensive mechanisms which render those useless?"

"We're screwed . . ."

\*\*\*\*

"They're behind schedule, again . . ."

"Push them harder!"

"We already have—they're puny, they don't last, and the mortality rate is getting higher. What a waste of food products . . ."

"What about giving them more advanced equipment to use? Are they bright enough?"

Sub-Commander Garoc carefully pondered his superior's question. "I would be careful how much we give them to use—the most advanced models have Wave technology. If that got into the wrong hands and was converted to weapons use, our edge over them vanishes—it's what made it possible to overcome their initial resistance during the invasion."

The Prime snorted. "If they couldn't figure it out

then, why now?"

*Be careful,* Garoc warned himself. *The arrogance of the Prime—like others in the High Command—led to problems on more than one planet takeover . . .* "Sir—given enough time and opportunity, anything is possible even for such pathetic beings. I recommend caution, and keeping our technology safe. If we even slightly delay reaping their resources and building the necessary support facility, it's a worthy trade-off for security purposes."

The Prime considered Garoc's point. "If our report goes out to Off-Planet Command showing less than projected results, they may send an inspector to find out why. You know what that could entail—they have the ultimate power of life and death over anyone involved in the conquest and administration of New Planetary Holdings. Do you want one of them breathing down your back fin?"

"No, Sir—of course you're right about this." It was best to mollify the Prime who was set on having his way.

"That is correct—I am right. Get the newer machines out in the field, and try to train these poor excuses for workers. If that doesn't work, perhaps we can make examples of a few of them to motivate the rest."

"It will be done, Sir . . ."

The Prime turned to other things as the Sub-Commander left.

He hoped he didn't make a mistake.

****

The Travelers moved out in the early morning leaving no trace of their presence. Heading north—the opposite direction from where they had their encounter—they hiked for most of the day before coming to a perimeter of jungle meeting open space.

They met no one.

Tag, as point man, reached the last of the large trees on the edge, and he took his time scanning the foreground for what he could see. Then he shifted to the distant horizon—only sections of tilled fields, growing unidentifiable crops.

So far? No immediate danger.

Next, he focused on the sky—other than plentiful bird life, there was nothing mechanical. "Well, I can't see anything concerning—or, much of anything else. Someone's crops are starting to grow in certain areas, so, presumably, the farmer will periodically be around to check them out . . ."

"Should we scan from a higher vantage point?" Of course, Rose would think of getting a bird's-eye view.

He nodded. "It wouldn't hurt . . ."

She was the resident tree climber of the group, her tall, lean, athletic body made for weaving in and out of branches. For fun back on the primitive world they visited, she once had a tree climbing contest with the guys. She managed to reach the top and back down before either of them had completed the ascent part of their climb. "I'll go," she offered.

They surrounded a large tree located near the edge, and Rose accepted Tag's leg-up. As she scurried up the tree with ease, she focused on the climb without sneaking a peek at the distant view. Good thing, too—about half way up, she was about to place her hand on the next available branch when a sixth sense screamed at her to freeze.

It was behind her, up, and to the left. With barely discernible motion, she twisted her head—eight feet away, a serpent coiled its body around a tree branch, making it difficult to determine length. Brilliantly camouflaged, one might mistake it for another limb on the tree.

Neither moved as they studied each other, determining distance, threat status, as well as initiating genetically hardwired fight-or-flight. Without moving her head, Rose shifted her gaze as far to the right as possible to find a landing spot if she had to leap suddenly should the snake decide to strike.

She quickly realized she had two things against her—it would likely move quicker, and she was in a reactionary mode. In that scenario, she had to play catch up—which might prove deadly. The only advantage was its size—a breadth of more than two of her hands around the thickest part of its exposed length. Because of its girth, she hoped it would move slower than a more slender variety.

Concentrating intently on an impending attack, Rose didn't notice sweat rolling down her face, dripping off her chin. The serpent, however, did. Its steely eyes shifted to the droplets moving on her face, a long, forked tongue flitting in and out to test the air. Just as she decided a strike was imminent, Rose bunched her muscles preparing for a leap to the side, and away.

Then it was over.

The snake calculated her as a low-level threat, not requiring a defensive response—mainly because it recently enjoyed a filling meal. Although Rose didn't know it, the serpent was a species not known for being aggressive unless hunting or for protective purposes.

As it slithered away, Rose clung to her position letting the sick feeling of anxiety pass.

"Hey—what are you doing up there? Having a nap?" Of course, from Tag's position, he couldn't see the snake.

"Keep your shorts on! I'm on the way up . . ."

The rest of the climb was uneventful. From her vantage point eighty feet above the jungle floor, she could see a considerable distance—further than Tag's position at ground level. Nothing moved. However, on the horizon to her right, she could make out low structures which could be housing or farm buildings—they were too far away to be clear.

After a ten-minute scan, she hurried back down, moving carefully but quickly past the point where she had the encounter. Within a few minutes, she was back safely on the ground.

The Travelers looked at her expectantly.

"Nothing's moving out there—in the far distance to the right I saw buildings, but they're too far away to make out what they are. Or, if anyone were around them . . ." Rose wasn't sure why she didn't mention the encounter in the tree.

Tag acknowledged her report, then looked at the others. "I suggest we rest here, and get something to eat. Once it's dark enough, we should head toward the buildings to check them out. I'd love to contact some humans so we can find out what's going on here—really going on here . . ."

No objections.

Once apart from Claire and Devin, Tag glanced at Rose. "Are you okay? What happened on the tree climb?"

"Let's just say I had an understanding with one of the local fauna in the neighborhood . . ."

## Chapter Three

They waited until dusk to set out across the open space. A fifteen-minute scan before they proceeded showed nothing of consequence and, by the time they drew near to the buildings, it was completely dark. Still, they could make out three structures, one of them with glowing lights inside. One looked like a barn, and the other appeared to be an equipment shed.

They settled in to watch the house for the better part of an hour. No one was outside and, luckily, there appeared to be no evidence of any Lizards in the immediate vicinity.

Huddled together, Tag spoke quietly. "We haven't seen who lives here, but I don't think a Lizard guy would set up a homestead way out here, alone. So, do we initiate contact tonight, or wait until morning?"

"Pounding on the door in the middle of the night," Claire surmised, "might freak them out. They could poke a shotgun in your face, and ask questions later . . ."

"Excellent point—morning it is."

They settled in for the night—as best they could in the open—alternating who stood sentinel. Dawn found them sitting in a cluster in the middle of a field about fifty yards away from the farm house. And, in true farming fashion, the occupants rose early to do chores.

A young, gangly legged, teenage girl exited the house with a dog, and headed to the barn—unfortunately, the dog picked up on their presence immediately. He came within twenty feet, stopped, and studied them while omitting a low-slung growl. Male and obviously a mixture of retriever and something else, he was gentle and friendly—yet, in the current situation, he went into protection mode.

"Hey, Buddy," Tag called out softly. "C'mon . . ." He held out his hand in front of him. The dog hesitated, confused as to what to do—but it must have sensed Tag was a dog person, determining he wasn't a threat. The animal approached, wagging a tail which never stopped until he came up to Tag, who let him sniff his hand before petting him.

Realizing the dog wasn't with her, she turned, and saw them sitting in a group on the ground with her dog lying on his back, Tag rubbing his belly. Startled, she looked at the house as though she may bolt for it.

"Hey!" Rose called out. "We mean you no harm—what's your dog's name?"

The question engaged the blonde-haired girl, and the fear on her face dissipated. "He's Grub—what are you doing here?" She looked at the dog soaking up the attention. "Some guard dog, huh?"

"Why is he named Grub?"

Finally, the girl smiled. "Because he never stops eating—it's a wonder he's not fat!"

Rose grinned. "I'm Rose, and these are my friends Tag, Claire, and Devin." Everyone remained seated in an effort not to spook her. "What's your name?"

"Millie . . ."

"Millie—are your parents home?"

"My mom is in there." She nodded her head toward the farmhouse. "They took my dad . . ."

"You mean the Lizard creatures?"

The girl nodded.

"Millie, will you go in the house and ask your mom to come out here, please?"

Without answering, the girl did so. Minutes later, a small woman—brunette, in her late thirties—appeared with Millie in tow. She approached to within ten yards and stopped to study the intruders, especially Grub lying next to Tag.

Finally, she spoke. "What are you doing here?"

"Well," Tag answered, "the first order of business was to meet Grub, and then we introduced ourselves to Millie. But, what you really want to know is why we're sitting in the field next to your house." He paused. "It's because we're new here, and we don't quite understand what's going on with the Lizard creatures . . ."

At the mention of them, the woman glanced quickly, scanning the area to see if they were being observed. "Well, let's not have you out in the open like this," she directed. "Come in the house . . ."

****

She pointed to a large farm table, inviting them to sit as she took a seat at one end.

Tag introduced each of them.

"I'm Glade—I understand you introduced yourself to Millie."

"We have—and, please—allow me to apologize for intruding. We're new here—we saw the Lizard creatures, but we don't know exactly what's going on . . ."

Glade looked at him with some surprise. "How can you not know? Everyone does!"

Tag managed a brief smile. "The Lizards came from a different planet, right?"

She nodded.

"Well, in a way, so did we—only a different version of this world. We've been to several, in fact. We arrived here three nights ago, so everything is new to us . . ."

Glade examined him carefully. Was he lying? It didn't seem so—he and his companions looked as if they were serious. "Okay—it's weird, but I get it . . ."

"Yeah—it's a long story with interesting twists. We can fill you in sometime if you'd like. But, for now, we need to know more about what's going on here for our own safety."

"Fair enough—the Lizards arrived almost eight years ago. It was a surprise attack, and a worldwide invasion—we never saw it coming, and reacted too late. Even if we were warned, I doubt it would have made much difference in the end—they were too advanced and powerful for us. Millions died before they totally crushed every military and police force across the world. They had technology which our side couldn't really penetrate, and they only had a few losses. Eventually, we had to surrender or be totally wiped out . . ."

"And, now?" Tag's voice was gentle and reassuring.

She grimaced. "They rule us—most people are slaves. A few are allowed to be free, but they're strictly controlled."

"Why are some free?"

Glade shrugged. "I guess they identified key occupations, and determined free people would be more motivated to serve them better. Any who don't comply with their rules are removed from that status immediately with no recourse."

Tag looked around the room. "That includes you as farmers?"

"Yes—it does."

"Millie mentioned something about their taking her Dad..."

She didn't answer as emotions took over, tears welling in her eyes. "It was a little over a week ago the Lizard bastards took him—they said he protested a new schedule for crop delivery. 'I can't make them grow any faster,' he told them. But they didn't care, and took him away—we haven't heard anything since. They told us not to ask, or we'd be taken next..."

Finally, Glade broke down. Rose and Claire comforted her as best they could while Tag and Devin headed outside. "If the Lizards have taken over worldwide," Tag noted, "things are going to be a challenge for us not to be in contact at some point..."

"Sooner than later, I'll bet..."

\*\*\*\*

Inside, Glade settled down and Millie made tea for everyone. "I'm sorry—I can't seem to stop crying these days. Everything seems so hopeless..."

"Don't be silly! You're entitled to emotions bubbling to the surface—it's nature's way to relieve stress." Rose knew enough about stress given the situation with her family.

"I know it's a bad time for you," Claire pointed out, "but you still have the farm and, most important, that pretty, young daughter of yours."

Glade nodded, but said nothing.

"So, those are positives," Rose smiled. "I'm sure we can come up with a few more . . ."

"Do you have anyone available to run the farm," Claire asked. "Is there livestock, or just crops?"

"We have a few head of cattle, sheep, and goats. They're in a large, fenced field beyond the last crop field to the north. There's a stream running through and the livestock feed off the land, so there's not too much to do now. But, we check on them occasionally."

"What about the crops?"

"All the planting is done—now it's a question of praying for sun and rain . . ."

"What about chores around here—can you manage?"

"Millie and I get some of them done as best we can—others we just don't get to . . ."

Claire sighed. "Okay, Glade—I'm going to have Rose stay in here with you while I slip out to chat with the guys for a few minutes . . ." She smiled at Rose, and went outside.

She found them leaning on a corral fence. "Hey—Glade's in a pinch with her husband gone. Apparently, they have some cattle, sheep, and goats not too far away. Right now, the livestock are self-sufficient living off the land, but, eventually, they're going to need some attention. The crop situation is pretty much the same story. What do you think about staying and helping her out? I didn't mention it to her because I needed to talk to you guys first—plus, since this is her home, she would have to agree, of course . . ."

Devin and Tag glanced at each other. "Actually, that option makes a lot of sense for her and us," Tag commented.

Devin agreed. "My uncle owns a farm, and I used to work there summers as a kid helping him out. I know a few things about what needs to be done, and when . . ."

She smiled. "Awesome—should we go back in and propose that to her?"

"What we don't want to do is put her and Millie at risk with our hanging out here," Tag cautioned. "We need to know what kind of watch the Lizards keep on this place—the best option would be for us to be invisible to them."

"True—however, she needs help. You heard if quotas aren't met, they'll come for her and the girl. Are we going to let that happen?"

"We can't be responsible for everyone we meet," Devin argued. But, once he uttered the statement, he wished he could take it back—Claire's glare was chilling. "Or, we could stay and pitch in—which would be a good thing all around."

Tag nodded. "Let's go back in, and discuss this with Glade . . ."

\*\*\*\*

When they were all seated around the kitchen table and Millie poured tea for them, Tag spoke directly to Glade. "We were thinking—perhaps—we can help each other if it doesn't cause trouble. We certainly don't want that..."

He had her attention.

"Maybe," he continued, "we can stay for a bit, and help you and Millie run the farm. And, we're not complete novices—Devin knows a thing or two about farming."

Glade took a long, slow breath before answering. "You would be helping us out because we have nowhere else to go—but, I have no money to pay you..."

"We don't want or need money—this would be our helping you run the farm and, in exchange, we would live here, for now. If we have a roof over our heads and something to eat it's a fair exchange..."

"I'm not sure..."

"Are you and Millie going to be able to meet the new quotas alone?"

"Well—no."

"Then, they'll take you away and you'll lose the farm, right?"

"Yes..." Glade's voice was little more than a whisper.

"Well, we can't have that..."

Her eyes filled with tears.

"If you want," Tag continued, "we'll leave, and you don't have to ever see us again—no one knows we've been here. But, what if we can help you meet your quotas? I'm not promising anything, but we might be able to look around to see what happened to your husband."

"You would do that?" Her voice quivered as tears finally fell.

"We'll give it our best try—but only if you want us to."

Glade was silent for several moments. Then, she looked at each of them. "Well, I guess you now have a home . . ."

"Excellent! Now we just need to figure out a strategy to minimize the chances of a Lizard's figuring out we have now joined the neighborhood . . ."

## CHAPTER FOUR

It was over breakfast the next day when the four Travelers, Glade, and Millie sat at the large kitchen table. "I presume," Claire began, "the Lizards speak a different language—we never got close enough to hear them..."

Glade nodded. "Correct. It's the weirdest collection of sounds—clicking, grunting like they're having trouble going to the bathroom, and growling—almost howling. You'd think it were three or four different languages spoken in the same sentence..."

"How do they communicate with humans?"

"It's interesting—they wear a pendant thing around their necks. It's really pretty slick—it acts as a translator, supposedly for any language they encounter. The voice quality of their speaking English through it is a bit tinny, but it's clear enough to understand."

"So . . . when you speak to them, it translates back into their gibberish?"

"Exactly . . ."

"How often do they come around?" Tag's question wasn't surprising to any of the Travelers—he always considered numbers and location first.

Glade thought for a few seconds before answering. "It's not a precise schedule—they drop in whenever they feel like it. I get the impression they sweep through a quadrant, visiting each independent operation. But—if I had to estimate—I'd say they come through every three to four weeks. As long as we do what's mandated, they pretty much leave us alone most of the time . . ."

Devin's turn. "When they show up, will there be more than one?"

"Yes—normally at least two, and sometimes three."

"Are they armed? Do they bring equipment?"

She frowned, trying to recall details for him. "Well—they arrive in one of their armored vehicles. It's kind of like a medium-sized truck with lots of protection. I don't think our bullets will penetrate it—plus, I heard they have some sort of technology that wards off anything fired at it—same with other vehicles or airships."

Tag glanced at Devin. "We haven't seen any of the airships yet . . ."

"I'm not surprised—they had a lot of them at the time of the conquest, but not so many nowadays. Maybe they sent them somewhere else to invade—I just don't know."

"Back to the question of weapons," Devin continued. "What are they toting when they come here?"

"Usually, I see a handgun strapped to their hips, like we would. Occasionally, one of them would have what looks like a rifle, although much different from what we carry. I'm not sure what else might be in their vehicles, if anything . . ."

"When was the last time they were here?" Tag waited patiently for an answer.

Glade fought to hold back her tears. "They took my husband about a week ago."

"Okay—that should give us roughly two weeks before they return. When the Lizards come here, do they search your house or outbuildings?"

"No—why?"

"Because, when they make their next visit, we're going to need a place to hide—it wouldn't be wise to use a place they search every time."

"Right—nothing is searched. They're more interested in intimidation and controlling us. I don't think it would occur to them we would do anything sneaky—they seem to think we're stupid based on how easy it was for them to defeat us."

"They got lucky, and had technology your people didn't have—that's why they won. If on equal footing, it would be interesting to see how a rematch would turn out."

She was surprised by the suggestion. "You mean to

fight them again? They're so powerful!"

"That's because you got whipped, and they've had humans under their thumb all this time. Nobody is unbeatable..."

Devin shifted his attention to Tag. "What do you have in mind?"

"Everyone has a weakness—it's just a question of finding what and where it is, and applying sufficient pressure in a timely fashion."

Devin glanced at Rose and Claire. "I know that tone—we're safe right now, so why risk it?"

"Hey, I'm really not suggesting anything specific—just thinking out loud."

"That's when you worry me most..."

Tag returned his attention to Glade. "What's your husband's name?"

"It's Kirv Lingar—why?"

"Oh, you never know—maybe our paths will cross. Now, if we're lucky, we know who to look for if the opportunity arises..."

\*\*\*\*

The room was small and, from what he could tell, the Lizards chained him to the wall for what he estimated anywhere from five to eight days—it was hard to keep track since they left a light on continually, and the room was windowless. Food? One meal of unidentifiable slop and water. Thankfully, the chains were long enough he didn't have to undergo the indignity of relieving himself where he sat.

Thinking of his wife and child was a saving grace as well as a torment, yet he knew he could survive and prevail over his circumstances due to his love for them. Worry and dread kept him awake most of the time—was his family still at the farm? Did the Lizard overlords harm them? How would they manage things on their own? True, Glade was strong, but this was asking a lot from her.

Kirv Lingar seethed with personal hatred for the Lizards, a simmering, violent passion churning inside of him. His normal peaceful and thoughtful character was thrown aside as various scenarios crammed his brain. *Just give me the opportunity, and you'll see how humans can react when you back them into a corner . . .*

\*\*\*\*

Most of the week sailed by without incident. The Travelers fell into a rhythm of helping with farm work and household chores, and evening conversations with

Glade and Millie revealed two strong personalities with well-developed core beliefs. Glade always tried to do right even during the most trying of circumstances, and it's what she was teaching her daughter.

Although he pitched in to do his fair share, Tag spent considerable time scouting the neighborhood—at least ten miles in every major direction—to get a feel for what the setting was and how free the Lizards allowed the local inhabitants to be. He avoided interaction with locals due to safety concerns for Glade and Millie, thinking it was best to maintain a low profile—on any given day, anyone would assume he was a traveler just passing through.

Of course, the secondary purpose of his scouting expeditions was to locate potential alternate hiding spots should they need to abandon the farmhouse and retreat. Luckily, he found several in different directions which would do nicely.

But, there was still much he needed to know. While working with Glade on farm equipment, he suggested a break to stretch their muscles. "Do you have much contact with your neighbors," he asked, taking a swig of water then swiping at his mouth with his sleeve.

She followed suit. "We used to before the Lizards came—since then, everyone minds their own business. Why do you ask?"

"Well—I wasn't sure if your neighbors were in the habit of dropping by. With our being here, it would be a little awkward if there weren't a cover story . . ."

"It's not likely—however, what do you suggest? Just in case . . ."

"I think something along the lines of we're freed, and we have valuable craft skills. We're in the process of passing through to a new location, stopping here for a bit of a break. The agreement is we help you out, receiving food and lodging in the meantime."

She smiled. "That sounds pretty close to the truth, if you ask me . . ."

"For disinformation," Tag chuckled, "it's usually best to stick as close to the truth as you can. Generally, it ends up being more plausible. The only fib part is the craft skills—however, I have to say my compatriots have a number of other skills which have certainly served us well, so far . . ."

"I don't mean to pry, but can I ask you a rather personal question?"

"Sure, go ahead—as long as I get to decide whether to answer it or not. And, yes, I do occasionally snore . . ."

She giggled. "Good to know—seriously, it's about your relationship with the two girls."

"Okay . . ." They were careful to appear as friends only—not couples—while staying with Glade and Millie.

"I take it there's more to it than your just traveling together?"

Tag had to laugh. "It's that transparent?"

"Well, it doesn't take a genius to pick out Rose's making doe eyes at you, and Claire's doing the same over Devin."

"I'll have to inform them remedial acting classes are in order . . ."

She poked him on the arm with a finger. "It's okay to be open with your relationships—Millie figured it out the first full day you stayed here. She's watched the farm animals and understands biology, and she knows love makes the world go around. At least it used to . . ."

"It still does—it's just not as obvious anymore with all the troubles brought on by invasion and occupation." Tag took another swig. "To change the topic for a minute, when the Lizards show up, which direction are they coming from?"

"Usually, they drive up the main road two farms over, then come cross country using a combination of country lanes or—literally—over the flattest ground they can find. What are you thinking?"

"When you mentioned our being transparent as couples, it made me think of how obvious the Lizards' approach might be. If we have enough warning, the four of us—who aren't supposed to be here anyway—can duck under cover so they won't know we're staying at your farm."

"What about the story we'll tell the neighbors if they see you and ask who you are? Won't that be good enough?"

"I'm not as confident with the Lizards—they're essentially a scheduled patrol which is going to be on the lookout for something different. Something out of place. A situation like that invites too many undesired questions . . ."

"Well, you should have enough time to hide—their armored vehicle makes a hell of a noise, and the ground around here is basically flat. Their normal approach is out in the open—so, unless someone is caught out in the fields away from cover, you should be fine. Even then, there's a fair amount of bushes and trees . . ."

"Have you and your neighbors ever considered an early warning system?"

"Excuse me?"

"The concept is when the Lizard patrol enters the neighborhood, a warning goes out to outlying farms they can expect a visit. If they have any reason to hide or divert something or someone, they have time to do it."

Glade considered the idea. "I'm not sure if the farmers ever needed such a thing in the past . . ."

"Think about it—we're here, and keeping that a secret is important. Have any of your neighbors had problems in the past where someone got into trouble?"

"Yes—occasionally . . ."

"Did the Lizards ever take anyone away like they did your husband?"

"Yes . . ."

"Well—maybe with a warning system in place, anyone who's at risk could conveniently vamoose before the Lizards arrive."

Glade nodded. "I can see where that might help . . ."

"Just a thought . . ."

"It can't hurt to talk to the neighbors—with Kirv taken away, they'll have heard about it. That fact gives me the opportunity to open the topic without appearing suspicious."

"Now you're thinking!"

\*\*\*\*

They came early.

Only one week after Tag and Glade had their discussion about a trip wire, early warning system, a Lizard patrol rolled across the area. Luckily, Glade already spoke to several neighbors who thought the idea had merit, and it was one of them who sent the message the Lizards arrived.

Most of the Travelers were close to the house and barn doing chores while Tag was out on a scouting mission. They prearranged to occupy a roomy storm cellar big enough to easily accommodate the four of them. Its entrance was through the barn, and they rigged it so the trapdoor in the floor wasn't obvious.

Rose, Claire, and Devin collected their backpacks—Tag's, too—and headed directly to the barn. Millie then made sure the trapdoor was covered with straw and other items after they secreted themselves inside.

It wasn't a long wait. For some reason, the Lizards skipped the farm adjacent to Glade's and visited her next. Their vehicle rolled into the farmyard, kicking up dust as it abruptly stopped in the middle. Doors opened, and they seemed to examine the immediate area before disembarking. Finally, the passenger door opened, and a Lizard in typical uniform and body armor exited.

Glade greeted them submissively. The Lizards didn't like to be kept waiting—it was part of their arrogance toward everything not of their kind or making. She saw enough of them on previous visits to recognize certain individuals. In the early days, Lizard creatures appeared so similar it was difficult to identify one from another, but she knew the name of the Lizard standing in the farmyard—Beal. He was particularly obnoxious, strutting away from the vehicle, making a slow circle as a show underlining the fact he was in control. Finally, he stopped in front of Glade.

With a sneer, he spoke through the translator pendant he wore around his neck. "Where is the younger female?"

"My daughter is working in the house." Glade learned one did not look them in the eye during conversation, and she kept her eyes fixed on his sandaled, huge, clawed feet.

"Make her come out here—I want to see," he snarled.

Glade turned, calling to Millie. Her daughter, of course, was watching surreptitiously from a window so she had no trouble hearing her mother call. She meekly stepped onto the porch, her hatred boiling for the mean-spirited creatures—especially after they took away her beloved father. Even at her age, she knew enough about her character to realize if she possessed a weapon at the moment, impulse control would be a huge challenge—a bullet in his brain would have suited her just fine. As it was, she turned out to be a good actress, hiding feelings of defiance deep enough to avoid undue scrutiny of her intentions.

"Have you kept production up as ordered?" The Lizard was demanding, as well as condescending.

Glade shrugged, her gaze still at the ground. "We're trying—it's hard since you took my man away . . ."

Beal snorted, giving her an inquisitive look to make

sure he wasn't being insulted. He found it somewhat difficult to understand the meaning behind words and some of the expressions of such pitiful creatures. If it weren't for the labor advantage and, as far as he was concerned, all should've been exterminated at the time of conquest.

Satisfied she wasn't being defiant, he considered her point about the male's being taken from her—it did make sense production would be more difficult with one less person. Nonetheless, Beal knew the mandate was to have the farms in the region produce enough to feed the large number of worker slaves involved in constructing facilities for resource harvesting and refining.

"Perhaps," he told her, "I should consider returning him here. That decision will require some thought . . ."

Beal took a last glance—everything seemed to be in order. He had five more farms to visit, and there seemed no reason to linger any longer. "Keep producing what you are told. If not, you will be in a bad position. Do you understand?"

Glade nodded. "Yes—it will be done."

Beal studied her carefully for a moment before returning to his vehicle. After he climbed inside and closed the door, the driver wheeled through the farmyard in such a manner, dust settled on Glade and Millie who stayed put until the vehicle was out of sight. They waited another fifteen minutes to ensure the Lizards wouldn't return, then both of them headed to the barn to give the all clear.

Tag witnessed everything. He was hiking back from his scouting expedition when he saw the vehicle rumbling across the fields. Taking cover within a small grove of trees close to the farmyard, he could clearly see the interaction—however, he was far enough away to be out of earshot of conversation.

By the time Rose, Claire, and Devin were exiting the barn with Glade and Millie, he strolled up. "I see you had visitors . . ."

"Yes," Glade concurred. "It's the usual crew that comes by . . ."

"Did they want anything in particular?"

"No—it's just a normal check-in to see if we're operating normally. Beal was as obnoxious as ever . . ."

"Is he the leader?"

"Yes—he commands even when more of them are around. I have the feeling he's in charge of the patrol group in this area."

Tag scanned the farmyard. "He must have been satisfied things are normal."

"Yeah—the usual arrogance and demands. Nothing's changed . . ."

Tag smiled. "Well—that's good. We remain below their horizon, and can operate without undue scrutiny."

"What do you have in mind?"

"Oh, a few things are percolating, but haven't quite gelled yet . . ."

## Chapter Five

They made him walk back on his own—thirty miles—but, he would take that hike any day because they let him go. Finally arriving home, stiff and sore, he thought of calling to Glade or Millie—but where was the fun in that? It would be much better to surprise them by walking in the door, unannounced.

He stood for a moment, hand poised on the kitchen door handle, when it opened from the inside and a tall, redheaded young woman stopped short of running into him.

"Who the hell are you," he asked, his voice registering concern.

Rose immediately figured who stood before her and, rather than get defensive, she smiled and offered a hand. "You must be Kirv! I'm Rose—Glade and Millie told me all about you . . ."

"Where are they?" He looked past Rose, scanning as much as he could see of the kitchen.

Rose stepped aside. "They're fixing dinner—surprise them!"

He teared up as he caught a glimpse of his wife and daughter and, within moments, everyone was trying to talk at once. Hugs were best because they were holding the man they thought disappeared from their lives forever and, upon hearing the commotion, Tag, Claire, and Devin arrived to join the celebration.

After the excitement died down and they made quick introductions, Kirv sat with the Travelers ready to ask questions. "First, I want to thank you for helping with the farm—Glade tells me you arrived out of nowhere at the most opportune time. As I understand it, you lightened their load for which I am appreciative . . ." He hesitated, looking at each Traveler. "What I want to hear is who you are as well as where you came from. Glade told me to ask you, then sit back and be amazed . . ."

He was.

After hearing the litany of events and circumstances the four young people experienced during the last several months, Kirv sat back in his chair, shaking his head. "I'm surprised you made it through—the odds were against you."

"It was touch and go more times than I like to think," Tag commented. "But, we hung in there and luck played a part. However, it wasn't all fun and games—Claire took a significant injury which still bothers her . . ."

"And," Claire interrupted, "Tag took a head injury

fighting the wild ones on the primitive planet. He was falling over from vertigo for weeks—if you didn't know he wasn't fond of the bottle, it looked like he was drunk all the time."

Tag laughed. "Slightly overstated, perhaps . . ."

Kirv grinned and returned his attention to all of them. "This portal event you described—it appears randomly?"

The four Travelers hesitated before Claire answered. "Yes, and no—it isn't there when we'd like it to be, and yet it appeared to save our asses more than once . . ." She glanced at Millie sitting on the other side of the table. "Sorry . . ."

Millie grinned. "Trust me—I've heard it before, especially when my dad talks about the Lizards. That's one of the nicer words he uses . . ."

Everyone turned their attention on Kirv.

He shrugged. "I get caught up in the moment thinking of what I'd like to do to those bastards!"

Everyone laughed, and they spent the rest of the evening comparing notes about what it was like in other worlds—as well as their current one—before and after the conquest. Finally, when the women announced they were going to bed, Kirv asked if Tag and Devin would do him the honor of having a nightcap with him. Of course, Devin was all over it and, even though Tag wasn't much of a drinker, he agreed. He wanted to talk to Kirv without the women.

When glasses were full, Kirv offered a toast. "To the day the Lizards are no longer on this planet . . ." Tag and Devin seconded the idea, drinking to honor that day.

"Why do you think they let you go?" Tag placed his glass on the table, his curiosity in full swing.

"I had many hours on the long walk back to here to think about that question—my final answer was they needed me. I think things aren't running as smoothly as their plan would like, and they have to answer to someone higher in authority—possibly off-planet. They keep harping on us about meeting deadlines and quotas, so I figure the pressure is on the local Lizard group to produce. If they don't, they'll have their clawed feet held to the fire . . ."

Tag glanced at Devin. "They must have millions of human slaves worldwide—can't they make that work?"

Kirv shook his head. "No—they have tens of millions, possibly hundreds of millions of slaves. No one knows for sure how many people were killed in the invasion, but, despite those huge numbers, I'm guessing the vast majority of slaves don't give a damn." He paused, thinking about the situation. "And, many might work covertly against the Lizards' interests . . ."

Aha! There it was! The opening Tag wanted. "Do you think people in this area would support a resistance movement against the Lizards?"

Kirv arched his eyebrows. "Yes—most would. The problem is no one wants to go it alone. If the Lizards singled them out, they would liquidate infidels immediately—families, too." He leveled a serious look at Tag. "A dangerous game . . ."

"Have you heard of any groups trying to do something of that nature?"

He shrugged. "Now and then, word comes of pockets of resistance, but we never know if they really do anything or they're crushed in the process."

Tag nodded. "I have to admit it's a tough go, especially since the Lizards have such an impressive technological advantage . . ."

"It's too bad, since human scientists were reportedly close to solving that problem just before the collapse . . ."

Tag sat up a little straighter. "Where were the scientists, and do you know if they survived?"

He shook his head. "I'm not sure if they made it—the Lizards would have slaughtered them if they knew about them. From what I heard, their labs were only several hundred miles from here . . ."

"Is there a way to find out if they made it? And, if so, can we locate where they are now?"

"It may take awhile, but someone has to know . . ."

Tag fell silent, and it was evident to anyone who knew him the wheels were turning. "Kirv—it's extremely important to find out. Will you please make the inquiries?"

****

Kyle allowed himself to do something which rarely happened—not because he didn't permit himself to indulge, but because he was so busy trying to figure out extraordinary challenges in understanding the cosmos.

He was daydreaming about his brother.

He reviewed everything he knew, confirming his brother experienced several portal travels—the good news was he knew Tag was okay and traveling with new friends, recently arriving at a new destination. Not knowing proved difficult, but, like most things in life, after a while the situation became less abrasive to his psyche.

The more he considered the multiple portal-trip experiences, Kyle was convinced it was likely a third party was controlling the events. If so, does the Controller decide on the destination for a Traveler, or is it random choice? And, if the Controller has a certain place in mind to deposit the Traveler, what governs that decision?

****

Beal inspected the barracks, surprised it wasn't as bad as he thought. He observed ranks of troopers standing at what they assumed was the proper station of attention, and he couldn't help but think what a sorry state of affairs.

The status of the Occupation Force on any conquered

planet was always filled with third-class troops and rejects from other venues—the best of the military were the Shock Troops sent in as the initial attacking force for planet conquest. Once they overwhelmed the defenders and mopped up, they were shipped out, refitted, provided replacements for any losses, and rested until the next planet assault. Behind them were the dregs which they left for Commanders like him—it was his job to manage the conquest, as well as strip out resources.

Not only was the quality of troops poor, they didn't have enough of them. Word had it too many successful planet conquests occurred, and there weren't enough troopers to fully man each new prize. He believed—considering how thin they were—his force should have six hundred troopers to be a full complement, and he had half that number. His area of responsibility included a half-million human slaves—no one really knew for sure because they died off easily, and nobody bothered to keep track. If the humans knew how thin his ground troops were, it could potentially turn into a major problem. Thankfully, they had weapons and machinery with Wave technology, giving them the edge to compensate for woefully inadequate numbers.

\*\*\*\*

Word came back quickly—there were a few research scientists left, and they were located approximately two hundred and twenty miles due south of the farmhouse.

Tag grinned as Kirv gave him the news. "How did you hear so quick?"

"Unknown to me, apparently there's a pipeline between the free people sharing information and warnings, if possible." He gave Tag a knowing look. "It appears not everyone rolled over in the conquest . . ."

"Outstanding! We need to access the pipeline . . ."

"Access the pipeline? Why?"

"I need to confirm with someone how far they got with analyzing the Lizards' technology . . ."

"Not sure I understand . . ."

"Because I plan on stealing some of it from the Lizards and getting it in the hands of those eggheads to see if they can crack the technology—you know, turn it back on those slimy, reptilian assholes."

Devin joined them, sitting quietly listening to the conversation. *Holy shit! Here we go again!*

\*\*\*\*

While the men planned, the girls prepped vegetables for dinner. "What do you do out here for friends," Claire asked Millie.

"I have a few scattered among the farms, but I don't get to see them much anymore. We talk on a communicator once in a while, but we have to watch what we say because the Lizards listen in sometimes."

"Well, that definitely sucks—girls should be able to talk about boys totally uninhibited, and to their hearts' content."

"I don't know any boys . . ."

"What? You don't know any boys?" Claire glanced at Glade. "Maybe, we need to fix that—with your Mom's permission, of course . . ."

Millie nodded slightly.

Glade smiled—she appreciated the interaction of Rose and Claire. They were only five years older than Millie, but both of them seemed mature for their ages. Yet, despite their adventures in multiple worlds, they took the time to interact with Millie and treated her as an equal. Already, Glade could see the confidence building in her daughter, and it was good for her. Besides, she could remember her own time at that age, hanging out with friends, talking about boys, and other things which seemed important at the time.

She wanted the same for her daughter.

****

"Tag, will you step outside with me for a minute?" In light of Tag's statement, Devin figured they needed to have a little chat. Noticing the girls in the farmyard, he steered his friend out the front door to a location out of earshot, and turned to Tag. "Are you out of your flippin' mind?" He'd been through a hell of a lot following Tag's lead in numerous sketchy circumstances in the last few months, but Tag's plan was insane.

"True—some may feel that way. From your question, I guess you fall into that category . . ."

"I do—as humans, we're under the radar here in a shitty situation. What we need to do is keep our heads down until we find the next portal ride, and adios our way out of this mess." He paused. "They have the human population as slaves, and the Lizards are working them to death!"

"Exactly—and that doesn't bother you?"

"Of course it bothers me—what the hell kind of question is that?" Devin started out somewhat calm, but his voice and temper were heading north.

Tag cocked his head slightly to one side as he looked back at his obviously frustrated friend. "How can you suggest we run away, leaving them to such a tragic existence?"

Now he was really getting pissed, and never before had Devin been so angry at Tag—or, anyone else—for a very long time. Sure, they had fighting situations recently where it was a basic survival thing, and they reacted accordingly. But, not only was Tag's idea sheer idiocy, Devin didn't like being called a coward. Maybe it was pent-up frustration, but Devin did something he would have never thought possible—launching a well-aimed punch as years of boxing and street fighting taught him.

Claire rounded the corner of the farmhouse, spotting the guys as Tag moved, realizing his friend was frustrated with him. The punch came as a surprise, but not so much that his years of martial arts training didn't make him react without really thinking about it. He stepped to his left, his right arm coming up with a high block, sweeping the intended blow off-target. The maneuver left Devin's arm and body motion coming forward with the expectation of making contact. When that didn't occur, his momentum carried him through, forcing him slightly off balance before he could recover, exposing his right side to an attack.

In a normal situation, Tag would exploit Devin's weakness to the fullest—however, he continued to move out of range before turning to face his friend who retracted his arm, recovered his balance, and turned to face Tag. But, before either could initiate anything further, Claire came at them at a dead run. "The next one who tries anything, I'll have their ass!"

Devin stopped in his tracks, waiting until she closed the distance between them. The diminutive young woman stood, legs apart, finger pointed at her tall and powerful man warning him not to move. "Tag, bugger off," she ordered over her shoulder.

Given the way he normally moved without making much sound, she assumed he was creating distance between them, so she waited to give him enough time to get out of range. "Devin, what are you doing? Tag is our friend!"

He shifted his gaze to Tag who was walking around the corner of the house, and out of sight. Then he looked down at the little lady who meant everything to him.

She gently poked him in the chest. "Come on—tell me."

He did.

"Okay, you had a difference of opinion—I get that. But why get angry, especially enough to take a swing at him?"

"Because he's right—we would be running away from helping out. The situation cries out for it—I know that, and didn't want to admit it. I guess the real anger was directed inwardly at me—if that makes any sense, at all."

"It does—so what do you need to do now?"

He looked down at her, smirking. "Yes, Mom—I need to make nice with my best friend . . ."

"Well, there you go." She stood on her tiptoes, and he bent over so she could give him a kiss.

When he left to find Tag, she turned, watching him walk to the corner of the farmhouse. "It probably wasn't your brightest move—taking on Tag, I mean. You know what he's capable of . . ." she called after him.

She shuddered at the potential downside of what could have happened.

## Chapter Six

Devin found Tag leaning against a split rail fence, watching sheep they rounded up the previous day. He joined him, then finally broke the silence. "You struck a nerve back there . . ."

"Ya think?"

Devin smirked. "You're my best friend—next to Claire and Rose, of course. And I kind of liked Jove and his sister, Lucy—so, based on the numbers, you come in fifth . . ." From the corner of his eye, he noticed a smile on Tag's face. "I'm sorry . . ."

Tag glanced at him and shrugged. "It's okay—I could've been more diplomatic rather than throwing it in your face."

"You were right, though, and, I knew it. But I didn't like the idea to begin with—however, the more I chew on it, helping is better."

"You don't have to go—or the girls, either. This can be a solo mission . . ."

"Right—like I'm going to let you go by yourself. You need someone to have your back . . ."

"Devin, you always have my back."

"Ah, shucks—stop, or I think I'll blush . . ."

Both men continued watching the sheep.

"Okay. And, thanks for joining in—it'll make things easier." Tag glanced in the direction of the farmhouse. "How do you think the girls are going to take the suggestion?"

"I'm not sure, but I vote for your telling them."

"Gee, thanks . . ."

\*\*\*\*

Everyone gathered at the kitchen table to discuss how to get their hands on the Lizard Wave technology. Of course, they didn't know its official name, yet they needed to call it something to provide human scientists with viable information about how the Lizards conquered the planet. Maybe they could do something useful with it to tip the scales back to their side—it was about time the human race in their current world caught a break.

"So," Kirv began, "we obtain a sample of their weapons—or, whatever. The question is how do we get it into the proper hands to make use of it?"

"I can take it," Tag offered.

"I'll go with you . . ."

Tag shook his head. "No—you need to stay here. The Lizards will miss your not working the farm, and they'll ask where you are, plus take it out on your family. So far, they don't know I exist—I can come and go without making a difference."

"I need to do something . . ."

"You are right now by providing shelter, food, and an operating base. Plus, you can get intel regarding Lizard whereabouts and help with the planning to liberate some of their technology."

Kirv's disappointment was obvious, but he understood Tag's reasoning. "Okay . . ."

"What about Millie and me?" Glade first glanced at her husband, then at Tag.

"You should be doing the same thing—I don't want to put you or Millie at extra risk."

Millie bristled at the Traveler's comment. "I'm not a little kid!"

"I know you aren't—you're a young lady who deserves

the opportunity to grow up to adulthood."

"What's the point if our planet is a slave world? I'd rather die trying to help free all of us than eek out an existence just hiding here . . ."

Tag glanced at Glade, noticing the hurt from her daughter's reference to their classification status. "The plan is for none of us to get harmed—nor a Lizard, if it can be helped."

"How's that going to work?"

"The plan is to sneak in, grab the tech stuff, then get out without getting caught. If everything works according to plan, we get what we need, and the Lizards don't even realize I was there . . ." Tag paused, thinking through each step. "And," he continued, "their not knowing the stuff is missing would be a bonus . . ."

Millie's eyes got big. "You can do that?"

"I can—however, I learned something very important with all of our recent adventures . . ."

"What?"

"Things rarely go according to plan . . ."

\*\*\*\*

They kept it compartmentalized.

Kirv started by asking for assistance from one of his neighbors furthest from his own farm, the neighbor honoring his request instantly. And that was just the beginning—word was out to discover information on Lizard movements as well as to document patterns and their handling of certain equipment. Kirv didn't give a specific reason, although some made private, educated guesses and the cooperation level was extraordinary—apparently, the masses were tired of paying homage to Lizard overlords. Slaves helped, too, when possible.

Within two weeks, they amassed a considerable amount of information which Rose, Millie, and Glade collated into a logical sequence—then the Travelers used that information to plan the mission. Because people in the area knew him, Kirv moved about freely, collecting adaptable pieces of equipment and materials they may need along the way.

Then it was time to finalize Tag's plan and, again, they gathered at the kitchen farm table. "Okay," Tag began, "as I see it, we'll be the active, moving parts. Kirv, Millie, and Glade—you'll be base support and logistics, also providing a cover story, if needed. This is just as important as what we're doing, yet it limits your exposure. You're the known entities, and need to be protected accordingly."

Kirv nodded, acknowledging Tag's assessment. "Where will you strike?"

"Actually, we have several juicy targets—the leading contender is a small Lizard base supported by a dozen of their troops—which is minimal, given the territory they cover. As an aside, we figured out from the information collected over a wide area, the Lizards are short-staffed.

Their numbers appear to be nowhere near what they should be, and that should make them vulnerable . . ."

"Where is it?"

"That's the other nice thing—it's about sixty miles from here, due south. Knowing that, we have two things in our favor—one, the base is in the same direction the liberated equipment will need to travel in order to get into the right hands. Two, it's far enough away from here that you should escape suspicion of being involved."

"However," Kirv observed, "those in closer proximity will be blamed . . ."

"Yes, unfortunately, that's likely. I don't see a way to prevent blowback if the Lizards discover the theft, so there's risk some will be hurt, or worse. If things go well, we may get away without any uproar, and it may take the Lizards time to realize their pockets were picked." Tag paused, looking at everyone at the table. "That's the ideal scenario—however, if we get our hands on something valuable that can shift the balance and they learn about it, there's no doubt they'll go apeshit trying to find it. They may sweep vast areas, so getting out of Dodge quickly is key . . ."

"Dodge?"

Tag smiled. "It's a saying in my country meaning to get the hell out—pronto!"

****

Beal sat at a table, guzzling what passed for an alcoholic beverage in Lizard culture. His immediate subordinate, Vanc, sat directly opposite him.

"Where did you hear this?" Beal took another swig.

"From one of my human sources—offer them scraps, and they'll do anything. They're so pathetic . . ."

"So—explain it to me again." Beal was conservative about risk, and protecting his tail ranked number one with him.

"The word is a human asks a lot of questions, convincing others to give him information . . ."

"What kind of information?"

"Details about our different bases, troop numbers, supplies, and equipment—stuff like that."

"Who's asking these questions?"

"That's the problem—no one knows. It's rumor. We haven't caught anyone snooping . . ."

Beal snorted. "Maybe your source is full of crap. Did you wring him out?"

"Extensively—but it didn't help."

"Then do it again . . ."

Vanc hesitated.

"Well?"

"It'll be difficult, Sir. The informant didn't survive."

Beal exploded! "What? You let your only link to the information die? What happened?"

"They're so frail compared to us, the interrogator went too far."

"Have him executed for treason—now! Then see if you can locate another source. Offer whatever enticement is needed . . ."

Vanc stood, saluting with a bent arm in front of his broad chest. "At once, Commander!"

As he left the barracks room, Vanc was grateful and relieved Beal directed his wrath at the bungling interrogator and not at him. Now he had the opportunity to dispose of that idiot before there was a chance for the real story to get out. It was he who ordered the interrogator to push harder, brutalizing the human informant—in retrospect, not a smart thing to do since the creature died.

\*\*\*\*

The mission clock started ticking.

They had as much information as possible without actually living on the small Lizard base with the beasts. They chose their target, and they'd learn the exact location of the scientists when connecting with a source who acted as a protector of one of the last vestiges humans had in the scientific community.

Now, all they had to do was steal Lizard technology, and get it to those who, hopefully, knew what to do with it. It sounded straightforward, but Tag knew there were pitfalls—a multitude of things could go wrong, a number of which could be random, a few unforeseen.

After finalizing plans, the Travelers were ready to leave by early morning. Rose and Claire faced Glade and Millie. "Thanks for giving us a place to live and a warm feeling of welcome . . ." Rose embraced the mother and daughter, in turn.

Claire turned to Millie. "You're a fine young woman with great character. Brave, too. Support your family, and I know one day you'll meet the right one for you." Then she faced Glade. "Thanks for being our friend when we had none in this world . . ."

Glade smiled. "You're welcome—it was our pleasure, and the least we could do for you. Not everyone would risk everything trying to rescue our world. All of you are amazing, and we thank you . . ."

The women embraced.

Tag and Devin took turns thanking Kirv for his help, wishing him and his family well.

Kirv shook their hands vigorously. "Good luck with everything—I don't think many people would attempt what you're doing for a society that isn't their own. With success of your plan, we'll build on our efforts here and organize our people to rally when the time is right. Eventually, we shall gain back our freedom and eliminate the Lizards . . ."

Tag shook his hand warmly. "I know you'll do it, Kirv—and don't be afraid to lead. You have it in you . . ."

****

"Well, these are going to be a pain in the butt . . ." Claire referred to the hand tools each of them carried—shovels and a pickax. The idea was to look like a young work crew moving to another job, passing for only a cursory look from curious humans along the way. More important, they needed to look like one more group of human slaves going about their work for the Lizard masters. Granted, the cover probably wouldn't hold up under closer scrutiny, but it might avoid causal questions or interest.

The plan was to cover the sixty-mile trek on foot to the target in three days—they didn't want to push harder by looking like they were in a hurry, attracting unwanted attention. Moving at a leisurely pace was more consistent with slave workers trundling along to get to their next workplace.

"I'll trade you the pick for the shovel, if you like," Devin offered.

Claire grinned. "No, thanks—I think you're a pick kind of guy . . ."

"Is that a good thing or a bad thing?"

Rose piped up. "Don't ask—you may be afraid of the answer."

Tag chuckled. "They're just envious because you have possession of the specialized tool . . ."

Devin stuck his chest out in a mock, proud gesture.

Claire shook her head. "It's his way of saying you're special..."

"So?"

She sighed dramatically. "Some connotations of 'special' aren't always complimentary..."

He gave Tag a beady-eyed look. "I can do without the non-compliments..."

Tag laughed, and their walk continued with light-hearted banter for most of the day.

They spotted only a few people in the distance. One or two waved, and they returned the gesture, but, luckily, no one got close enough to strike up a conversation. The last thing the Travelers needed was to provide their cover story of workers on the way to the next job.

Even better, they saw no evidence of the Lizards.

By early evening, they scoped out possible locations to pitch camp for the night. It wasn't too much into dusk when they found a suitable place—off trail, about one hundred and fifty yards. There was water, and jungle cover was thick enough to conceal them—it was perfect, but only after Tag and Devin scouted the perimeter, pronouncing the site suitable.

As they had to do in previous worlds, they set up a rough bush camp—no one had bedding, so setting a blanket on the ground was as complicated as it got. No campfire. They couldn't afford the risk of attracting attention.

"I wonder what culinary delights in the dried food line await me tonight," Devin commented, rummaging through his pack.

Tag was following suit. "Yeah—the suspense is killing me..."

"How far do you think we came today," Rose asked.

"We made good time—maybe a bit over twenty miles, or so."

"Then we'll need the whole three days allotted for travel to the target?"

"Yep—plus, we may want to be a bit more careful as we get closer. It's important to scope out what the setup is around the target—if things go south, we need to be somewhat familiar with the lay of the land so we can get out. It would be nice to have an idea of suitable ambush sites if the Lizards are onto us, and in close pursuit. If it takes an extra day to check it out, so be it..."

"Well," Claire commented, "so far, things have gone according to plan..."

That was about to change.

# Chapter Seven

Two more days of continuous travel with only short rest breaks as well as eating dried food on the fly brought them within striking distance of their designated target. Again, they encountered few people along the way, and Claire figured it was one of two things—the Lizards eliminated a substantial portion of the population at the time of the conquest, or large groups of humans were slaves working in other areas.

Maybe both.

Their journey, however, wasn't problem free—on the second day, an encounter with a Lizard almost turned deadly. Up until then, they managed to duck into cover when spying the odd Lizard patrol in the distance. The element of surprise, however, occurred for humans and reptilians when the Travelers were navigating thick, dense jungle following a narrow path. Devin in the lead, Claire and Rose followed single file with Tag acting as rearguard ten paces back. As their pathway intersected another, suddenly a Lizard trooper appeared trudging along the adjoining trail, and it was only due to good luck Devin and the soldier abruptly halted moments before an imminent collision—Claire and Rose bumped into Devin in succession, and Tag was far enough back to stop before he came into view from the other pathway.

It was a good thing they rehearsed for such a situation.

Devin immediately looked at the ground, slouching and grounding the tools he carried over his shoulder, the girls following suit. Out of sight, Tag moved into the thick jungle cover, figuring if the encounter went south, his being an element of surprise couldn't hurt.

The Lizard soldier initially looked startled by the sudden appearance of the three humans seemingly out of nowhere. But, he quickly recovered and assumed the usually haughty persona of the conquering-species overlord.

He activated the translation device. "What are you doing here?" Even with the mechanical, tinny sound, his arrogance was apparent. Glaring at the three puny humans, especially the male, he waited impatiently for an answer.

"We have been ordered to survey a location for a hunting camp," Claire responded. Kirv advised them the Lizards adored hunting, the chase and kill their favorite recreational pastimes. So far, the reptilians limited the activity to non-human species, and the Travelers didn't want to be first-time targets.

"The jungle is too thick here," the Lizard snapped. "Why do you not see this?"

Keeping her submissive gaze on the ground, she answered. "We were told to come in here—we did not question the order..."

The beast snorted. "Who sent you?"

She shrugged. "I don't know who it was—you look the same to us." Behind her, she heard Rose stifle a snicker which almost slipped out.

The Lizard swiveled to look at Rose who covered up the slip by coughing out loud. Satisfied he wasn't being defied, he refocused on Claire. "Why isn't the male talking for you?"

Claire understood immediately—Glade told her the Lizard society was male dominant with the females in the background. "He's strong by our standards, but not very bright—a simple greeting stretches his vocabulary."

The Lizard eyeballed Devin, then shook his head and chuckled. "Your kind is dull to begin with—if he's stupid by your standards, I'm surprised he could get this far."

Claire nodded her head in agreement. *Yeah—but, not so dull than to fool your sorry ass...*

"Move!" The Lizard motioned with his weapon to get out of the way, heading down the path in Tag's direction, marching past him, unaware of who hid in the bushes.

When the heavy footsteps faded to nothing, Tag slipped from cover, a quizzical expression on his face.

Claire pointed to Devin. "I was simply stating the

obvious—and, even the Lizard beast could see the dim light in the window of our friend here..."

"Well—thank you very much for that..."

"Hey, it worked! Right?"

"True..."

"Well, there you go."

Tag clapped Devin on his back. "Thanks for taking one for the team!"

Devin grunted. "I'm glad everyone's so amused..."

\*\*\*\*

They thought that was the end of it. Unknown to them, however, all human encounters outside defined slave worksites were reported to the Planetary Control Center—the hub allowing the reptilians to monitor movement of individuals from the conquered population. The Lizard they met on the jungle trail arrived at his destination an hour and a half after the encounter and, by the time he checked in, downed a drink, and shot the bull with his cronies, another two hours slipped by. Before he went off shift, it finally sunk in he was to file a report of three, unsupervised humans wandering alone in the jungle. He chuckled at the thought of revising his report to read two female humans and one idiot male.

As often happens, bureaucracy was particularly inefficient. It marched on at its own laggardly pace and, eventually, the report reached the point where it was disseminated throughout the regional military command.

Beal reviewed recent human encounters that were different from the slave farms dedicating their workforce to construction duties. Of particular interest were isolated reports from human resources hoping to gain favor from their overlords. Once he connected several reports in sequence, they indicated a group of four young humans—two males and two females—moving in a southerly direction. Interestingly, an occupation soldier—obviously a third-tier individual—met them in the jungle, but he didn't fully check out the three humans he encountered.

Beal wondered if they were the same humans spotted several times north of his location. It was in such situations he cursed the withdrawal of most of their airships for future invasions on new planets, leaving them hamstrung for quick reconnaissance of a wide area. Everything was left to ground forces which were particularly thin since they were stripped out for the same reason as the airships. Everywhere he looked, they lacked sufficient force to properly control what they conquered. *Why go after something if you can't look after it?* To Beal, it seemed his race should stop the expansion of their empire.

In his position as Regional Commander of the largest occupation force, one might expect Beal to remain in a central command post, allowing his forces to get their claws dirty dealing with the surviving human population.

However, he liked to get out as much as possible to obtain a firsthand feel for what was happening in the field. On a whim, he would often join a patrol to see with his own eyes the state of affairs—relying on substandard troops to accurately report was a constant battle from the administrative end.

As he contemplated the issue, Beal became aware of someone hovering in the doorway. "Enter, or go away..."

Vanc stepped into the room.

"Report."

"Commander, there's no further information regarding the group of four young humans you showed interest in—they may have been workers traveling to join a construction group, or surveyors. That said, I checked and found no evidence of orders for a potential hunting camp in that area of the jungle..."

"The jungle is too thick there—anyone can see that."

"Agreed—it's likely a cover story."

"But why would they need a cover story? That's the real question..."

"Perhaps they only appeared to be worker slaves..."

Beal seriously considered his second-in-command's suggestion. *Free humans. A cover story. Heading south. What are they up to?*

****

The third day of their trek was uneventful. The Travelers approached the area of the small Lizard base in the early evening, finding a comfortable, safe location out of the way. Devin and the girls rested and had something to eat while Tag scouted the immediate area to make sure no threats existed—after that, he joined them.

They waited until total darkness to scope out the Lizard barracks. The jungle thinned, but they still had sufficient cover to conceal their approach, and one Lizard soldier stood guard, doing a less than stellar job. He got up occasionally, walked fifteen or so paces, then headed back to a seat designed to accommodate a large tail. Then, he promptly fell back asleep, snoring loudly.

Devin glanced at Tag. "How close do you want to go? With this clown outside the door, we could saunter in, ask for a beer, and he still wouldn't notice . . ."

Tag arched his eyebrows. "Let's not test their ability to hear and wake suddenly. I'm comfortable viewing from this range—it appears they only have one entrance and exit to the building. Good from a defensive position—however, it's easy to trap them inside. If we were here to execute an attack, they would be conveniently bottled up, unable to respond effectively . . ."

Devin shook his head. "After all the action and tactics deployed in the last world, it makes me wonder how the reptilians managed to conquer this one . . ."

"Obviously, we're not looking at their A team—give a sub-grade soldier a huge technological edge, and he's still tough to take out even though he might be an idiot."

"But—we aren't here to take them out."

"Nope—just a quick in and out liberating some of their tech stuff, and we're out of here."

"How?"

"Observe their patterns. Learn what may be the ideal stuff we need, and watch for an opportunity."

"And if that doesn't come?"

Tag shrugged in the dark beside his friend. "We'll just have to create one, won't we?"

\*\*\*\*

Kirv sat at the farm table, candlelight creating a soft glow as he relaxed, thinking about how they could stick it to the Lizards. Previously, the idea would never have occurred to him—now, after his detainment as well as encountering the Travelers, he couldn't sit still and do nothing.

He needed to strike back.

Of course, if found out, consequences could boomerang, possibly hurting him and his family, but the risk was worth it to gain a small step toward freedom for his world. He and Glade discussed it, both agreeing they needed to do their parts.

So, he faced a choice—act alone as a family group, but, potentially, make less overall impact, or rally some of the neighbors he could trust to effect change by a coordinated effort. Successful or not, surely the Lizards' reaction would be heavy-handed—or, heavy-clawed in their case. If they couldn't determine who was responsible, Kirv anticipated they may strike back at random targets to make a point. He considered reaching out to free people outside his area, motivating them to act accordingly—even contacts in the slave ranks could prepare many humans to be ready to act when needed. Up until now, an information pipeline was the extent of involvement, and it became clear it was time to act. There was no doubt about it—casualties were a part of war and, on his small scale, he was about to start one.

****

Tag and Devin kept watch throughout the night, spelled by one of the girls so there were always two sets of eyes studying the objective. Finally, Tag pulled them back to their small base camp in the jungle. "Okay, what do we know?"

"They have a dozen soldiers as previously advertised by the information pipeline," Claire responded, "and, most of them look to be unbelievably lazy. If Callie saw this, she'd order them deported back to their planet!"

Rose agreed. "The problem is they don't go far from their base because they're lazy and disinterested in their duties—they need to be lured away."

Tag grinned. "Exactly! There are two scenarios I'm considering, so jump in with your thoughts—one, we create a diversion away from their small base and have one of us slip in and pilfer the technology when they're rooting around in the jungle. Two, we lure one or two away, or catch them on a patrol and somehow liberate what we need."

"The second choice," Devin observed, "would mean they'd know immediately we have their technology, and the chase would be on . . ."

"Correct . . ."

Devin thought for a moment. "With choice one, if we get lucky and they don't see us and don't notice the theft right away, we could put some distance between us before they find out . . ."

Tag nodded. "That's the preferred option—we know, however, the perfect situation hardly ever plays out. We need to be fluid in thought and action . . ."

Claire glanced at him. "Okay—what's going to be the distraction to draw them away? And, who are the lucky ones to set that up?"

"We could draw straws . . ."

"Really?" There was no mistaking her sarcasm.

Tag ignored it. "It's hard to know what the trickiest part will be—if all the Lizards bite on the distraction and leave their base, then one of us will have an easy time infiltrating to pick up what we need. That's if they leave some goodies behind." He paused, thinking of how things might play out. "If, however, some stay back, getting in and out undetected will be a challenge. In any event, the distracting group will do their thing, and take off before the bad guys arrive . . ."

"So you think the hard part is going to be the theft from the barracks?"

"Yep . . ."

"And, who gets that enviable task?"

"I seem to be the most likely choice . . ."

"Should two remain here to search, or should Tag search and one provide backup?" Devin wasn't quite sure of the particulars, but it seemed to him they needed to divide their duties.

"Good idea . . ."

"If things go south at the base," Devin continued, "an extra weapon to fend them off could be huge . . ."

"Agreed . . ."

"Well—what's it going to be?"

Tag thought for a moment. "I think we pair off into teams of two—Team One stays and lifts the tech stuff, and Team Two makes a lot of noise somewhere so the Lizards investigate." Tag paused. "I should be the one to do the search—Claire is the best shot of the two girls, so she could cover me, if needed. You and Rose could do your thing out in the jungle to attract attention. When it's time to get out, both of you are tall and can run faster and easier than Claire."

"Okay, what's the distraction going to be?" Up until then, Rose remained silent, thinking through Tag's plan.

"We'll have to work that out . . ."

# Chapter Eight

It was always a long shot—still, no response bit deep into the hope of making progress. Usually a free thinker who seemed to effortlessly float complex ideas on a cosmic scale, he felt constrained. Frustrated. Blocked.

Several weeks flew by since they constructed a mathematically-based message, sending it on its way to the portal's Controller—if there were one—through the ether of space. He knew his chances of communication were slim—yet, with no result, why did he feel cheated when the odds were so astronomical? Nonetheless, it hurt to not accomplish such a simple goal—free Tag from the cycle of portal trips. By nature, Kyle was an upbeat person, so wallowing in self-recrimination only added to his frustration.

He was stuck in a loop.

But, as often happens with pets and owners, Lego seemed to recognize his master's dissatisfaction. The big furry oaf wandered into his office, exploring the room before resting his head on his master's lap.

Kyle massaged the dog's ears and jowls where he loved to be touched. No need to be gentle—the one hundred and forty-five pound animal preferred the roughhousing over a light pat. The quiet moment made Kyle recall when he and Tag first got Lego—after losing their parents in a car accident, three months old with huge paws, the new addition seemed to brighten things for their traumatized family.

Now, they were down one with Tag's disappearance.

"Hey, good lookin'—what are you boys up to?" Jackie smiled as she watched the tender moment between owner and dog.

"Thanks for the compliment."

"Really? I was referring to the dog . . ."

"Ouch!"

She giggled. "Okay, what's up?"

"Well, to be truthful, I was stuck, feeling frustrated and a bit sorry for myself until Lego arrived to cheer me up."

"Excellent! Why don't we continue on that theme? The two of you can come with me to the gallery, and you can help with setting up for the showing. Lego can sit back and give his critical analysis . . ."

"How so?"

"Simple—no reaction is a negative. Tail wagging and

excitement will be construed as a thumbs up."

"Hmm . . . Lego, the art critic. Who knew?"

\*\*\*\*

The plan was simple—create a big kerfuffle in the jungle to draw the Lizards away from home base. Then, sneak in, lift the tech, and get out. Next steps? Link up, head south, and hope the reptilians didn't notice or wouldn't be able to catch them. They figured simple would be best, except for the likelihood of numerous variables throwing a monkey wrench into the works.

Everyone in position, Tag and Claire were close to the Lizard barracks under cover in the evening's failing light. They would be hard to pick out of the jungle underbrush, especially if the reptilians were concentrating on the distraction. Devin and Rose were located a half a mile from the barracks in a small clearing—previously, Tag and Devin thoroughly scouted the immediate area to plan the best evac route once it hit the fan. False trails in place, hopefully the Lizards would follow them during the confusion.

The deception was predicated on the small amount of powerful explosives they brought with them from their last world. Military grade, the blast would be enough to get the attention of anyone in the vicinity, and the Lizards would react to what was going on in their own backyard.

At least, that was the plan.

Claire's nerves shredded when nothing happened. Did Devin and Rose have a problem with the explosives? Worse, were they found out by the Lizards? Fidgety, she was about to ask Tag a question when the jungle reverberated with a loud explosion, rattling the door of the barracks building.

The outside guard fell out of his chair and, before he could regain his feet, the rest of the Lizard soldiers poured out of the barracks, stomping the guard in the process. If their mission weren't so serious, Tag figured they could've sat back with popcorn and watched the show. He shook his head, considering the alien species that now ruled this version of Earth. *Really?*

Within moments, six of the nine soldiers disappeared into the jungle, running toward the sound of the explosion. Three of them were unaccounted for, but Tag didn't have time to worry about it. "Okay, I'm going in—take your station, and shoot at anything that's reptilian."

She cocked her handgun. "Got it—do your thing..."

Tag moved swiftly through the barracks door, gun in hand just in case they miscounted and one of them lurked inside. The interior of the small building was a shambles—it was a pigsty to start with and, when the Lizards left in a hurry after the explosion, they knocked over chairs and tables in the process.

He kicked furniture aside and began searching, first noticing a chest with a clasp holding it shut—one good bash with the butt of his gun and it fell open. Inside, he spotted a hand weapon, its charge of whatever form of ammunition, and two other devices he didn't recognize. Nothing else appeared readily available to grab, so Tag collected the items and exited the barracks, running toward Claire's position.

He stopped beside her and slipped the items into his pack, tightly fastening it. "Did you see anything?"

"Not a damned thing . . ."

"Outstanding! Let's boogie out of here . . ." Tag led the way, making sure he didn't lose the short-legged Claire in the process. The Travelers set a meeting place for linking up with Devin and Rose, but they had a head start, running immediately after the charge detonated—their distance to travel, however, was greater. Even so, without unforeseen problems, all should arrive at the same place around the same time.

Of course, there was a backup plan—if they failed to link up at the primary location, they had two more fall-back choices. If none of those worked, everyone was to keep moving directly south—each had the coordinates of their ultimate destination.

Everything appeared to be going to plan, except for one little detail—the sudden appearance of a Lizard soldier blocking the path in front of Tag. Apparently, one of the three missing Lizards from the detachment wasn't missing anymore . . .

\*\*\*\*

Running through the jungle on a preselected path, Devin considered it extremely fortunate the explosives they brought with them from the last world came with a delay timer. With the force of the explosion just set off, being too close would've landed him in the trees in pieces.

He heard Rose running effortlessly behind him. Both were tall and long-legged and, with a clear path they were rapidly chewing up distance to the rally point. Their part of the plan accomplished, he hoped Tag would have enough time to grab the tech stuff and get away. More important, he worried about a scenario of Claire's having to get into a shootout to cover Tag's searching the barracks. So far, he hadn't heard any gunfire—however, they were making noise while running, and they were too far from their friends.

Within ten minutes, Devin and Rose reached the primary rally point.

No sign of Tag and Claire.

\*\*\*\*

The Lizard warrior appeared equally surprised as Tag and, after a moment's initial shock, he moved, reaching for a sidearm. With his weapon partially drawn and before it rose to level firing position, Tag moved closer and kicked at the clawed hand. The Lizard fumbled the weapon, yet it didn't hit the ground. Tag quickly leapt up and kicked out again, this time connecting solidly—the gun sailed into the underbrush, lost from sight. The Lizard and Tag followed its flight path until it vanished from view.

Then, each fixed their attention on the opponent.

Approximately six feet across, the trail left little combat room to maneuver. Tag stepped back out of range once he knocked the weapon away, hoping not to use his own gun—he didn't want other Lizards to zero in on their position at the sound of gunfire.

If their combat turned hand-to-hand, it was going to be tough. His opponent was huge—at least eight feet tall and weighing in at three to four hundred pounds. Not having been so close to one before, Tag hadn't appreciated how bloody massive they were.

"Should I shoot the bastard," Claire called out. Obviously, taking the time to ask the question, she appreciated what the sound of gunfire would accomplish—more bloody Lizards.

"Not yet," he responded, never taking his eyes off the reptile. "Let's see what happens—you'll know when to fire, if needed . . ."

"Be careful, Tag . . ."

"No shit!"

The Lizard activated his translation device before running into the human in front of him and, once the explosion occurred, he figured questioning humans might be needed. He understood the interchange between the male and the female, although hugely surprised the puny human dared to confront him. What was especially disconcerting was the ease with which Tag disarmed him. However, the Lizard, Qwei, felt comfortable battling the small opponent—it had been quite awhile since he had been in a hand-to-hand combat situation. But, after sizing up the human standing ready in front of him, Qwei smiled and drew his combat knife, then moved forward.

Claire's eyes widened at the size of the bladed weapon. "That thing looks like a friggin' sword!"

Tag heard the murmured comment, readily agreeing with her assessment. He decided to leave his own knife sheathed—leaving his hands free would be better. And, if needed, he could draw it quickly.

The Lizard thrust his knife down at Tag's stomach as two huge strides forward ate up the distance between them, the force of the blow and size of the weapon capable of splitting the human in two.

That's if it connected with the target.

In an extended position with his right arm and leg forward to deliver the momentum of the thrust, the tip of Lizard's huge blade sliced air—and it was only a split second later Qwei caught movement from the corner of his right eye.

His right knee joint flared in pain.

Tag struck with maximum power, his kick landing on the exposed right knee of the Lizard. If it were a human, such a side impact should have blown out the leg and disabled the opponent—but the beast was still standing, turning toward him.

Before the large blade could reach him, Tag mustered another kick to the same knee joint, this time a frontal attack. He heard something give in his opponent's leg, but the Lizard still stood before him, although a defined limp was evident. Qwei found it increasingly difficult to have his right leg support him, and the little opponent kept buzzing around him before he could land a counterstrike.

Then, a third blow.

His leg severely compromised, Qwei was down on one knee trying to keep track of the human attacker—not so easy with searing pain in his knee.

Once the Lizard faltered, Tag easily spun out of the way, pivoted with maximum momentum, and carried through with a spinning kick to the throat. Even with its being down on one knee, Tag had to aim high to connect with his target.

The Lizard warrior's throat wasn't as sturdily built as the rest of him—in fact, it was something of a soft spot in the otherwise robust individual. The crushing blow snapped tissue, bone, and cartilage, audible to everyone on the trail.

Qwei wasn't sure what happened—he couldn't breathe, and choked on blood flooding into his collapsed throat. He was only vaguely aware of the human male standing in front of him, watching him die. Qwei knew it was happening, and he was strangely curious why things didn't seem to hurt anymore.

Several minutes later, the massive reptilian lay dead. Thankfully, agony was spared at the end, yet there was no doubt it was a nasty way to go. It made him remember a recent time he confronted an enemy soldier in their last world—a female with a combat knife tried to skewer him, and he was forced to kill in a similar fashion.

It wasn't pretty.

The result of the skirmish evident, Claire quietly moved forward and stood beside Tag, gently placing her hand in his. "You had to do it—he would've been merciless..."

"I know. I find it tougher—more personal—when it's face-to-face, rather than potting away with a gun hoping to hit something."

Despite their circumstance and true to herself, Claire remained on course. "C'mon—let's go. The others will be waiting for us..." She pulled him away, pointing him down the trail. Only once did she glance back at the formidable beast now lying pathetically strewn across the trail.

She shuddered at the thought of how easily it could've gone the other way...

# CHAPTER NINE

Devin wanted to press on to the secondary rally point since Tag and Claire hadn't shown up. He was nervous hanging around, waiting, even though it was only five minutes. Maybe the fact they were still close to the diversion location had something to do with it. "I think we should continue on . . ."

Rose thought for a moment. "No—let's wait a few more minutes . . ."

Hanging around wasn't his style, but he acquiesced. "Okay—five minutes. That's all . . ."

As he was about to let Rose know it was time to go, he heard someone coming down the trail, approaching their small clearing. "Shhhh," he ordered, placing his index finger to his lips while drawing Rose into cover until they could see who it was.

Within twenty seconds, Tag and Claire entered the clearing, stopping to look for their friends.

Rose reacted first, running to hug Tag who was looking the other way, and Devin followed suit with Claire.

"Well—you two certainly know how to make things go boom," Claire commented. "The noise shocked the outside guard, and he fell out of his chair. It was hilarious!"

She stopped talking when there was no reaction from Devin and Rose, mainly because both were focused on Tag who was gazing into the distance.

"What's going on," Rose asked, concern starting to form.

He didn't answer, and continued staring into the jungle.

She glanced at Claire, arching her eyebrows.

"We had a bit of trouble on the trail," Claire explained. "We bumped into a Lizard . . ."

Rose nodded for her to continue.

"There was a fight . . ."

"Oh . . ." Rose turned her attention back to Tag, hugging him. "Hey—you've been in this situation before. What's different now?"

Tag finally turned his attention to her. "I don't know—and, you're right, it's not my first time. There have been many—too many. But, even though he was a loathsome creature, it was depressing to watch him die, the life slowly oozing out of him. For some reason this one's affecting me more—I don't know why."

Rose gave him a kiss. "Tell you what—we've gotta go now. Let's get somewhere safe, and we can talk about it more if you like."

He snapped out of it at her prompting. "Okay—let's head south, and keep moving until it gets fully dark. We need to get as much distance as we can if they figure out we borrowed their technology . . ."

****

It was midmorning of the following day when Vanc reluctantly entered the Commander's office. He hated being the bearer of bad news, and his superior's temper was legendary.

Beal looked up. "Sub-Commander—why are you here?"

Vanc paused briefly. "A report came in from outpost 1138 . . ."

The frown on the Commander's broad face encouraged him to continue.

"There was an attack on the outpost . . ."

"And?"

"One dead."

Beal smirked. "What do I care about another dead human? They die like flies here . . ."

"Not human, Commander—the casualty is one of ours."

The Commander sat up a little straighter. "Explain!"

"As I said, an attack came—an explosion in the jungle. When the detachment rallied to investigate, they found only the evidence of the discharge, nothing else."

"How did the soldier die?"

"Not from the explosion—he was found on a jungle trail, two time units away from the other site."

"What killed him?"

Again, a pause. "Not from weapons fire, or a puncture wound of any sort. His throat was crushed . . ."

Beal sat silently, thinking. *My species is twice the size and several times stronger than humans. How could such a thing happen?*

He finally noticed his subordinate's nervousness. "Anything else?"

Vanc knew he couldn't delay any longer. "Yes—a holster weapon, range finder, and a hand-held anti-grav unit are missing from their barracks." He waited for a few seconds, then added, "The weapon and anti-grav have Wave technology."

Beal froze. *Missing Wave technology! If it falls into the wrong hands, it can prove disastrous!*

And, it could get worse. When the Prime and New Planetary Holdings heard about it, someone's head would roll—literally. Beal didn't want to think about word of this getting back to Off-Planet Command. The whole mess happened in his district, on his watch, and it wouldn't matter to those above him the incident occurred at a small, isolated outpost.

He would be responsible.

Vanc stood quietly to not attract attention. He could see the Commander's thought processes register, knowing full well there were stories out there of garrison units on some planets being executed for less.

The Commander glared at him. "Get an investigative team out there, and take a half section of troops with you—I want the full story of how this happened. The area within ten micros of the barracks as the source point is to be quarantined. Nothing goes in or out, unless it's our troops."

"Yes, Commander."

"And, Vanc? Unless you want both of us executed, find those missing Wave items!"

They stared at each other wondering if that were a possibility, or a probability at the moment.

\*\*\*\*

When it got to the point of crashing into trees in the dark, Tag called a halt. "Let's find someplace off the trail to bed down. We need to rest, eat, and be ready at first light to get going. The Lizards might be searching in the dark for us, and they'll make up the distance we covered if they come our way . . ."

As it turned out, luck was with them.

But that didn't mean it would last . . .

\*\*\*\*

Tag took the last overnight watch, monitoring until early-dawn light filtered through the jungle canopy. "Okay, everyone—up and at 'em. It's time to go . . ."

They didn't need much prompting. The tension from the previous day plus the worry about being tracked had them on edge and, after a quick bite to eat, they discussed their plan. "We have roughly one hundred sixty miles to cover," Tag advised, "carrying the contraband we liberated from the Lizards. Right now, we don't know if they're aware they were ripped off—but, let's assume so. We need to be hyper-vigilant of being tracked—yet, balance that against moving quickly enough to keep ahead of the chase. I don't know the Lizards' pace, and it won't matter if they move with their vehicles and sweep ahead of us. So, there may be a net of them searching for us in any direction."

"What about airships joining in," Claire asked.

He shook his head. "We haven't seen any before, and reports are they don't have many available. However, for something this important, they may use what resources they have in reserve—I would. And, we have no idea if they have satellite viewing capabilities, or anything of that nature . . ."

"Hardly any challenges at all, then . . ."

He smiled. "That's the attitude! Look on the bright side!"

"It's going to be a long road," Rose observed. "We should get going . . ."

\*\*\*\*

The investigative team worked as best they could throughout the night, but the jungle search had to wait for morning. One order of business they could accomplish was to direct the immediate arrest of the outpost leader. The officer in charge of the half-section of troops took the detainee out into the nighttime jungle—directed by Commander Beal before they left—ordering two soldiers to place the former outpost leader against a tree—then both troopers brought their Wave rifles to bear and opened fire. The nature of the technology could be used for offensive or defensive purposes, and the beams converging on the victim blew his body apart. If one were to inspect his remains under daylight conditions, nothing bigger than a baseball remained.

No chance of identification.

When they had sufficient light, the investigative team carefully examined the area surrounding the barracks, as well as the clearing in the jungle where the explosion occurred. Human footprints were abundant in both areas—there were, however, several sets of footprints from both locations which led in different directions. Each set appeared to peter out into the jungle when they led off-trail. Initially, it was difficult to determine where the perpetrators went, or if they separated, taking their own ways out of the area.

The previous night, the half-section leader directed several squads to use motor transport to jump ahead in various directions to head off the humans. They randomly chose where to set up their watches since they had no idea where the targets went—a crapshoot, at best. Squads of Lizard troops figured they had major trails covered, and the squad leaders met the previous night before heading out to their respective areas. The consensus was they didn't have enough troops to cover each possible trail—not to mention none of them were too excited about sending out single soldiers considering what they heard about the dead Lizard trooper with his throat crushed. Not one of them could figure out how a puny human could do such a thing, and they also didn't have a clue about the size of the human force staging the raid.

One thing, however, was sure—whatever they ran into, the squad leaders wanted decent troop numbers and Wave tech weapons to meet the threat.

Block and ambush was more their style.

\*\*\*\*

The path limited movement to single file, their direction choice resulting from a decision to keep as low key as possible—if they had to sacrifice a bit of speed for stealth, that was okay.

So far, so good.

In the lead, Tag was happy with the pace and distance they covered. The narrow trail ran straight south with only the odd bend here and there to avoid boulders, or particularly heavy foliage. Still, he had to be careful not to wear out Claire—she wasn't completely healed, and her pace was slower than her fellow Travelers. So, a steady, distance-eating pace worked—if they ran into trouble, all of them being out of breath and exhausted wouldn't leave them in very good shape to repel an attack, or react to an emergency situation.

Every two hours they took a ten-minute break—just long enough for a small drink as well as a handful of dried food. As they rested, each wrestled with personal thoughts. *Were they clear of the pursuit? Did the Lizards notice the missing items? Would they run into them around the next bend? Where would they camp for the night?*

With his own mind occupied with similar thoughts, Tag almost missed the tip-off they weren't alone on the trail—and, it was a testament to their hard-won experience during the last several months that none of them uttered a sound once they saw his raised fist.

He stood, listening intently to sounds approaching from ahead—then, a hand signal indicated to get off the trail and seek cover. Instinctively, they moved in unison to the same side and, as quietly as possible, disappeared into jungle cover.

It didn't take long for the source of the sound to appear.

A sub-squad of four Lizard troopers stomped down the narrow trail, their girth nearly filling the path as they marched in single file. The four humans could see enough through the foliage to distinguish the enemy soldiers were equipped with large, rifle-type weapons of a strange design. They were also armored with vests, headgear, and leg guards—the consistency of the protective gear seemed to have its own light source, shimmering on the shadowy jungle trail.

One of them emitted a grunting sound followed by several clicking noises—the file leader growled back which seemed to shut up the original Lizard. They continued on down the trail the humans just traversed, oblivious to the fact they were walking over trail signs of their targets.

When the Lizard procession was gone, the Travelers stepped onto the path.

"If that's their language," Claire commented, "I figure the original speaker was probably doing the universal thing all troopers do—bitching about something."

Devin smiled. "I think you're right. We were lucky we didn't bump into them on the trail . . ."

Tag agreed. "I have to admit my mind was wandering, and it must've been the talking which alerted me to them. Thank heaven for whining soldiers . . ."

"Did you notice their protective gear seemed to be lit up? At first, I thought it was shimmering in the light, but it's mostly shadowy in here. No—it definitely had a light source, as if it were energized in some fashion." Rose glanced at Tag for confirmation.

Tag nodded. "I noticed it, too. It might be their high-tech systems aren't just for offensive weapons, which I bet those rifles are. The armor they had on might somehow protect them more than usual. If so, they'll be hard to bring down if we get into a firefight with them—it's probably what led to their easy success in the original invasion."

"If," Devin interjected, "the foursome behind us has friends still ahead, we're within their defensive net. This can get ugly . . ."

"Agreed—I'm betting you're right. Well, there's no going back and retracing our steps because we know for sure we're blocked by the unit that tromped through here—unless we stay behind and shadow them. But, that's a regressive step. I say push on carefully, fully prepared to hide or run depending on circumstances. We have to slip through them—I don't think we have the firepower to fight our way through . . ."

"That's my thought . . ." Devin raised an eyebrow. "Do you want me to take point, and you can watch my butt for a while?"

"Okay—lead on. We'll space things out a bit more between us to give room to move freely. But, keep in visual contact of each other . . ."

# Chapter Ten

Vanc didn't hesitate. His Commander's tone and body language were more aggressive than normal, and he knew it was from the pressure they were under to retrieve the stolen technology quickly—before the report filtered up to the highest rank on their conquered planet. He shuddered to think of what Off-Planet Command would do.

"Report."

"The investigative team determined the explosion in the jungle was merely for distraction purposes to draw the stationed troops away from the barracks."

"Which it effectively did . . ."

"Yes."

"Continue . . ."

"They confirm three items are missing, two of which are Wave tech equipped."

"What about the search?"

Vanc shook his massive reptilian head. "Nothing yet."

"Send another half-section of troops," Beal ordered. "I want the area blanketed."

"Commander—even if we sent everyone we have in this district, the jungle area is too large and the targets of the search could have gone in any direction. It's not possible to effectively cover the multitude of trails in the area . . ." Saying such a thing to his superior was a risk, but necessary.

Rather than explode in anger at having that fact pointed out, Beal took a few moments to consider the crappy situation. "Place a request for three airships to be allocated for the search . . ."

"Sir, the Prime has direct control over all airships on the planet. Having so few, he won't give us three."

"I know he won't, but asking for three may give us at least two, which is manageable—one won't do us much good."

Vanc recognized the Commander's frustration, so it seemed the right moment for a piece of good news. "There is one thing, Sir—the outpost leader was executed last night."

Beal nodded acknowledgment, pleased the execution would make a statement to all forces under his command.

Failure and negligence brought extreme consequences, and he knew the same fate awaited him if the situation weren't rectified by recovering the stolen technology.

He turned to his subordinate. "Vanc, do whatever is needed to create enthusiasm among the units involved in the search and retrieval operation."

"Yes, Commander." Vanc realized he was dismissed.

As he exited the room, the Sub-Commander understood he had total authority to use any means he could think of to motivate the units involved—including extreme measures outside the normal course of already harsh discipline within the Lizards' military structure.

\*\*\*\*

Dodge and weave. Run and hide. They performed various permutations of that dance for the last four hours, but not without incident—several were close calls. So far, however, the Lizards didn't know the Travelers were skulking through their neighborhood trying desperately to slip through the net of blocking troops.

It wasn't a situation of the Lizards having so many soldiers that sheer numbers were a problem—in fact, it was just the opposite. Even though they scattered their troop deployment within a large area, they could appear anywhere, anytime, making their appearance difficult to predict. Then there were the airships—that made things a tad more difficult. Thankfully, the jungle canopy and ground foliage gave the Travelers plenty of cover, making the aerial sentry more of an annoyance. Nonetheless, despite the challenges, they made slow and steady progress. By late afternoon, they had another ten miles under their belts—half the distance they planned because the Lizards were actively seeking them.

"I noticed fewer of them in the last hour—hopefully, we reached the back end of their search net," Tag observed as they stopped for a short break about a hundred yards off the small, main trail. "It's a good time to plan the next leg..."

Claire shrugged. "We've seen this before—just as we think we're in the clear, another unit pops up. I'm not sure if they set units into a staggered pattern, or it simply worked out that way."

"They might move units," Devin added, "leapfrogging them ahead of us..."

"If it's purposeful, it indicates they know we're in this sector. Unless we left a clue somewhere, they shouldn't have any idea of our numbers, or which direction we took from the point of the heist." Tag paused for a bite of dried fruit.

Rose's turn to weigh in. "If they had us localized to one area, wouldn't their airship be hovering, waiting for us to be flushed out?"

Tag shot his better half an approving smile. "Good point."

"So, do we operate from the theory the Lizards don't have a friggin' clue and are covering all directions as best they can, hoping to get lucky?" Devin looked expectantly at Tag.

"Yep—with that in mind, is everyone ready to go for the next leg?"

Nods all around.

\*\*\*\*

"I hate tromping through the jungle in this heat—what are we supposed to be looking for, anyway?"

"Somebody says an outpost lost its Wave stuff, so we get to go find it."

"Why can't they find their own damned stuff?"

"Good question—the word is someone high up has his tail in a knot. Apparently, the outpost leader ended up on the wrong end of a Wave weapon over it—bits and pieces spread all over the jungle . . ."

"Yeah—they're serious, alright. What happened?"

"Rumor has it humans stole it . . ."

The Lizard trooper walking beside his squadmate looked at him carefully to see if he were joking.

The doubting look didn't go unnoticed. "It's what

I heard—and, my source is in a position to know about such things."

"Who would have thought puny, meek humans would dare such a thing? And, for what? We overcame them completely . . ."

"Well, obviously that fact hasn't sunk in for some of them . . ."

"Then we need to find the humans, recover the Wave items, and end up heroes—maybe we'll be awarded something."

"And, if we don't," his squadmate pointed out, "maybe we'll end up as spatter in the jungle."

A sobering thought.

\*\*\*\*

Exhausted by the trek and constant tension of being hunted, the Travelers made it to late evening without being intercepted. Once they located a suitable overnight spot, they collapsed, coaxing tension to drain from their bodies. Eventually, Rose suggested they should get something to eat and drink before falling asleep.

"Good idea . . ." Claire dug into her pack, searching

for something tasty. "We didn't see any patrols for the last two hours—I think we might've slipped through their security net..."

"That's a nice thought," Devin agreed, "but we still need to be careful. They may be sending troops ahead of us, or setting up an ambush. We'll never know for sure until we clear this area..."

"Even then, if the Lizards get a whiff we've come this way, they'll track us wherever we go..."

Tag nodded. "That's a valid point. But, are they effective trackers? We don't have any idea and, eventually, we're going to run out of jungle at some point. Then—unfortunately for us—it's open territory..." He waited a few moments to let his words sink in. "So, if it's harder to track us in the jungle, what happens when we move to different terrain? Then, of course, we're in a position of being more exposed..."

Devin agreed. "We better have a cover story in case someone asks—human or Lizard."

"We can't say we're just on a scenic tour, and ask where they suggest we go for dinner." Even though Rose was joking, there was an element of truth to her statement.

"Very funny," Claire chuckled, "but, talking about food, it's going to be tight on supplies at the rate we're consuming. I know we decided to travel light for speed purposes, but if we keep slowing down like today, we may be out before we locate the scientists..."

Devin patted her hand. "It's not as though we haven't lived off the land before—look at how we made out just fine in the primitive world..."

"I know, but we didn't have Lizard troops on our asses, pissed off because we borrowed some of their stuff. It's not like they don't have more . . ."

He grinned at her. "In a pinch, we could look to a farm for some help on the food end of things."

Tag glanced at Devin and Claire, then at Rose. "We lucked out with Kirv's family. Remember, they warned us most farmers are good, decent folks, and they might be helpful. However, there are some humans who are informants for the Lizards to get more favorable treatment. Trusting the wrong person could burn us . . ."

"If it comes down to it," Rose commented, "we'll just have to be good judges of character."

After a bit more conversation, the Travelers curled up and tried to get some sleep. By consensus, they agreed not to post a guard—the spot they picked was well off the small trail. A good thing, too—everyone needed to be as fresh as possible for continuing their trek in the morning.

\*\*\*\*

Three hours later, the squad of Lizard soldiers deployed on a rare night patrol using light-capture technology so they could see in the dark. The squad of eight moved down the same trail the humans traveled, moving past their sleeping targets—at one point, the distance between the two groups was less than one hundred yards.

Unfortunately, the Travelers didn't move far enough off-trail. Even so, the Lizard squad leader was pissed off at one of his troopers responsible for operating the unit's tracking device that could detect live animals—and, humans. They'd show up as if they had a neon sign plastered on them—get within a hundred yards, and the system would light up like a Christmas tree. The only problem was the trooper responsible for tracking forgot to recharge the unit, so he carried an ineffective device at the moment they passed within range of the peacefully sleeping humans.

Luck? Yep . . .

\*\*\*\*

Every day was the same with no change in venue—even worse, he had no choice about what to do. He didn't know the date nor time because his watch lost power long ago, so he took an estimate from the sun each day. Not that he really cared—what did it matter?

The man laboring in the sunshine would be surprised to learn his enslavement was a little over eight years—it seemed much longer. Drudgery numbed his mind to the point where everything he did was an automatic response, repeating the menial tasks his masters ordered him to perform every hour of every day. But, what could he do? Such was the life of a slave on the planet Earth conquered by the Lizard warriors, and he was one of millions forced to live the same. Many gave up and were executed, or were simply worked to death. But, those numbers paled in comparison to the billions of humans killed outright at the time of the conquest—they fought as best they could, but to no avail.

It was over in a matter of weeks.

For a short time, an underground resistance of survivors carried on the fight, but they were soon rooted out with deadly efficiency by the front line, combat shock units of the enemy. Once the last effective human fighters were eliminated, the elite Lizards were shipped off-world to be replaced by their third rate occupation force. It was then grim reality set in for human survivors.

Cletus was a strong man, always had been. Pre-conquest, people used to look at him and immediately assume his powerful physique and good looks were all he received in the way of natural gifts. It wasn't until they interacted with him that his real gift came to light—he possessed a powerful intellect, too, with the motivation to use it.

Back in the days of his freedom, Cletus was a soldier with extraordinary talents. An officer in his country's military, he was instrumental in planning the defense against the invasion. Commanders over him followed his suggestions, which delayed the inevitable for a week or two—but, in the end, greater military technology won.

When the final collapse came, Cletus ensured his survival by not revealing his background. If the Lizard overlords knew of his military skills, elimination would've been swift. They didn't fancy leaving potential threats to stir up trouble, and they liked the slave population to be nice. Placid. Compliant.

For years, Cletus harbored the notion some day he would help in the uprising of mankind to repel control by the Lizards. Unfortunately, that reality never occurred and his hopes withered under the brute force of daily labor.

Yet, somewhere deep inside, it never died.

# Chapter Eleven

Tag awakened first, as usual. His internal clock seemed to adjust to first light, and his morning ritual was to go from a sound sleep to instantly awake ready for action. But, that morning was different—he lay awake, sorting through a strange feeling he couldn't quite pin down. At first, it was fuzzy, but it slowly increased. *Strange*, he thought, *if it were only a dream, it should fade, not get stronger . . .*

Whatever it was, he was certain the feeling revolved around Lizards and close proximity, but not the experiences of the previous day. If he had to explain it, several Lizard warriors passed by close to their location—in a line—all of them looking for him and his companions.

Tag shook his head a little bit, as if he could shake it

loose to fully form. It were as if he were viewing it from an aerial perspective, hovering above the treetop canopy.

"Hey, are you okay?" Rose sat up, putting her arm around his shoulders.

"What? I'm not too sure, to be honest—I had the strangest feeling of observing something, although I was asleep."

"What was it?"

"Lizards—and they were close by during the night. But, they're gone now . . ."

She didn't say anything—she just hugged him.

"Maybe I'm cracking up. Maybe, you should move so you're not too close to a nut bar . . ."

"Nut bar?"

He chuckled, again realizing the subtle differences in their home worlds as well as what each took for granted regarding customs and speech. "It's a saying in my world—at least where I'm from. It describes a crazy person . . ."

"I've known it all along! But, someone's got to stay with you, so you don't hurt yourself."

"Very funny. Seriously though, this is such a strong feeling. It's unlike anything I've experienced . . ."

She smiled, and put her head on his shoulder.

"Maybe it's your feminine side coming out—you know, women's intuition . . ."

"Great. Just great." He paused. "Please, don't tell

Devin that . . ."

\*\*\*\*

He didn't let the junior officer finish his report before interrupting. "Yes, or no—did they find the missing Wave tech items?"

A pause. "No, Sub-Commander."

"Then don't stand here blathering about steps you've taken which haven't solved the problem. Find the missing items and the humans responsible—and, don't come back until you've done so. You have two solar periods to get it done—if you can't, I'll find someone else who can. Any further failures will see you removed from rank, the military, as well as a member of the living."

"We're trying . . ."

"Get out!"

When the junior officer left with his tail between his legs—literally—Vanc turned to look out the window. No trace of the humans responsible for the theft. False trails in the jungle led nowhere. More troops and two airships rendered negative results. There was no doubt time was running out for all of them, and his neck might be on the line next.

However, in spite of the odds being against him, a thought popped into his mind as a possible solution—it was risky, but they were coming to that point.

Mercs.

Somewhere, there were a few of them on the planet. If he could get them involved, perhaps they would have better results. Mercs were the nastiest of his kind, and he never had direct contact with one. Nonetheless, rumor had it they had their ways of getting things done when regular means weren't working. Maybe they were just what he needed—things were getting desperate, and it was time to use any means possible. Why not? Beal sanctioned whatever it took to get results, so why shouldn't he enlist the Mercs' support?

The only problem was cost—if they didn't get paid enough, he'd be the next one they hunted. And, the price was fluid depending on efforts expended.

\*\*\*\*

He shifted feet, strode back and forth, and positioned his head in a near horizontal view. "Okay, what," Jackie asked, shaking her head at the theatrics.

"I'm not sure . . ."

"Why don't you try standing on your head? Maybe that will enlighten you . . ."

"Well, okay—will you steady my legs? I never could

hold that position for long . . ."

"Very funny. It's interpretive—a modern abstract. You don't have to figure it out—feel it. It's an interesting piece."

"Exactly, a piece of . . ."

"Kyle! That's not very nice—please don't make comments like that when the artist is here for the showing!"

"Okay—I promise . . ."

"What type of art do you like?"

He thought for a moment. "Maybe, something with lots of color, especially vibrant reds and oranges—you know, with kids and puppies. Things like that . . ."

Jackie glanced at him, noting the twinkle in his eye.

She punched him in the arm. "What do you really think?"

"Actually, I'm impressed. Your showing is going to be a success. I'm very proud of you!"

Jackie gave him a big hug. "I couldn't have done it without you . . ."

****

The biggest of the bastards was also the meanest, reveling in going out of his way to make things miserable. Over the years, Cletus witnessed a handful of slaves reaching the breaking point, finally attacking 'the Provoker'—that's how he thought of the guard.

Twice, Cletus reached that point before his intellect kicked in and overrode the burning, raw emotion. He knew any attempt on the guard would be hopeless—only a convenient way to commit suicide. Stupid, really—but everyone had their breaking point.

He had his orders—backfill around the foundation of a newly constructed building that would house a factory. Normally, it shouldn't take long—parked on the side of the lot was a piece of machinery which could've done the job in a couple of hours, requiring only the operator. Instead, the Provoker had eighty human slaves working with shovels in the hot sun, backfilling by hand—before the sun reached midday, three workers passed out. The guards poked them with electrically charged prods, but to no avail. Cletus figured at least one of the prone humans was dead.

*Maybe,* he thought, *if someone in charge over the Provoker knew about the deliberate inefficiencies...* Cletus figured wishing for worse to be done to the Lizard was too much to hope for. Still, as the concept took root, he spent the rest of the workday focusing on ways word could reach the proper authority—unobtrusively, of course. For a slave, it might be impossible, but there could be another approach. *The other guards . . .* he thought. *Are any of them jealous of the Provoker? Afraid? How much do they hate his guts?*

Cletus figured the situation might present an opportunity for one of the guards to stick it to the Provoker, possibly moving into his position as lead guard. Realistically, it depended on ambition of the individuals—certainly, none of them would do it for humanitarian purposes. They cared little what happened to the slaves and, in all of his years of captivity, none of the Lizards ever made an attempt to befriend a human slave.

So—if not for humanitarian purposes—greed, vengeance, ambition, and sheer spite were powerful motivators. *Maybe one of the guards will take the step to report the Provoker . . .* Cletus knew the trick would be to plant the seed of his concept in such a way the guard figured it was his own idea—if so, would he be willing to act on it?

Keeping a sharp eye out for evidence of dissatisfaction would be the key. The offshoot benefit to Cletus was the fact he now had a mission—something to look forward to each day, rather than succumb to the same dreary, meager existence.

\*\*\*\*

They pressed forward on the second day after the heist, and the question was to balance the necessity of getting the hell away from the location, and getting busted by the Lizards. Go overboard on one, and it could be curtains.

The Travelers were up first thing in the morning

and, by agreement, they pushed on until midday before breaking for something to eat, meager as it was. There was no sign of the Lizards, but that didn't mean the buggers weren't out there.

"Do you think we cleared them," Claire asked.

"It's tough to know for sure, but, so far, so good. We still need to be careful, however—they could be lurking anywhere."

"We're going slower than planned, right?" Rose looked at Tag to answer her question.

"Yep . . ."

She leaned back against a tree trunk. "Well—I guess a schedule doesn't really matter, considering humankind on this planet spent the last eight years in limbo . . ."

"Keep in mind," Claire pointed out, "we have no idea of their technology, and we're only hoping it can be sorted out by the scientists—and, that's only if we can connect with them. Remember—they've been hiding from the Lizards all this time. And, they may not have access to much in the way of equipment anymore. The truth is this could be a gigantic bust, so don't get your hopes up . . ."

"Thank you, Miss Ray of Sunshine, for all of your words of optimism and encouragement . . ."

"Tag, you know this is a long shot . . ."

He paused before answering, then looked directly at Claire. "Yes—it's a long shot. We have a bunch of variables, any of which could go sideways—but, we have to try. Otherwise, all of these people are doomed. It doesn't seem to us anyone else is stepping up, except Kirv and his family—and, they're farmers with no experience in this sort of thing. In the last few months, we've been through all sorts of crap, somehow managing to come out the other side. We can try to help, or walk away and look for a portal ride out of here."

Claire shook her head. "Alright, already—you don't have to go heavy on me. I was just making an observation this isn't an easy thing to do, and nobody's walking away. We need to be realistic, that's all . . ."

Devin looked from one to the other. "Are you two done? All of this controversy is interfering with my digestive process of this lovely cuisine . . ."

Rose laughed. "Yeah—it's pretty good alright! All three bites, or so!"

He was about to respond when Tag signaled to be quiet—everyone froze, listening intently. In the distance, they heard running engines and, as the seconds ticked by, the sounds grew steadier.

They exited the trail, locating a spot to have their break, and it was off the trail enough to be out of sight of anyone. However, the trail wasn't large enough to accommodate the size of approaching vehicles.

"Why don't you stay here, and Devin and I will scout what's up," Tag suggested to the girls.

They nodded and, within a few minutes, they had the answer—the trail intersected a larger road, suitable to accommodate military sized motor vehicles, four of which were passing in front of them.

"Those vehicles could handle a fair amount of equipment—or, about ten to twelve Lizard troopers each." Devin scooted further back into foliage cover facing the highway.

Tag did the same. "It's possible they could be moving human slave workers..."

Devin glanced at his friend with a quizzical look.

Tag shrugged. "Yeah—I know. Not bloody likely. Lizards would march them somewhere watching from the comfort of their own vehicles, not caring how many humans didn't make it."

"It has to be military—so, the question is where are they going, and for what purpose?"

Moments later, they had answers to their questions. The convoy of trucks pulled to a halt just before a bend in the road, roughly a hundred yards from where they hid. Lizard troopers began emerging from the back of the last two vehicles and, once out, the vehicles pulled away from the area. Twenty troopers gathered together to receive directions from the pair of Lizards commanding them.

Tag signaled to Devin, pulling back and moving quickly to where they left the girls.

Claire raised an eyebrow when they arrived.

Devin answered her silent query. "We have trouble—there's a decent-sized road close by. They dropped off two squads of Lizard soldiers, and it looked like they were being given last-minute directions—which, I'm assuming, are orders to find us. This is going to get intense, and fast..."

Tag nodded. "I'm guessing they're the last group to cover the outer perimeter of the search grid. We covered a fair amount of territory, so far, and they have to know we'll be on foot. I think they'll start moving back toward the barracks we hit, hoping to scoop us up in their net. If we can get past them or, in this case, let them move past us, the way south may be clear . . ."

"So, what do we do?" Again, Rose looked to Tag for an answer.

He hesitated. "Movement is easier to detect than finding a stationary, hidden target—that's us. Unless they end up landing on top of us, I suggest we dig in like ticks somewhere in good cover, and hope they sweep by us."

Devin glanced at Tag. "What if we have to break cover and scatter?"

"Good point—if we get separated, once you're clear of them, continue moving south. Try to estimate ten miles from here and, if safe, wait an hour for a linkup between us. If that doesn't work try, at the twenty-mile mark. If still unsuccessful, we know the ultimate destination for locating the scientists, so keep traveling and we'll rendezvous there."

Each nodded, then moved further from the trail, locating good cover in thick foliage. The trick was to have it dense enough to camouflage them, yet accessible enough so not to hinder a speedy exit.

It required steely nerves to remain motionless and perfectly quiet as the four of them listened to the Lizards' approach. The buggers weren't just sticking to the trail as they hoped—rather, individual Lizard soldiers moved through the underbrush toward their hiding spot. That was the bad news—the good news was they could clearly hear their approach as massive bodies made a racket knocking aside branches as they advanced.

The line of Lizard soldiers—spaced roughly twenty yards apart—continued moving toward them, and the Travelers watched intently as the closest trooper moved to their position, all of them hunkering down further on the jungle floor. The closest Lizard—who initially appeared as if he were going to stomp on top of them—ended up veering slightly to his right to avoid the thick area where they hid. Without turning to watch him move past, they listened carefully to the sound of his diminishing footsteps.

No other troopers were in sight, their line seeming to have swept past their position.

They began to emerge from cover when one of those random chance things in life interfered with their plan. Tag cleared the bush cover, waiting for the others to join him, and it was then he discovered something unwelcomed. The first trooper who stomped close by their position made so much noise, he covered the sound of a second trooper who stopped twenty yards away from their position, partially obscured behind several tree trunks. The second trooper paused to sneak an illicit drink from his stash when one of his superiors wasn't around to catch him.

He was in the process of taking another snort, when he suddenly observed the four humans emerging from the thick cover not far from him. Startled, he must have made a noise because all of them instantly fixed on his position.

There was a moment when the two members of opposing species stared at each other, competing to see who was the most surprised.

Then . . .

# Chapter Twelve

Tag reacted first. He drew his handgun, firing three shots in rapid succession, each hitting the intended target in the torso. The only problem was the reactive Wave tech armor the Lizard wore dissipated the impact of the bullets. He staggered, somehow managing to stay on his feet, but the bullets didn't even penetrate.

There was a bright side, though—the Lizard soldier sneaked shots for several hours, and the potent liquid had him partially gassed. His reaction time slowed considerably, plus the element of seeing the human as well as the impacting bullets on his armor served to disorient him. Eventually, he drew his handgun from its hip holster, pointing it in the general direction of the quickly moving human. Well behind Tag, he fired the Wave tech-equipped weapon.

The result was spectacular!

The Wave beam missed Tag by a considerable margin, intersecting with the trunk of a massive tree. The three and half foot diameter trunk burst apart, and the tree started to topple.

Tag moved, but the Lizard didn't quite make it out of the way fast enough. Lucky to escape the tree's trunk flattening him like a pancake, branches connected, sending him sprawling, face down, pinning him—at least for the moment.

Tag didn't wait to see the end result. The loud noise of his shots as well as the Wave beam slamming into the tree, echoed through the jungle. Concerned the loud sounds would attract the attention of remaining Lizard troopers, Tag yelled at the Travelers. "Scatter!"

Running hard, he angled toward one of his friends who showed fleeting glimpses of movement between trees and bushes. Within fifty yards, he caught up with Claire running all out, small branches whipping her as she pounded along the jungle floor.

"It's Tag," he called to her. "Keep running as fast as you can! I'll watch our backsides!" She never looked back, or took time to acknowledge him other than putting on a small burst of speed. He sneaked a glance, and didn't see an immediate pursuit—yet, he knew it would come. The Lizards' search net would now focus on their location—and, them.

*Take care of Rose, Devin,* he thought as he ran ten paces behind Claire. *Take care of both of you . . .*

\*\*\*\*

As it turned out, the Mercs were close by in another Lizard camp, so Vanc made arrangements for their immediate relocation to Beal's headquarters. In fact, he was in a meeting with their leader when word came of a potential break. A squad on the southern, outer perimeter of the search grid made contact with a human male—with shots exchanged, Vanc knew he must intensify the search.

He didn't know if the human were connected to the theft of the Wave tech items, but the fact was they had zilch for other leads, and concentrated pursuit was necessary. The chance of another rogue, armed human loose in the region was unusual enough, but couple that with the missing items, and it would be a hell of a coincidence if they weren't related.

He shut off his communicator and turned to Zarn, the Merc leader. "We have a possible lead to the south—follow it. Bring me the missing items and the human, if you can take him alive—my assistant will give you the coordinates."

The Merc leader nodded acknowledgment of the mission. "It will be done—have our reward ready when I return."

Vanc watched Zarn leave his office, shuddering at the Merc's ferocity. By nature, Lizards were a vicious, mean-spirited species, and Vanc had a greater than normal share of violent behavior in his past.

The Merc scared the hell out of him.

\*\*\*\*

She made good progress with her long legs and matching stride. On the decent-sized trail, Rose chose speed over cover—but, after a fifteen-minute run at full bore, she had to slow the pace considerably. To stop would be an invitation for capture or worse, and she couldn't get the magnitude of the discharged Wave tech weapon out of her mind. She hadn't seen anything approaching its raw power from a handgun, so staying ahead of a Lizard equipped with force such as that was number one on her agenda.

While keeping a decent, steady pace, she had an opportunity to scan the area, searching for a glimpse of her companions. Nothing. *Where the hell are they?* Sure, Tag ordered them to scatter, but all of them should be heading in the same direction. The problem was the thickness of the jungle cover—one of them could be in sight on a parallel path under normal, clear conditions, but, at her current location, Rose had to hear someone before she could see them. *We'll link up at the first meeting point,* she thought as she continued to run.

She didn't want to think of no one else's showing up. Going all the way south alone to find the scientists wasn't an attractive proposition for her.

*C'mon guys—show up!*

\*\*\*\*

The Lizard, who must have been attracted by the gunfire, damned near ran over Devin. At the same time, both rounded a large, fallen tree partially blocking the path. Devin reacted immediately by drawing a large combat knife he received from the Future Warriors from the last world.

He witnessed the negative results of Tag's shooting the Lizard, and he wasn't about to repeat that folly. Two steps brought him immediately in front of the Lizard soldier, and a quick, lateral move propelled him past the right side of his opponent—at the same time, he drew the combat knife across the exposed throat of the startled Lizard who didn't anticipate the brash move by the mere human. Devin knew the reptilians had an esophageal soft spot from previous hand-to-hand combat when Tag defeated another Lizard by crushing his throat.

The large, razor-sharp blade did its work well.

The Lizard soldier clutched his throat in an attempt to quell the cascading green blood, but all he achieved was its flowing through his clawed hands.

Devin kept moving away from the beast not looking back. He knew he struck a mortal blow—more important than checking the status of his incapacitated opponent was putting distance between him and the Lizard. As he ran south on the path, the rhythm of his feet hitting the ground matched his most important thoughts. *Where are Claire and the others?*

****

Apprehensive at first, the more he got into it, the easier it was. Of course, he still had to proceed with an element of caution—why invite difficulties? Still, a certain amount of risk was inherent in taking positive steps toward the ultimate goal of freedom. He still had the fire for it—the majority of the survivors did not.

Without furthering the interests of his farming enterprise as he should have been, Kirv spent the last two days canvassing his neighbors in an effort to winnow who would seriously be willing to join him. The objective? Create opportunities to fight back against the Lizard overlords. As it stood, a direct confrontation with a few volunteers would be sheer folly with no chance of success. However, a subtle approach to undermine the existing status quo without identifying the source was the trick.

To further that goal, he initiated contact within the local slave ranks which had a tenuous pipeline. Farther away, word traveled to more distant, free people, and it was time to act—to take back. Like any endeavor, a movement had a beginning. A spark. However, nothing would catch fire without the fuel readily available in combustible form.

Kirv provided the spark—was it enough to take back his world?

****

Beal listened to his Sub-Commander. The reported incident to the south with a human confronting his troopers was a positive. Interestingly, two troopers were dead—one to the north of the raided outpost, and one to the south. That part was confusing—which way was he going? North, or south? Evidence indicated the dead trooper to the north had been that way longer than the one to the south.

Then, there was the semi-drunk trooper who described a confrontation with a human—shots fired by each, a falling tree, and a branch stabbing the soldier in the ass.

*Idiot!*

Again, that episode happened to the south. So, was it one lone, rogue human who appeared lucky enough to best his soldiers? Or, were there more of them? He didn't want to think of an outbreak of human resistance—if it caught on, his kind would have a major challenge containing it because of their few numbers. *Damn the Off-Planet Command for stripping away too many soldiers from the Occupation Forces!*

Vanc stopped talking, waiting for his Commander to catch up with the situation.

Beal refocused on his subordinate. "A risky move to bring in the Mercs," he agreed. "They're particularly nasty business. But, your instincts might be right—something tells me this prey has teeth, and an uncanny ability to extricate out of difficult situations. The Mercs should cancel that advantage—I certainly wouldn't want them after me. Carry on, and report progress . . ."

Vanc nodded, and turned to leave.

"Vanc, this better work!" Beal called out. "The cost of hiring Mercs is high, but I'll gladly pay to get out of this bind. Failure is not an attractive alternative . . ."

"They're Mercs—how can they fail? The target is only human . . ."

****

At first, he overheard it from others whispering, cloaked in darkness in the slave barracks. "There was a resistance—strike at the Lizards however you can. Watch for the sign . . ."

Rumors often permeated the slave population with ninety-nine percent turning out to be pure bull. However, there appeared to be something different as the ideas swept through the captive human population of the work camp. They endured so much to survive—surely, they finally deserved something good.

Cletus listened carefully to what was being said, and by whom. Once he had the gist of it, his focus turned to who began the rumor—the source. Figuring it out wasn't too hard—a few key questions, and he learned the source's identity. Nirva—a young woman working in the kitchens, charged with keeping the slave workforce alive and useful for the Lizard overlords.

She had regular contact with the free farmers on the outside when they brought their product to the work camp's kitchens. One of the providers was Kirv, and it was because of a hushed discussion with him, the excitement began to grow. But, it was never good to trust rumor—Cletus needed to talk alone with her to verify the seriousness of her story.

It was easy enough to arrange. He approached the human work-gang boss the next morning, volunteering to get the rations for his crew for that day. The boss readily agreed—Cletus was a hard worker, never giving any trouble. And, he owed him. Several years ago, Cletus saved the boss from a cave-in—buried and unconscious, the large slave dug him out before he suffocated like several other slaves who didn't make it. Cletus never talked about it, or asked for any favor afterward.

Within the hour, Cletus arrived at the kitchen with the slings to carry his work-gang's meals—then, he sought out Nirva. Occasionally, he saw her around, offering a brief smile before moving on to another task, never having the opportunity to have a conversation.

He waited by the entrance to the kitchen for two women to leave, and he had to bend slightly to clear the overhead of the doorway. For a large man, he approached quietly. Her back to him, Nirva didn't know he was there until he spoke directly behind her.

"May I bother you for a moment?"

Startled, the young woman jumped, whirled around, and pointed a large kitchen knife at him.

He stepped back two paces with his hands up in

mock surrender. "I promise to eat all of my veggies before I eat dessert!"

She shook her head, still trying to calm her racing heart rate, and didn't catch the gist of his comment. "What?"

Realizing he gave her quite a start, an apology seemed appropriate. "Sorry for scaring you—it wasn't my intent. I came to ask you something . . ."

"Cletus—what is it you want?"

"Well—putting down the large knife is a good start."

Nirva looked down at what she was holding, realizing she was gesturing with it at the poor fellow. "Sorry," she mumbled as she placed the knife on the counter.

"How do you know my name?"

"Someone once told me who you are . . ." She managed to awkwardly cover up the fact she previously sought out another woman for the sole purpose of finding out his name, and details.

"I see—what did she say?"

It was getting very uncomfortable for Nirva. She was a quiet, shy woman who didn't talk much to men unless it involved kitchen business. "You came to ask me something—what is it?"

He could see she was getting flustered and wondered why. Something else he noticed—Nirva was quite attractive. Even with her brunette hair drawn back out of the way and clothed in a simple dress, she looked fetching. Never having the opportunity to get this close to her, it never sank in before.

She decided to rescue him. "I asked you why you want to see me . . ."

Finally, it registered he had a mission in being there—the very pleasant distraction got him off his game plan.

# Chapter Thirteen

None of them had a watch that worked—something to do with portals not liking timepieces. It didn't matter, however, since they became proficient at figuring out time by the position of the sun—nighttime? Not so much. That was a bit more difficult unless they had a moon.

Rose knew she was there for well over an hour, and no one showed. Hers was the first rendezvous point, although, technically, it wasn't specific—Tag suggested ten miles south, wait an hour and, if no link-up, then move on to twenty miles south. However, in the jungle without a precise coordinate, they could be hundreds of yards—if not miles—apart, and not know it. Without radios or other forms of communication, the only thing she could do was yell—and she couldn't do that without attracting the Lizards.

She decided to give it another fifteen minutes and, if nothing, then move on. Sitting in a jungle listening to living sounds wasn't particularly disconcerting, considering they spent a number of weeks in the forest living off the land in the primitive world. In the jungle, though, it was different, and the spooky thing was the Travelers were being actively hunted.

And, she was alone.

If something popped out of the jungle in front of her, it could be one of her friends, an animal, or a Lizard warrior—she could take her pick.

Fifteen minutes came and went. All she saw was a pair of fawns wandering by, and Rose had no doubt mama was close. "That's it—gotta go!" Staying made her feel more exposed, and she'd rather be moving.

Backpack in position, she headed due south—hopefully, she would find someone at the twenty-mile mark.

\*\*\*\*

Tag and Claire made good progress—the last week allowed Claire to heal more, and it showed in her stamina. Considering the action they encountered, their part of the jungle seemed uninhabited except for indigenous wildlife.

Finally, they reached a point where both slowed independently, then stopped. "Ten miles?" Tag glanced at Claire.

"Yep—by my estimate, we should be here."

No Rose. No Devin.

"If you want to take a load off," Tag offered, "I'll sweep the immediate area—maybe I'll see them . . ."

"Okay by me . . ."

Silently, he disappeared into the jungle.

She perched on a good-sized rock, pulling out a snack and water bottle from her pack. Sitting alone and with Tag's being gone, it seemed like one, big-ass jungle! But, she couldn't think of anything other than Devin—without him, she felt a cavernous void. *Okay—where the hell are you? And, Rose? You can appear anytime now . . .*

Tag was only moderately worried. The Travelers were separated before in other worlds, and everything worked out fine—there wasn't any overriding reason the same thing wouldn't happen. Granted, in other places, they didn't have oversized, butt-ugly Lizards after them, and he hoped Rose and Devin were traveling together. However, if separated, both possessed excellent survival skills.

Forty-five minutes later, he returned to Claire, who was still sitting alone. She looked up when he suddenly appeared before her. "Nothing, huh?"

"Nope, everything is clear—let's give it another half an hour to be sure, then push on to the twenty-mile mark."

"Roger that . . ."

\*\*\*\*

Estimating distances? Devin sucked at it—why, he didn't know. He navigated the reasonably dense jungle on the lookout for Lizards, but he had no idea how far he'd gone—it was nothing more than a huge guess on his part. When he had a feeling he reached the ten-mile mark, he did the same as Tag—he canvassed the area.

Nothing.

After an hour, he decided to press on to the next rendezvous point—twenty miles, due south.

*Great. I probably botched this estimate, so now I get to estimate another ten miles from the point of where I couldn't figure out the initial ten mile meeting place. Fantastic! This just gets better and better . . .*

\*\*\*\*

There were only three of them—usually, that's all

it took to be efficient and deadly. The military vehicle transporting the Merc team to the last-known encounter with the rogue human rolled on, no one speaking, its two military members focusing straight ahead, not attempting to engage them in conversation.

It was safer that way.

Soon, the vehicle stopped, and the Mercs disembarked—no acknowledgment or thanking them for the ride. As far as they were concerned, the crew existed only as part of a transportation device—nothing more.

A noncom met the team, leading them to the site of a Lizard trooper lying on his side on the jungle floor. A squad of soldiers stood back from the body, happy to give the Merc team space to examine the fallen Lizard.

Zarn didn't touch the corpse, but he leaned over enough to discern the single, side-to-side, broad slash to the throat. No other marks—no defensive wounds, or marks on his body armor. It appeared the encounter was brief—a large combat knife took out the trooper with a quick swipe, and that was it. Green blood pooled under the corpse, and there was no evidence of the trooper's firing his weapon.

Also missing? Human blood.

The Merc leader nodded in silent appreciation for the efficiency of the kill—it was impressive for a human. *Perhaps,* he thought, *the hunt will be more interesting than the usual, dull routine of finding runaway human slaves . . .*

****

When Kirv again visited the slave camp to deliver his produce to the kitchens, the young woman he spoke to on his last visit met him. She assisted in unloading and carrying items into the kitchen and, when they were done, Nirva turned to Kirv. "Will you stay here for a moment? There's someone who wishes to speak to you as soon as you're ready . . ."

"Of course . . ." Moments later, a large man strode through the back entrance into the kitchen—Nirva stood watch outside, having previously sent the other two kitchen workers on tasks away from the building.

Cletus approached the smaller, sturdily-built man, extending a large hand which was grasped by a strong, equally callused one. "I understand from Nirva you had a conversation regarding—anti-Lizard interests . . ."

A bit wary, Kirv nodded. "I spoke to her, yes." His tone remained non-committal, and the large man smiled at how carefully the farmer chose his words.

"I'm Cletus, unfortunate slave for the past eight years. Before that, I had certain aptitudes that may be of value if circumstances go a certain way . . ."

Kirv smiled back. *He's an intelligent one,* Kirv thought, *but he can cause trouble if he's in league with the Lizards. It's happened before . . .* The potential for turning one over to the Lizards could work both ways, but someone had to make the first move, exposing himself to risk.

He figured it might as well be him. "Yes—I spoke to her about resistance to the status quo." There. His neck was on the line.

The large man smiled again. "Good! It's about bloody time someone started the process. What can I do from the inside?"

It was Kirv's turn to smile. "Well—here's what's going on . . ."

\*\*\*\*

The area was beautiful and even the gruff, unrefined Lizards appreciated the setting as extraordinary. To keep it pristine and undamaged by guests who might be careless, the authority of New Planetary Holdings, appointed Warders—reporting directly to the Prime—who had the ultimate responsibility for everything occurring in the conquered world.

There were eleven more regions protected by Warders on the planet, most of them located overseas. Before the conquest, only one other existed in what was previously the North American political sphere. There was one in the east several thousand miles away, and one in the western quadrant of the continent, its quality defined by mountains, magnificent waterfalls, and forests.

Warder areas in other regions of the planet featured their own unique qualities which attracted the attention of the Lizards as recreational locations for Lizard overlords—but not the lowly, Lizard troops. The Warder-controlled areas catered only to the elite leaders, and off-planet guests paid exorbitant amounts to join them.

It was all about the hunt.

The Warders ensured the wildlife was not over-hunted, and the quality of the species available was of the highest standard—those two things made the Warder-controlled regions famous, even to the off-world Lizard elites.

What did they hunt?

Humans.

\*\*\*\*

"I see we sent two airships to Commander Beal's sector—why?"

Sub-Commander Garoc addressed the Prime. "Sir, we talked about this several days ago, and you gave your approval . . ."

"Being in the position as the supreme authority for

the administration of this conquest, I find it hard to keep track of everything requested. It's like a river that won't stop flowing—tiresome, actually. I can't recall why they needed airships..."

"As I recall, Sir, it had something to do with finding missing equipment..."

The Prime turned from the window, his eyes meeting Garoc's with a steely glare. "What kind of equipment?"

"I'm not sure they specified the details, Sir."

"Don't you think it would be a good idea to find out those missing details?"

"Of course, Sir. I'll do it right away..."

The Prime thought for a few moments. "Garoc—there's something about this that makes me uncomfortable. Take a headquarters shuttle, and meet Commander Beal in person. You have my authority to do whatever is required to sort this out. Have the staff cut those orders for you..."

"Yes, Sir!" Garoc answered enthusiastically, looking forward to getting out of the Administration Center and into the field—while wielding the Prime's authority! As he turned to go, the Prime had more to say. "And, Garoc—take a complement of headquarter guards with you. Six should do. If you think there's a problem, you'll have the guards to back up your authority."

The Sub-Commander bowed formally. "Thank you, Prime. I will find answers, and report..."

"Do that."

\*\*\*\*

So far, so good. The good news was there weren't any Lizards on the ground in her immediate area. The bad news? She just ducked under a large tree for the second flyover of an airship—maybe two—using a search grid, and she figured she was one of its targets.

Rose waited until the sight and sound of the airship diminished, taking comfort in the jungle canopy cover—chances of spotting her were slim. However, hiding under a tree until the airship passed made her feel less exposed.

By her estimate, she was at the halfway mark between the designated rendezvous points. The trouble was without their traveling in the area before, they had no idea about what landmarks there were to fix her position. Plus, estimating the designated mileage would be different for each of them, especially Devin. The girls remarked before about his difficulty with estimating distances, but neither mentioned their observations to him. Apparently, he operated under the assumption none of them noticed and, if alone, his chances of getting close to where he needed to be weren't particularly good.

Certain the airship was gone, Rose headed south.

She missed Tag.

\*\*\*\*

"I thought you knew where we are!"

"Roughly—yes. But, the jungle's so thick here, it's tough to get a fix..."

Claire raised an eyebrow at Tag. "Where's a GPS when you need one?"

From scanning the jungle, he focused back on her. "According to Kirv, that would require satellites—of which they have none left. The Lizards took them out at the time of the conquest."

Claire was quiet for a moment. "Tag—I'm worried about Devin..."

"Unless you haven't noticed, Devin can take care of himself..."

"I know, but it's not that. He knows directions, but he has trouble with measuring distance. You set ten and twenty mile meeting points directly south—he'll figure out south, but he won't have any idea of how far to go. How are we going to link up with him?"

Tag nodded. "I've seen that issue with him—but, if he's on the correct line south, we have a chance of intersecting with him. Granted, it's tougher in the jungle—but, according to Kirv, the jungle thins out soon. So, in the open, finding each other will be easier..."

"Easier for the Lizards, too," she pointed out.

"True." Another thought occurred to him. "Hey! He could be with Rose. She's pretty good at finding her way around!"

"Let's hope so..."

****

*Sure—he says ten miles and, if that doesn't work, then twenty miles. That's perfect, if I can figure it out. I might as well just walk straight south, and hope I bump into someone who isn't about to shoot me.*

The trail he was on seemed fairly straight and in the direction he wanted to go, so he could make good time. Periodically, Devin paused for a minute to listen carefully—especially for anyone tracking him from behind. So far, his tail was clean.

He was only mildly concerned for himself, figuring they would eventually link up—most of his thoughts centered on Claire. Was she alone, too? Hopefully, Rose or Tag—or, both—accompanied her. The four of them had been on enough adventures and faced more than their share of adversity in the last several months, and he realized they grew considerably in confidence, learning to apply their abilities to difficult circumstances.

They would need all of that, and more. Their mission was difficult enough—more so, if having to go it alone.

*Hopefully, it doesn't come to that for any of us . . .*

## Chapter Fourteen

Vanc hurried into his superior's office without his usual deference of waiting at the door to be invited in, causing Beal to look up from the reports he was scanning. Initially annoyed by the unannounced interruption, he conceded anything distracting him from the mundane task was welcomed. But, that feeling disappeared as soon as the expression on Vanc's face became apparent.

"Commander, we have a situation . . ."

"What?"

"A contingent from the New Planetary Holdings Headquarters of the Prime just arrived."

Beal blinked, stunned for a few moments. "For what purpose?"

"It has to be for the missing Wave tech..."

"But, how would they know of it?"

"I'm not sure, Sir. We kept the report vague regarding why we needed the airships—someone in their office must have gotten curious..."

Beal was silent for a moment. "When they learn what it's all about, it'll be bad for us."

"Yes, it will—but, if we try to deflect things further, the situation will be much worse. Perhaps, we come clean immediately, but stress the situation is under control."

"But, it isn't..."

"True, Sir. But, we do have the Mercs on the job—if they don't perform, maybe we can deflect the blame on them for not recovering the missing items."

Beal considered his subordinate's idea, quickly assessing the pros and cons. "That's an idea—still, having them quickly find the missing items for us is certainly the best outcome. But, you're right—blaming the Mercs may help us." He paused, then looked directly at Vanc. "This'll be a sticky situation if those items aren't returned..."

"Sir, should I show in the headquarters contingent?"

Beal sighed. "Yes—let's get this over with. We can't start off by insulting them when our fate may rest in their claws."

\*\*\*\*

He had to be incredibly careful.

If the Provoker heard a whisper of the topic, anyone caught listening would likely be executed on the spot. Cletus went only to those slaves he determined were the most trustworthy, although when favors and rewards were potentially available to snitches, anything could happen.

On the other hand, the ultimate reward was freedom.

Since his pledge to Kirv, he carefully spread the word—be ready to act. The response he received was heartening, and individuals agreed to do what was necessary when the time came—even at the cost of their lives. Most shrugged the possibility off as fair trade for the opportunity to work toward freedom. Others uttered their preference for making the attempt, rather than a lifetime of slavery.

Then there were those who wanted revenge.

Without specifics, Kirv advised the Travelers were on their way with stolen Wave tech, hoping to link up with remaining scientists. The mission was to crack the secrets of the advanced technology, and turn it back on the Lizards—then, they'd stage a slave revolt to be implemented by Cletus. They would distract the Lizards, drawing away as many of their troops as possible from the hunt for the humans who stole the technology. It was a worthy plan, and word filtered through—the Lizards were too thin on the ground to properly control the conquered planet. If they could spread them thinner, there was at least a chance of success . . .

On his end, Kirv had discussions with selected neighbors linked to the existing pipeline. Up until then, it was limited to passing information only, but Kirv pushed for it to become active by spreading the word and recruiting others. The purpose? Expand the slave revolt with free people by supporting their efforts with supplies and equipment—filching from the Lizard storehouses were definite targets, too. Glade and Millie did their parts by talking to farmers' wives and young people.

Finally, the wheels were turning, and all it needed was the spark to ignite the revolt. It was a given people were going to die, and the chance of success was slim. The Lizards were powerful and their technologically advanced, but they managed to leave themselves vulnerable.

Now was the time to take advantage of their arrogance.

\*\*\*\*

The airships were gone—at least for the last hour. That pain in the butt, however, was replaced by a patrol of four Lizard military troopers who recently tromped by. Luckily, she pulled off the trail to readjust her hiking boot a few minutes before their arrival and, when she heard them coming, Rose managed to find excellent cover providing a good vantage point to observe the procession.

They appeared to be conducting a search, but it was perfunctory at best. She could see and hear them arguing about something, although it was hard to tell with their strange combination of grunts, clicks and growls. Whatever the discussion, it distracted them, and they rolled by her without noticing.

She waited well past the last, fading sound to ensure the area was clear. They headed in the direction opposite to her path, so once she got moving again, she would be pulling away from them. It was disconcerting, though—the Lizard troops were searching further south than she preferred. But, once she thought about it, she realized there was an upside to the reptilians' stomping down the trail she just used—they wrecked all evidence of her being there, and trackers would have their work cut out for them.

Inching from cover, Rose scanned the area in all directions, then silently reentered the trail heading south. Another couple of miles, and she should reach the twenty-mile mark for the second shot at a rendezvous with her friends.

\*\*\*\*

Five miles north of her, heading south and following clear evidence of a human's recently passing down the trail, the Mercs came upon a four-trooper military Lizard patrol. Zarn heard them coming, of course—yet, it wasn't until he saw them he realized they completely destroyed the human's trail. Footprints? Gone.

Not known for his sparkling personality, he snarled at the patrol leader. "Get out of my way! Idiots! You spoiled the trail—if I can't find our prey, I'll come back and choose you to die instead!"

The patrol leader bristled at the threat, cursing out a response.

Weapons from both sides leveled into firing positions, the troopers fully understanding nine Wave tech weapons discharging in the confined area would be devastating. The standoff ended when one of Zarn's companions warned they were wasting time, and their prey would be putting more distance between them. It was a smart move—the suggestion seemed to diffuse both sides, giving them an excuse to back away from the confrontation. Zarn lowered his weapon, and roughly shouldered past the patrol leader who growled discontent at the lack of respect.

It was all for the best—the patrol leader didn't relish fighting the three Mercs. Even though they possessed twice the manpower, messing with the Mercs and coming out alive was a crapshoot. He watched them head south, then turned his patrol north, grunting at his troopers to keep up.

Zarn cursed again as he examined the trail. The human's footprints were effectively wiped away by the clumsy patrol, and all he knew was the human was traveling south—chances were good it would continue in the same direction.

So would he.

He picked up the pace since he didn't have footprints to track. *Surely, some evidence will appear,* he thought. *The best situation will be a sighting, allowing us to move in for the kill.*

Beal's directions prioritized recovering the missing items as the primary mission, only indicating a desire to confront the thief. But, the Merc leader didn't share the feeling.

He always looked forward to a kill at the end of a hunt.

\*\*\*\*

"Well?" Claire looked to Tag for confirmation of their location.

"I guess we're at the twenty-mile mark—give or take."

"Now what? This spot is so imprecise—their estimate could be off by a couple of miles. And, if they're using a different trail, they could be to the right or left of us by a wide margin . . ."

Tag quickly scanned the area. "True—why don't you be the focal point and stay here to observe this trail? I'll scout the area to see if they turn up elsewhere—keep in mind we might be the first to arrive, and they're still on a trail heading south."

"Okay, I'll hang out. It hampers us because we can't call for them because of unwanted attention—unless either of them use this particular trail, it's going to be difficult to reconnect."

"Agreed—it's too bad we didn't have more time to sort out a meeting spot with greater precision."

"That would have been nice, but you did the best you could under the circumstances . . ."

"I guess—anyway, give me an hour to check things out, and I'll be back."

"Roger that . . ."

Within seconds, he vanished into the thick jungle ground cover.

\*\*\*\*

Devin stood on a trail listening intently for movement around him—other than animals and birds, he heard nothing he considered a threat. Yet, something was out there, tingling his sixth sense—danger was coming, and it hadn't arrived. Something new was in the mix.

Something evil.

That was cause for worry—not so much for himself because he'd deal with whatever it was as best he could. He worried for the others—if they weren't alert, surprise could be deadly.

\*\*\*\*

"Well—tomorrow's the big day!" No matter how much she prepared, Jackie still wasn't sure if she covered all the bases. "I'm not sure I did everything right..."

"Relax! You know what you're doing, and it'll turn out just fine."

"I hope so..."

Kyle put his hand over hers. "Hey—it's your first show, and you have the jitters. It's perfectly understandable..."

"What if no one comes?"

"I'll be there, and I predict you'll have more people than you expect—just watch!"

"I have a feeling I forgot something..."

He chuckled. "Undoubtedly, you have. So what? You have a fine-looking gallery, and beautiful pieces in the show. Two up-and-coming artists will be there, and you have refreshments organized. Not only that, you got the word around the community—those are the essentials. Now, the best thing you can do is take it easy."

"I guess . . ."

"You need to have a little faith—just like you point out to me about Tag. Keep the faith, and good things will flow from that . . ."

\*\*\*\*

The Lizard guard was undoubtedly the meanest the slaves ever encountered in their eight years of captivity—and that was saying something.

Cletus's work group was tasked with removing rocks from an area designated to be a factory construction site, the team consisting of over four hundred and thirty slaves, directly controlled by only two guards. Despite the enormous difference in personnel, the Provoker's base character and addiction to violence ignored the warning signs as well as the potential for things to turn against him.

It started when one of the slaves hurt himself trying to roll a large rock out of the way—the boulder rolled back, crushing his hand. Two slaves helped him extricate his damaged limb, and another slave with experience in dealing with injuries stopped to attend to him.

That's when the Provoker lashed out.

Observing the work stoppage by several slaves, the Lizard didn't wait to find out the cause. Instead—as soon as he was within range—he extended the prod touching the back of the slave attending the injured man, dropping him in his tracks. As the slave writhed on the ground, the Provoker laughed, stinging him twice more in rapid succession.

Cletus snapped. The revolt wasn't supposed to start for another twenty-four hours, but seeing the cruel event unfolding in front of him, he wasn't about to wait on a schedule. He took four large steps toward the Lizard guard who was turned away from him and, as momentum moved him closer and without thought for his own well-being, Cletus raised his shovel and followed through with one sweeping strike. Eight years of frustration and anger came out in a rage, lending incredible force to his already powerful stature. The blade of the shovel connected with the back of the Provoker's head, stunning the Lizard, causing him to lurch to the side.

Cletus didn't hesitate. He spun in a complete circle, shovel extended, timing the apex of his swing to connect the blade with the Lizard's throat. The edge of the blade did its work, partially severing the Lizard's head.

The other Lizard guard happened to be within sight of the incident and, before he could draw his handgun, the slaves swarmed around him. After a brief struggle, they managed to overwhelm the massive reptile and, once on the ground, several strikes with hand tools and rocks crushed the guard's skull.

Hearing the commotion, two nearby guards fired on

the slaves with their Wave tech weapons, killing thirty-four before they were overpowered and beaten to death. The slaves surprised a third guard while he was sleeping, and he never knew what hit him. In the aftermath, there were no wounded—once hit by a Wave tech discharge, even a grazing wound ended up severe enough to finish off a target.

The slave revolt had begun.

\*\*\*\*

Word soon reached Kirv and his family. Cletus arrived at the farmhouse accompanied by a group of slaves—five, including Cletus—each equipped with the Lizard guards' handguns.

"I thought the plan was to go into effect tomorrow," Kirv commented as they stood in the farmyard. There was enough stress knowing the revolt was to start the following day, and it was more than a surprise when Cletus showed up early.

"An incident occurred which accelerated the timetable."

"Well, then—we'll have to fire off messages informing our comrades the revolt is underway." He paused. "What can I do?"

"We can use something to eat, plus supplies to take

with us. Our group consists of former military, police, and National Guard members—all are committed to organizing groups for the coming fight."

Kirv nodded. "Good. I'll ask Glade and Millie to bring out something to eat. Then, we'll put together something for each of them to carry . . ."

"Much appreciated . . ." Cletus thought for a moment. "Do you have any maps of this region?"

"Sure—in the house, I have regional maps issued by the Agricultural Board before the conquest. You can have anything you need . . ."

"I sent hundreds of former slaves in all directions to spread the word as well as cause whatever grief they can among the remaining Lizards. However, none of them have weapons capable of harming the reptiles from a distance—they need to physically overwhelm the bastards by hand-to-hand fighting. Many will perish . . ."

"Is that any different than being worked to death?"

"Not really—better, if it has to happen. At least, they'll be dying for a cause . . ."

## Chapter Fifteen

Technically, by rank, Commander Beal was senior to Sub-Commander Garoc. However, with a directive giving him authority signed by the Prime of the planet? Beal might as well be the lowest rank possible—he knew he must cooperate fully with Garoc, who would report back to the Prime. There was also the little matter of the six New Planetary Holdings headquarters guards accompanying the Sub-Commander—it was unwise to forget about them.

Three individuals sat in a meeting room, Garoc on one side of the table, Beal and Sub-Commander Vanc on the other.

"So, Commander—what's going on with our precious airships you're using?"

Beal looked across the table, struggling to keep the

frustration out of his tone. "They're assisting in a search."

"I understood that from the original request from your headquarters. Searching for what, exactly?"

"Missing equipment from a remote barracks on the edge of my territory . . ."

"What kind of equipment?"

There is was—the cruncher. Beal tried to minimize the issue by turning to Vanc. "Sub-Commander, what's the list again?"

Prepared because he and Beal discussed it beforehand, Vanc pulled out a paper. "Let's see—it was one handgun, one range finder, and one anti-grav unit."

Garoc busied himself flipping through a file and, upon hearing the list, his head snapped up as he stared at Vanc. "What kind of technology are they?"

Vanc stared back. "The handgun and anti-grav unit are Wave tech powered."

The visitor from Planetary Headquarters choked slightly, then cleared his throat. "Wave tech! You let this out of your control?"

"We executed the outpost leader who was responsible."

"I don't give a shit about him—who took the missing items?"

"It appears to be humans . . ."

A full minute of silence.

"A report will go out immediately," Garoc stated,

"to the Prime about this serious problem. If the humans crack the secret of Wave tech, our advantage will be gone—potentially, they could use it against us. If Off-Planet Command hears of this, others will share the fate of the outpost commander."

"Understood."

"What have you done to retrieve them?"

"We stripped as many troops from guard duties over the slave population as possible to join the search," Beal interjected. "We have, of course, the two airships released to us. And, we just brought in a Merc team to chase them down."

"Whose Merc team?"

"Zarn's..."

"Good—they're effective as well as relentless. Brutal, too."

"Exactly."

Garoc summed it up. "You should fervently hope these resources find the missing items quickly. This could get very ugly for everyone concerned..."

\*\*\*\*

*Okay—I'm at the twenty-mile mark, or as close as I can figure it. Where the hell is everybody?*

Devin turned in slow circles, his eyes closed, focusing on anything sounding like it didn't belong in a jungle. Nothing. *Great. Just great!*

He hadn't encountered anything other than wildlife since his dustup with the trooper. *Okay, the deal is we wait an hour for the others to show up. I can do that . . .*

Two hours later he sat, completely alone.

*Fabulous—I get to do a trip to the south all on my own. What could possibly go wrong?"*

Devin reentered the trail, heading south.

\*\*\*\*

Rose sat, waiting, thankful she didn't encounter any more Lizard patrols during her hike to the twenty-mile mark. If no one from her group showed up, she realized it would be a long trip south on her own—the trick was to be watchful without driving herself nuts, spooked by every sound.

"Hey, Big Red—goin' my way?"

Rose leapt off the fallen tree trunk, spinning to face

the voice. "Tag! You scared the crap out of me!" Within seconds, she was wrapped up in his arms, worming her way closer, wishing he would never let her go.

Finally, he whispered in her ear. "I get the distinct feeling you're happy to see me."

She pulled away enough so she could see his face. "Tromping through the jungle on my own with Lizard patrols on my butt wasn't my favorite experience—I wasn't looking forward to heading all the way south on my own."

"Speaking about being on your own—have you seen Devin?"

"Nope—I haven't seen him since we split up. What about Claire?"

"She's with me—I left her just off a trail close by while I scouted."

"What happens if we can't link up with him?"

"There's no choice—we head south to the final destination, find the scientists, and, hopefully, see him there."

"Can we wait for a little while, in case he shows up?"

"Only for a bit more—we can't linger too long. The area is crawling with Lizard patrols, and Claire and I spotted airships cruising overhead."

"I saw them—a patrol, too."

Tag grimaced slightly. "I'm not sure how, but I sense something else is on our tail, more deadly than we've seen so far."

She searched his face, noting concern. "Terrific—Claire is going to be upset about Devin if we have to leave without him."

"Pissed is more like it . . ."

"It'll be extremely hard for her—she'll feel as if she's abandoning him . . ."

"I know. Let's go get her—we'll wait a bit to see if he shows. If he doesn't show up soon, we have no choice but to get going . . ."

\*\*\*\*

He scanned Garoc's report a second time for its contents to sink in. *Wave technology now in the hands of humans . . .* The fact several Lizard trooper deaths were attached to the missing items was of no importance to him. *If Off-Planet Command learns of this, we'll be in deep trouble.*

The Prime began to imagine effects of a visit by an inspector sent to sleuth out the situation—clearly, it would compromise his position as the leading authority on the planetary holding. At the least, he would be removed from office, and returned to the home planet to explain his failure. The worst was the termination of his life and, possibly, those of his family within two generations. Such was the vengeance of his kind for dereliction of one's duty.

A junior officer interrupted his mulling over morbid possibilities.

"Yes?"

"A new report, Prime—it's marked urgent."

He took the envelope, dismissing the officer. It didn't take long to scan the report and, within moments, he knew his fate was sealed. Unwittingly, he let the paper slip through his clawed hand as he turned to look out the expansive window.

Upside down on the floor, the one-page report was terse, informing the reader of the commencement of a full-scale, human slave revolt.

The situation in Beal's territory was out of hand.

\*\*\*\*

The Lizards took great pains to create the hunting preserves, keeping them in pristine condition. Appointing Warders to manage the highly-coveted areas, dozens of human slaves worked endlessly to clean and manicure what, at first glance, looked like a wild area—

closer inspection revealed deadfall cleared, and bushes trimmed. That particular preserve measured a fenced area of almost two hundred square miles. It was stocked with all indigenous wild species and, if there were diminishing numbers, they were immediately topped up to desired levels—and, there was one indigenous species, but not wild. Of all the choices available for the hunt, it was, by far, at the head of the list—the off-planet elites of the Lizard culture unanimously chose humans as their favored prey.

The leading Warder of the Wash Hunting Preserve was responsible for selecting specimens—human or otherwise—and for stocking the preserve. Kwatz realized it took care and ingenuity to keep Wash as the first choice, as well as ahead of the other preserves on the planet. His commissions were generous, not to mention his elevated power and prestige simply because of the preserve's preferred designation.

Lately, however, there was a problem with the quality of human specimens arriving for his consideration. The supplier bordered on negligence given the large number of specimens Kwatz felt compelled to reject. The object of the hunting experience for his clients was to face only exceptionally healthy specimens in their prime—intelligent, physically robust individuals made for the most desirable opponent. That term, however, was a misnomer since the Lizard hunters were, of course, armed, but prey was not. Losing an important, powerful client due to a hunting accident would be disastrous to their carefully cultivated reputation.

Walking between rows of the current, potential candidates for human replacements did nothing to foster the impression the supplier heeded the previous warning to improve the quality of his stock. Kwatz needed ten specimens to replenish numbers—as far as he could determine, only six were acceptable and, of those, two were marginal.

"You dare bring this rubbish before me?" Kwatz sneered as he walked among the candidates. "I told your superior to improve his quality—he didn't comply. I'll take six, but at a reduced price matching the reduced quality. Perhaps now my meaning will sink in . . ."

The representative bowed. "As you wish, Warder. I'll pass along the message." He knew not to anger the Warder any further—he was a lucrative client, and any fallout over quality control would affect his share of the commissions.

The guards removed all but the six selected human subjects before Kwatz took one more turn around the small group, carefully inspecting the new merchandise he just purchased. But—he wasn't the only one sizing up the situation.

One among the humans selected was a predator in his own right.

\*\*\*\*

Zarn cursed yet again. The miserable, Lizard military patrols on the trails were, in some cases, totally obliterating the traces of the human target. *Idiots!*

As far as he could tell from infrequent glimpses of minute trace evidence, the human was still heading south. Where trails converged, it took his team much longer than normal to sort out which way the target headed, slowing his hunt considerably.

Zarn's reputation hinged on always being successful in half the time it took other Merc teams, yet their competition was always in the background. Falter, and the role of being the primary clients' choice would disappear, their attention focusing on other teams.

If it continued, he knew it was possible he and his equally frustrated team members may turn their sights on the bungling military patrols—a few blasts from their Wave tech weapons may sharpen the attitude of the patrol members. However, Zarn knew his client, Beal, wouldn't be pleased at the loss of his guards at the hands of the Merc team.

\*\*\*\*

"He's not going to make it, is he?"

Tag wasn't sure if the question were rhetorical or not. "I'm sorry, Claire. It doesn't look like it . . ."

Rose tried to soften the blow. "Devin's a big boy—he can take care of himself. You've seen him in action plenty of times . . ."

"True..."

"And, he knows the ultimate destination. We're headed to the same place, so we'll just meet up there."

"I guess..."

Tag took a turn. "Remember when you were snatched by Ranj? Devin just about went nuts—but, he hung in there and we got you back. It all worked out..."

"Ranj turned into our friend, and I was at no risk from him."

"That may be, but we didn't know that—he looked like any other big, bad alien."

"What Tag's saying," Rose commented, "is we've all had our ups and downs in the last few months, and we came through it. Devin will, too. In fact, we might run into trouble heading south while he waltzes along with no problems."

At her friends' prompting, Claire got back into her normal, sassy mode. "Okay, enough with the cheerleading stuff—I get it. We'll just have to see him down the road."

"Ladies, I think it's time to turn our wagons south—shall we?" Tag grabbed his pack, hoisting it on his back.

Claire looked behind them with one last hope she'd see Devin coming toward them.

No such luck.

# Chapter Sixteen

He hunted before from the perspective of tracking prey, but, in those instances, the target was armed as well as prepared to end his life if given the opportunity. To him, it seemed like a reasonable balance in the scheme of things—making things too easy led to a boring experience. Now, he was the prey, given nothing with which to defend himself. They expected a chase, of course, but with a predictable result. *The Lizards call this a sporting event? What a bunch of schmucks!*

However, Reese had a different approach to the equation. Let the Lizards come with their special tech weapons and superior attitude—but, when it came to the nitty-gritty fighting in the weeds, he'd show them some old-fashioned down and dirty. Pre-conquest, he was an expert in Special Forces Recon techniques, but there wasn't any way to compete with the Lizards' Wave tech weapons—however, give him space to maneuver, a large combat knife, a couple of the slimy bastards, and he'd show them how to party.

Turned loose with the rest of the new purchases at the command of the Warder responsible for the Wash Hunting Preserve, he quickly moved away from the other five humans who were running as fast as they could to put distance between them and the release point. What they didn't know was the visiting Lizard hunters would be using smaller versions of the airships to jockey from point to point while the human prey exhausted themselves in a futile attempt to flee.

Reese simply cleared the immediate area, hunkering down to craft backwoods weapons of his own. The Lizard guides had so ingrained in them the humans would run, chances were they wouldn't look around the corner from the hunting lodges. They wouldn't even know he was there until he chose to get up close and personal.

****

Try as he might, worrying about Claire just wasn't something he could get out of his system. He sure as hell hoped Tag was with her—Rose, too. But, even with Claire's savvy and experience, it was a tough planet for being on one's own.

Devin kept to a narrow trail heading south—well,

maybe a tad east of true south. Traveling for several hours, he wasn't sure, but it seemed as if the foliage were getting thinner. He knew from Kirv's report, the jungle eventually petered out into a large, more populated agricultural region—and, he looked forward to moving into a more open area. Yes, he would be exposed, but the view would give him a better idea of what was out there rather than stumbling into someone on the next bend in the trail.

Plus, he may see his friends.

\*\*\*\*

"Shut the door." His voice normally commanding, Beal stated his order quietly.

Vanc did as requested, turning to look at his superior. If the Lizards had eyebrows, he would have raised one in a silent query. Instead, he waited until Beal organized his thoughts.

"I don't like the fact we have six of the New Planetary Holding headquarters guards backing up Garoc. The Prime must have his report by now—if an order comes through removing me, they'll haul me back there. Anything can happen after that, none of it good . . ."

Vanc remained silent for a ten count. Part of him

sympathized with Beal's situation insofar as the taint might rub off on him as Sub-Commander of the region. A purge might get down to his level—however, the other way to look at it was from the perspective of opportunity. If Vanc stayed in place and Beal were removed, then it could be a chance for advancement. "What do you propose, Commander?"

Beal hesitated, not sure if he should take Vanc into his confidence. "Perhaps, we should take preemptive steps . . ."

"Such as?"

If he were to pull it off, he needed Vanc's help—therefore, Beal felt he had little choice in the matter. "Gather a platoon of our fully-armed guards, and deploy them in a way to cut off the headquarters guards from Garoc. If he gives even a glimmer of trying to take over, eliminate them all. We'll make it look like an accident later . . ."

Vanc stared back at his Commander, not at all sure how to play this one to his advantage.

Either way, it was a dangerous game.

\*\*\*\*

Returning from an extended patrol combing the jungle for the human or small group possessing the stolen goods, the patrol leader questioned what was so important to warrant troops and two airships. Interestingly, they weren't informed of the details of what was missing—but, it had to be important if there were secrecy and dedicated resources.

After tromping through the jungle for the last thirty-six hours, his troopers were exhausted. Only six miles from their barracks, all were looking forward to rest and a decent meal. The result?

The Lizards were vulnerable.

\*\*\*\*

Timing is everything.

Cletus deployed his ever-growing group of slave escapees in a classic ambush pattern around the jungle trail, instructing them to wait until the signal. Then? Attack the middle of the ten Lizard patrol members—by doing so, all members of the patrol would be equally exposed to the ambush at the same instant.

Five humans, including Cletus, possessed Wave tech handguns liberated from the dead work-gang guards. The purpose of attacking the patrol—apart from the opportunity to kill their Lizard oppressors—was to get human hands on the rifle version of the Wave tech weaponry carried by each Lizard trooper parading by the hidden attackers.

When the fifth and sixth in line were directly in front of him, Cletus discharged his Wave tech handgun. In a morbid way, the result was spectacular—the blast obliterated the fifth trooper in line, effectively blowing his torso and upper body apart. The detached legs actually took two more steps despite not having a neural command from a shattered brain. Before the sixth trooper could bring his rifle weapon into firing position, Cletus fired a second shot. Moments later, he heard Wave tech discharges along the trail, two from troopers with rifled versions who managed to get off shots before being struck. As a result, several humans were killed.

The first and tenth troopers were assaulted by multiple humans armed only with farmhand tools, knives, and roughly-crafted spears. Sheer numbers and pent-up rage from years of bondage suddenly released in an unstoppable wave and, although three humans died in the attack on the front and rear of the patrol, Lizard troopers were eventually overwhelmed and struck down. Considering enduring a long, eight plus years of slavery, the humans took less than a minute to totally subdue the hated Lizards, none of which survived.

The humans regrouped with Cletus, fifteen Wave tech weapons now at their disposal. There was discussion about the discharge of the weapons attracting the attention of the Lizard command—some were concerned more Lizard warriors would concentrate on their immediate location. Cletus, however, viewed such a scenario as further opportunity to ambush additional Lizards as they surged into the area to investigate.

Fortunately, he preplanned and selected secondary and tertiary ambush sites for that specific purpose. The surviving human attackers moved into those positions, relishing the opportunity to inflict further damage on the Lizard garrison.

*Bring it on*, Cletus urged. *Bring it on!*

\*\*\*\*

Kirv, his family, and several of his farmer neighbors supplied three more former human slave groups which passed through after Cletus left. The groups were smaller, yet just as determined to do whatever was required to extinguish as many Lizards as possible from existing on their planet.

They brought with them rumors of wide-scale slaughter of individuals or small human groups caught by the Lizards who were incensed by the revolt. Work gangs in other regions—not yet included in the uprising—were being systematically exterminated, which led to their fighting back instead of meekly submitting. Ironically, the Lizards' attempt to quash the spread of the revolt was, in fact, fueling fires in new areas. On the plus side, rumors abounded of Lizard groups being ambushed and destroyed.

It was savage fighting to the death.

\*\*\*\*

He knew his term as an authority figure on the Planetary Holding was at an end, and there was little he could do about it. However, as one of his last acts before the arrival of the inspector from off-planet, the Prime felt he needed to strike back—to blame someone. His target? Commander Beal. He allowed Wave tech equipment to be stolen by humans, causing the region under Beal's command to be in full, open revolt.

It all centered on Beal.

The Prime determined the Commander should pay the ultimate price for his shortcomings. Why wait for the inspector to arrive? In his mind, it was better to be proactive by striking first. So, he took what he considered appropriate action by issuing an order for the arrest and execution of Commander Beal.

Inclusion of Sub-Commander Vanc was simply an afterthought.

\*\*\*\*

He raised a glass of fine red wine. "A toast! To the amazing success of your art show opening! I think even you were surprised . . ."

She clinked his glass with her own. "True—I was kind of hoping, but also kind of scared no one would turn up or like it. Does that make sense?"

"It does—it's new territory for you from an owner's standpoint."

Jackie eyed Kyle with a serious look. "What did you think?"

Kyle put a hand over hers on the table. "I'll be honest—there were several pieces I didn't like too much. The bulk of them, however, were very good. Excellent presentation, too."

"Thanks—with art you're not supposed to necessarily like them all. If a few pieces appeal to you, mission accomplished . . ."

"It would be nice if Tag were here to help celebrate."

"Yes, it would. But, he hasn't met me . . ."

"It doesn't matter—I know he'll love you. Just wait—one day he'll walk in that door, and you can see for yourself."

"You know I'll pray for that day . . ."

Kyle squeezed her hand. "Me, too . . ."

\*\*\*\*

He waited, patiently.

The last flight of a small, four passenger airship was fifteen minutes earlier, and he heard it land in the clearing not far away from his cover. Of course, he purposely left tracks to lead them to his immediate area—nothing too obvious, just enough to be detectable by the guide tracker leading his guests to an easy kill.

Once he constructed a roughly-made spear and stone-edged, cutting hand tool, Reese moved from the relative closeness of the Warder's guest area into the heart of the hunting range. The comparative difference between his primitive weapons versus the Lizards' hunting rifles was extreme—still, he felt the advantage was his.

They hunted for sport.

He was well trained for war.

****

The order for Garoc came through the communicator, its pinging alerting him to the incoming message. Once read, he set out to find the guard Commander of the headquarters unit and, after five minutes of trying to find and communicate with him, Garoc returned to his quarters. Once he cleared the entranceway, he was suddenly surrounded by troopers—Beal's guards.

Sub-Commander Vanc entered behind him. "Garoc—these guards will be taking you to a place for your safekeeping. With the humans' revolt causing problems, your safety is at risk."

No fool, the headquarters Sub-Commander knew his safety was far from ensured. "I feel secure with my own guards—where are they?"

"Redeployed for base security..."

Garoc knew the spiel—they were under arrest or worse. "Perhaps, I should contact the Prime and request more headquarters guards be sent to help."

Vanc smirked. "Thank you for the offer, but that won't be necessary. We can handle things from here..."

"The Prime will find out what you're doing..." Garoc hoped his desperation didn't show.

"He can think what he wants—what's presented to him will be a slightly altered version of events. One more palatable for him..."

"He'll see through that..."

"Possibly. But, from what we hear, the Prime is on the way out. He'll be too busy looking after his own welfare to worry about what's going on here—including your fate."

Resigned to his eventual demise, Garoc rendered a half-hearted smile. "Go ahead and enjoy the moment. There's something coming you don't know or see—unfortunately, I won't have the pleasure of watching it unfold."

Vanc motioned for his guards to remove Garoc under previously-issued orders—his headquarters guards were already eliminated.

Finally alone, Vanc wondered about Garoc's warning. *What the hell does that mean? What's coming?*

****

The Merc team picked up the pace once they cleared an area beyond where the garrison patrols fouled up the quarry trail. Now, they had a fairly clear view of human footprints heading south—three sets, the larger most likely a male. Another set could be a male with a smaller footprint, or a female with a larger foot. A much smaller set was very likely female.

Zarn studied them only from an interest perspective, gender causing no concern—all were targets. He figured it was easier to bring back proof of their deaths to Beal rather than shepherd walking captives all the way back to the Commander's headquarters. Plus, it saved time.

It was all about efficiency.

# Chapter Seventeen

The trail opened within a mile, and they were making good time with enough room for two to walk side-by-side. Tag suggested the girls walk ahead of him while he stayed ten steps behind—that way, he could see in front and monitor behind them should a threat appear. So far? Smooth sailing. Of course, if Devin were with them, things would be ideal, but the three of them were managing.

Still, Tag sensed an element of danger, but it remained veiled. He couldn't determine form or its direction, but there was no doubt something sinister loomed. "Maybe we should pick up the pace a bit," he suggested, not wanting to alarm them.

Claire, as usual, didn't buy it. "Okay—what's up?"

He hesitated, but both girls turned, studying him.

"I'm not sure—the vibes I'm getting indicate something nasty is out there and, possibly, not too far away. It's hard to tell, but I'd say it's behind us—I figure maybe we should put a bit more distance between us just to be safe."

The gals traded a look, nodded, and picked up the pace.

After half an hour, Tag called a stop. He stood quietly, focusing on their surroundings.

"Well?" Rose tried not to make the question seem too urgent.

"I can't be sure—they're impressions only. But, I think we're being tracked. Whatever it is, it's a good distance back, but slowly closing the gap. It's nasty, and we don't want to tangle with it—or, them. I can't tell how many..."

"What can we do?" Claire glanced around them, uncertain of the threat.

"We can try doubling back, or constructing trail puzzles—however, I get the impression these are pros. Doing that will allow them to catch up to us..."

"How about an ambush?"

"Possible. Keep in mind, however, they may be wearing Wave tech protective body armor, and our weapons won't penetrate it. Only a headshot or hand-to-hand fighting will work—even so, both will be a challenge for us."

"We can run, alternating with fast walks, to keep the distance between us—or, better yet, increase it," Rose suggested.

Tag glanced at Claire. "Normally, even with your height and leg-length challenges, you can keep up with us at a steady run. I'm concerned if you're recovered enough from your injury . . ."

"I can give it a good try—I'm feeling stronger every day. Let's run, and check it out . . ."

Tag studied her for a moment, then agreed. They set a moderate running-speed pace for twenty minutes, followed by a brisk walking pace for ten, and Claire seemed to do just fine.

\*\*\*\*

Almost an hour behind them, Zarn studied a change in footstep patterns of their quarry. "It's obvious they started to run . . ."

"How did they know we're following?" One of his team members knelt down, examining the tracks.

"I'm not sure—it looks as if they stopped here, moved around, then headed off at a good pace."

"If they're fit enough to keep a good running pace, we can't match them—it's the downside of our bigger bodies," the second Merc pointed out.

Zarn nodded. "Let's follow to determine their pattern of running versus walking. If it's mostly walking, we'll be okay—if they're running more, we'll need to call for transportation."

"Land vehicles are too big to follow this path..."

"True. We'll have to get off this trail into a more open area, use a ground vehicle, jump ahead, then try to guess correctly where they'll pop out of the jungle. We may need an airship..."

"Beal will never give one..."

"He will if he wants us to catch them..."

\*\*\*\*

"Garoc and the guards have been taken care of..."

"Permanently, I presume?"

"Of course."

"Good—now let's hope the Prime doesn't send anyone else to investigate for a while."

"He'll be too busy guarding his own tail—if an investigator arrives, things will change dramatically. For all of us..."

Beal sat, contemplating the disturbing scenario.

"What's the status of the slave revolt?"

Sub-Commander Vanc paused, figuring out how to word it. "It's not good—we have them partially contained, but in a widening area. We lost over thirty troopers so far—worse, they were stripped of their weapons. So, we have more humans running around with our own weapons being used against us . . ."

Beal scratched at his leathery skin in frustration. "Have the armory issue Wave tech battle shields—they'll cancel the effects of the captured Wave tech weapons . . ."

Vanc nodded his agreement, then switched topics. "Speaking of captured weapons, a request came through from Zarn's Merc team. They want an airship at their disposal to find the humans who stole the original missing equipment . . ."

"It hardly matters with the revolt and the humans' having weapons. So, the answer is no—he can't have an airship. We need to cancel his contract because it doesn't matter now."

Vanc knew better. "It's not that easy—his team will want to be paid."

"For what? They didn't catch the target . . ."

"Sir, it won't matter to them—they'll come back to collect."

Beal pondered that for a moment or two. "I'll have to deal with it later—there's too much going wrong here at the moment . . ."

****

The trail widened as the closeness of the jungle began to melt away. He wasn't particularly claustrophobic, but having more space made it easier to breathe. Funny—he didn't notice the subtle feeling of constraint until it was gone.

Devin paused on the pathway to take in his surroundings, something he did each hour. Soaking in the immediate environment allowed him to free up his senses to detect anything of concern—since linking up with the other Travelers, he developed an increasing ability to detect what wasn't obvious.

His thoughts turned briefly to Claire until his intuitive radar picked up a blip. There was something moving out there not too far away—something different. It felt as if it didn't belong . . .

He remained still, trying to tune in on what he was feeling. Something was definitely not right, and it was approaching.

Decision time.

If he got out of there, which direction should he take? Or, should he find a place to hide, then dig in? With that choice, however, there was a possibility of their detecting him.

He'd be trapped.

\*\*\*\*

They landed four.

As the small airship lifted off to return to a holding area, three Lizard clients from off-planet looked to their hunting guide. Considered a tame, trustworthy human captive, he scanned the area. Pre-conquest, Logan was a hunting guide for rich individuals who wanted to get their thrill by taking down big game. Deer, elk, antelope, and bear were preferred targets—with the Lizard bastards, however, their favorite targets were human.

Logan cooperated completely as he tracked his human clients. When a Lizard insisted on human quarry, Logan did his best to divert them away without looking too obvious. He figured it was his small way of resisting the conquerors—plus, it was a good way to keep his ear to the ground because his Lizard clients often talked openly about many things. Things they had no business discussing . . .

He often shook his head at their arrogance as they expected him to follow their directions using the universal translator. In the next breath, they completely ignored him as though he were deaf or incapable of understanding them when they left the translators turned on. Theirs was amazing ineptitude, and he wondered how the hell they managed to conquer his world. His current group? Each wanted to bag a human.

Logan turned, indicating to the hunters to follow. He set a course through dense cover, his small frame easily sliding by the numerous branches and bushes covering the section. He could have taken an easier route, but he relished the difficulties and cursing elicited from the big-bodied Lizards.

The beauty of small victories.

Within thirty minutes, Logan noticed human tracks—nothing too obvious, just random traces. They looked fresh, so he was alerted to a possible human presence close by. Of course, he said nothing to the three Lizard hunters who were thoroughly pissed by being scraped by the foliage.

Following the subtle signs, Logan spotted an ideal ambush area—if a human had weapons as well as the fortitude to try them on the Lizard hunters, it could get interesting. Unlike the garrison troops, the hunters wore no protective armor—none of them anticipated their prey could potentially turn on them. They figured with their hunting rifles, any game could be dispatched well before it became a threat.

Logan paused moments before entering the potential kill zone, waiving on his clients with a comment that a target might be under cover close by. He aligned them just enough off to the right so their flanks were exposed to what he figured would be the most likely location for any attack—he couldn't be sure, but something was telling him to be wary of the area.

Two Lizards eagerly entered the clump of bushes, trees, and boulders—the third was behind simply because there wasn't room for all three to enter at once.

Within seconds, all hell broke loose.

A discharge from a hunting rifle. Grunts. Screams. One of the Lizard hunters staggered backwards into a small open area, a roughly hewn wooden spear protruding from his throat. He took three steps, pivoted left, then dropped like a rock.

Then, two things happened.

The third Lizard hunter turned, desperately trying to escape the ambush. But, when his back was turned, a human male appeared from the thicket holding a Lizard rifle. As the Lizard approached Logan, the hunting guide raised his weapon, firing two shots into the Lizard's prominent forehead.

The forest fell silent.

The male human nodded, raising his rifle to acknowledge the help from Logan. Then they slowly moved toward each other, stopping five feet apart. The unknown male motioned with his head toward the Lizard Logan shot. "Not liking the clientele?"

Logan looked at the dead Lizard, then back at the man standing before him. "Not much—lousy tippers."

The man laughed, and offered a hand. "My name's Reese. Thanks for the assist . . ."

"I'm Logan, former hunting guide to these assholes," he commented, shaking Reese's hand enthusiastically.

Reese quickly sized up Logan, liking what he saw. "I'm about to embark on a little payback—want to come along?"

"Hell, yes!"

\*\*\*\*

It made no sense. The farms were there to feed the Lizards' slave workers. Why destroy them now?

Kirv, Glade, and Millie left just after dark, heading south. He wanted to travel at night to put as much distance as possible between his place and them, but not without sorrow. Kirv and his family spent many years building up and maintaining everything he had—it was disappointing to walk away from it.

They received word earlier in the day of neighboring farms being surrounded by Lizard troops, killing residents, as well as burning buildings, equipment, and fields. Apparently, one farmer was caught aiding slave workers who revolted, and the Lizards went apeshit—now, they were wiping out other farms in the region. Kirv knew the Lizards were taking losses, figuring they were desperate to regain a semblance of control—but, he didn't want his family sitting in an exposed position, undefended, waiting for the coming onslaught.

Time was short, so they were well served by having the foresight to fill backpacks ahead of time for each of them just in case everything derailed. As they trekked along a narrow country road on the way to the surrounding jungle, the family could see the backlit night sky reflecting fires to the east and north of them—neighbors' homes were up in flames.

So—the decision had to be made. Where to go? Once they cleared the area, which direction should they choose? What would be their ultimate destination?

# Chapter Eighteen

The officer finished his report, and stood silently waiting for a response. Silence. Did the Prime hear? The officer understood circumstances were heading toward the dire end of the spectrum, but he expected the supreme authority on the planet to take things in stride. He expected him to order something be done to rectify the situation, not be overwhelmed! That worried him greatly. Stuck on a conquered planet with a threadbare garrison and its indigenous human population starting to run amok wasn't a comforting thought.

Eventually, the Prime spoke. "Thank you for delivering the report from the analysis group—obviously, matters are sliding out of control in Beal's region. Losing contact with Garoc is unsettling, and we must react accordingly."

He paused, looking at the floor before he continued. "Send out a directive to all regional Commanders on this planet to suppress any hints of unrest in their areas. They now have full authority to take whatever preemptive action is required to stamp out resistance by the humans before it gets a foothold. We cannot afford another district to become unraveled like Beal's . . ."

"Yes, Prime."

"Order in the Planetary Reserve Force to visit Beal's headquarters, and bring him to me. They are to take control of the situation in his region to suppress the opposition, even if it means elimination of the human population there—this can't be allowed to spread to adjacent regions."

"Of course, Prime."

"I don't want to be forced to take the next step by requesting reinforcements from Off-Planet Command. This is our own mess, and we have no choice but to clean it up ourselves . . ."

The officer nodded acknowledgment of the orders, and left the Prime's office to carry out the initiatives.

Alone again, the Prime turned to the window. *How much time do I have left to appreciate the beauty of what lies before me?*

\*\*\*\*

His two team members stood waiting, occasionally exchanging glances. It had been several minutes since he ended the communication link.

Zarn looked at both. "There will be no airship, nor ground vehicle provided for us."

Again, the two team members exchanged a glance. "Then how do they expect us to find the target," the larger one asked.

"They don't."

"What's going on?"

Zarn sneered. "Sub-Commander Vanc, unfortunately, advises Commander Beal canceled the contract."

The other two Lizards stared back in amazement.

"The question is," Zarn continued, "do we continue on, complete the assignment, and go to Beal for payment? Or, do we turn around, and visit with Beal?"

"And, ask for payment now?"

"Of course . . ."

"We go back to Beal now, he pays, and we teach him a lesson!" The larger Lizard's eyes glowed with anticipation.

Zarn considered his teammate's suggestion. "There's a downside to that approach . . ."

Previously silent, the smaller team member pointed out the obvious. "But, we wouldn't have finished the contract terms, and that will reflect on our reputation for always being successful."

"Correct—so, the decision is what is more important—a potential smear on our reputation, or proving to other clients not to play games with us?"

All three contemplated the situation.

The smaller Lizard spoke first. "Let's finish the job, go back, get paid, then make an example out of Beal . . ."

Zarn smiled. "Clearly, the best solution."

The large Lizard shrugged his agreement.

"So be it. Let's find the targets without aid. We'll confiscate transportation when we find it—then there'll be a reckoning with Commander Beal."

They moved onto a different pathway leading to the west which would soon empty into an open area—perhaps then, they could find suitable transportation.

****

"I'm not training for the Olympics."

"You have Olympics, too?"

"Duh . . ."

Tag chuckled. "Sorry—no offense meant. That's one

of those things we didn't compare between our different versions of Earth."

"I know—just yanking your chain!" Claire smiled at him as they jogged along the track.

The trio alternated who ran side-by-side, and who hung back. Currently, Rose was the lone wolf loping along ten yards back.

"So, I take it your comment referred to a desire to slow down . . ."

"Correct. I know we want to put distance between us and whatever is following. But, if we're too pooped to bug out if they catch up to us, we could be in trouble."

"Agreed—let's take a breather."

They slowed to a fast walk—by unspoken consensus, no one wanted to stop.

"So what do your Spidey senses tell you?"

He looked down at Claire, and smiled. "I think we're maintaining the same gap. I don't feel whatever's out there gained on us . . ."

Rose moved closer when they went into walk mode. "There's a long way to go before we get to the scientists' neighborhood—if we're shadowed all the way, it's going to be a lot of stress. At more than one point, we're going to have to stop and rest. Is that when they catch up?"

Tag didn't want to leave her without hope. "Probably—however, we know they're coming, and that makes a huge difference. Taking someone by surprise allows a big advantage—if we can be ready when they come, it should balance things out for us."

"It better," Claire murmured, "because it's a long road where we're going."

\*\*\*\*

The second encounter went just as well as the first—Lizards ambushed, dispatched, their weapons liberated and dispersed to the good guys. The third ambush, however, wasn't the success he hoped for—the Lizards weren't stupid, or they wouldn't have conquered Earth. The third group obviously heard what happened to the other patrols, and they were ready to mix it up. Six surviving Lizards managed to clear the ambush site—four didn't make it at the cost of twenty-three humans destroyed. Equipped with shield devices, the Lizards neutralized the effects of the humans' Wave tech weapons, and the four Lizard deaths were a result of hand-to-hand fighting when the humans maneuvered past the shields to inflict damage up close and personal.

After the action ended and his men regrouped, Cletus saw an unknown, male human approaching from another trail.

"Are you Cletus," the man asked.

"Yes—what's up?"

"I've been moving through the area advising every

group I can find—the Lizards started massacring slave groups and farm families at random. I don't know if it's payback for the revolt, or a decision to eliminate everyone in this region."

"How did you know to ask for me?"

"Kirv sent me. He said you were probably too busy busting the Lizards to hear about the rest of the people in this area."

"Well, he was right—we've been hammering them pretty hard." Cletus paused. "What about the slave camp down by the river—anyone left?"

"Not many—a few service people, and the kitchen staff hung around. If the Lizards return to it, the remaining slaves will be toast."

"Nirva!"

The man didn't understand the sudden worried look on the large man's face.

Cletus turned, calling out to his second in command. "Morris, get everyone together now—we're heading back to the old slave camp . . ."

"Okay, Boss." Morris began to stir the fighters to get up and get moving.

*I need to be there in time—she has to be alright!* It was a thought that would haunt him until he found out.

Cletus fretted as his force of fighters moved into position to start the trek back—they weren't moving fast enough to suit him.

****

They took an easterly route moving quickly away from the kill zone in the hunting preserve, and it was early evening when the two men arrived at the perimeter fencing.

Reese glanced at the former hunting guide. "The Warder has to know by now he's shy three clients . . ."

"Absolutely—one of the other hunting guides is a Lizard with reasonable skills. The trail puzzles we left behind will only fool him for so long." Logan didn't seem particularly worried by the prospect of being tracked.

"Do we have a concern about their coming after us?"

"Not particularly—first, they don't have a lot of extra staff to run the Wash Hunting Preserve. Second, the Warder may try keeping quiet the loss of three off-planet clients. Bad for business . . ."

Reese chuckled, appreciating Logan's dry humor. "Let's head a bit further east to see what opportunities arise to cause the Lizards real problems . . ."

"I'm in! Lead on . . ."

****

Decision made.

It was simply a matter of staying tucked into his hiding spot, relying on whatever might be tracking him to mosey on by. He took extreme care to move through the trees before he came to ground again. The idea was to not leave any evidence of his moving into cover—after all, there was no point in making it easy for them. On the other hand, if there were some wild animal and he were upwind? Not good.

It didn't take long. There were three of them— Lizards. But not decked out like garrison guards—they were different, and something he hadn't seen before. The lead tracker took considerable time scoping out the trail as well as the immediate area where Devin headed for the trees by climbing a vine. The other two walked ahead, checking for evidence the human was near.

Zarn signaled his team, continuing to study the ground and lower bushes for signs. "Clearly, it left the ground—this one is wily . . ." He knelt down. "See where everything on the ground just ends? It used the trees, which limits the rate of travel unless it were some kind of monkey." He paused, scanning the area. "Chances are the prey is close by—maybe within sight, but hiding in cover. Fan out from here—move laterally to see if we can flush it out."

Devin watched as the three Lizards separated, starting an obvious search grid.

*Damn!* He weighed the commitment of staying put, and toughing it out—there was, after all, a chance they might miss him. If he tried to run, they'd be on him in seconds.

If he could give back the following fifteen minutes

to time, he would've. He remained immobile while the search pressed closer to his location and, eventually, one of them came within four feet of where he lay. The Lizard scanned the area in each direction—nothing. You see, the beauty of his hiding spot was the entry—Devin dropped into a small opening from above without disturbing anything, leaving no evidence he was there.

Finally, they moved from view. But, Devin knew enough to stay put for a while in case the buggers were hiding out of sight, waiting for him to make a fatal mistake.

Patience was key.

As it turned out, he decided to wait until it was almost dark on the jungle floor before he cautiously ventured from his sanctuary.

He was alone.

Devin continued to move south on the trail—however, given the chance to switch to a different, intersecting trail, he would gladly take it even if it didn't head directly where he wanted to go.

\*\*\*\*

The focus shifted to the upcoming nuptial, but he found it difficult to proceed with the plans—the idea of Tag's missing his wedding was more than he could consider. More than he could accept. If, tragically, Tag's life ended—Kyle could accept his not being there. But, when he learned Tag was still alive, it created a barrier for Kyle's moving forward. Earlier efforts to figure out how to bring him back were an incredible, statistical longshot—but, he had to try.

And, Jackie knew he'd never give up.

Things shifted for him—sometimes day-to-day, other times week-to-week. Driven and optimistic, he believed if an alien could solve the wormhole problem, why couldn't he? Then, there were the down times—the concept was so complex it was insurmountable. Still, there was one thing he knew deep in his soul—he'd see his brother again.

It was simply a question of when.

\*\*\*\*

They talked it over, deciding to continue south, and Kirv, Glade, and Millie agreed the other directions offered nothing in particular. Heading in the same direction as their recent house guests gave them a sense of purpose by potentially helping locate the scientists—but, they'd have to link up with the Travelers somewhere along the line.

Kirv was aware of the Lizards' search grid in an attempt to locate the original theft's perpetrator, but he didn't know if it were still in effect given the recent skirmishes between escaped slaves and Lizard forces. Rumors were flying concerning ambushes, Lizard losses, and human interventions on a growing scale. So, he led his family directly east for a day to break free of Lizard patrols in the search grid—then they turned south.

With the family dog, Grub, walking just in front of him, Kirv took comfort from the fact the animal's more acute senses would pick up on lurking Lizards as they pushed south.

One thing Kirv knew—the dog would react strongly to any hint of a Lizard.

He hated those bastards.

# Chapter Nineteen

They lost the trail, but Zarn knew the prey was somewhere close by. Unfortunately, a certain amount of skill or blind luck continued to aid the individuals' eluding them—until their fortunes turned as his team worked its way west to open space, picking up evidence of three humans moving south on an intersecting trail.

He studied the footprints. "We saw these before, closer to where the thefts occurred . . ."

"Should we follow them?"

"Of course—they may be holding the technology. We need to find someone responsible for all of this, so we can end things and have our visit with Beal."

"I'm looking forward to that . . ."

"Don't kill him at first sight—we need to get paid first. Then we'll make an example of him..."

The large Merc bowed his head. "As you wish—but I want the honor of the kill."

"And, you shall have it. Now—let's follow these three, and get this done..."

****

They approached as evening light started to fail, and he directed his fighters into a semicircle as they closed in on the former slave camp. The kitchens were on the near side, and Cletus was nervous about Nirva's well-being and whereabouts. It was weird, too—he didn't realize the level of affection for her until the Lizards' rampage.

Scouting revealed no reptilians, but it didn't mean they weren't inside the buildings. They passed carefully through the outer ring of low-slung structures, checking each for occupants. Then, his fighters continued to penetrate further into the heart of the camp close to the kitchens. He signaled everyone to hold while he and Morris studied the immediate area, and Cletus heard safeties being flipped off multiple weapons as tension increased.

The kitchen was twenty yards away—a subsidiary

kitchen attached at a right angle, facing away from them, and all appeared quiet. Cletus glanced at Morris crouching beside him next to a large, free-standing planter with vegetables growing inside it.

"What do you think?"

His second in command shrugged. "It looks peaceful enough—no telling for sure if the Lizards are here until we sweep the entire camp, one building at a time. I'd like to take it slow and easy until we're sure . . ."

"Okay, send details to each side of the camp. I'll stay with the main body—we'll do the kitchens first, then move to the center."

Morris smirked. "You got any particular reason to pick them?" He knew of the leader's interest with the head gal running the kitchens.

Cletus nodded. "Yes, I do—and, if I find her, I'm not letting any asshole Lizard do her any harm."

"I guess you better find out then—I'll take care of the rest of the search."

Cletus agreed. He rose, moving in the direction of the main kitchen, followed by ten of his fighting team. A greater bulk of their force spread out into wings, searching buildings.

Fifty paces out, a door opened, a person emerging with a large bag. The sudden appearance of activity drew the attention of everyone as eleven weapons fixed on the target.

"Hold!" Cletus ordered his troops as he continued to sight the target.

The woman turned, almost dropping the bag in fright.

Nirva!

He ran over to her. "Can I take that for you?" Without waiting for an answer, he relieved her of the bag, passing it to one of his men.

"You came!"

Cletus enveloped her in his arms.

"For you . . ."

They embraced for a time neither could define.

Finally, Morris jogged over. "Sorry about this, but we're about to be up to our asses in Lizards . . ."

"What's going on?"

"A reinforced patrol coming in from the jungle on the other side of the camp—they'll be here in ten."

"Is contact imminent?"

"No—our forward scout team is out of the way for now. But, we have to decide real quick—fight or withdraw."

Cletus glanced at Nirva.

"Pass the word to pull back—let's keep some separation until we get under cover of the jungle. We go in for twenty minutes to the ambush spot, then deploy. If they stumble in after us, we'll give them a greeting . . ."

"Cletus . . ." Nirva didn't like the sound of their plan.

"Stick with me no matter what happens—it can get

hairy later on."

She smiled. "Like glue . . ."

Cletus grabbed her hand, guiding her back the way he and his troops entered the camp.

From a bird's-eye view, the Lizard force moved in from the opposite side of where the human group detached and melted back into the jungle. Movement of each group was unknowingly simultaneous as if they were partners in a dance. The Lizard scouts didn't catch a whiff of the human presence as they moved only to the central portion of the camp, calling a halt to rest after deploying into defensive positions.

They never knew their targets were only paces away.

\*\*\*\*

"I'm not sure."

"What do you mean?"

"I don't know if they're still following—I can't feel it, but that could be wrong."

"Really? Don't tell me your mojo is failing . . ."

Tag glanced at Claire resting on a large rock by the

side of the trail. He did feel a bit flustered, but the smirk on her face made him laugh. She enjoyed teasing him, and it usually resulted in his not taking himself too seriously.

"Okay—I'm pretty sure we're clear for now. After our break, I'd like to keep moving at a good clip to put more distance between us and the Lizards."

"Absolutely, Fearless Leader . . ." Claire stood and saluted.

He glanced at Rose who looked back with an eyebrow raised, and a shrug of her shoulders.

Tag detected Claire's false bravado. "He's going to be fine—we'll see him at the final rendezvous point."

"I know . . ."

"Why don't we start moving again, and see how far we can go before dark?" Rose thought it was a good idea to get things moving before the conversation turned maudlin.

Tag and Claire nodded and Rose took the lead, setting a decent jogging pace to eat up distance. They knew heavy-bodied Lizards moved moderately fast for very short distances—that's the reason they traveled by transport. Good news for the Travelers. However, the bad news was the Lizards had stamina, keeping up their slower pace for long periods.

Not good.

****

It was three days traveling east from the perimeter fence marking the edge of the Preserve, when they first spotted what they were looking for—tracks of Lizards passing to the south.

Logan, an expert hunting guide and tracker, easily picked up their trail. "For Lizard bastards, they move quickly—three of them. Interestingly, there are fresh tracks of three humans . . ." He paused, making certain he was reading the tracks correctly. "I'm figuring one male and two females, also moving south . . ."

"The humans are being hunted?"

Reese looked at Logan for confirmation.

An affirmative nod. "Well—this may be the opportunity we've been waiting for. If they're tracking humans as quarry, they may not be too careful when checking their six—if they do, at all. We could slide in behind them and say howdy . . ."

Logan chuckled at the image. "Yes, that's exactly what we should do! It's not a precise thing, but I'd say the Lizards passed this way within the last two hours. They don't move too fast, although they have pretty good stamina for a longer, slower chase. If we can maintain a good clip, we should overtake them sooner than later . . ."

Reese smiled. "Lead on—let's find some Lizards and ruin their day!"

"I'm all over it!"

****

The massive Merc breathed heavily as he dropped back, his chest expanding and contracting as he struggled to inhale and exhale. Too bad for him, it was a losing proposition—he sounded like a blacksmith's bellows on steroids.

Annoyed, Zarn finally had to call a halt before the big one had a cardiac. "We're closer—I can feel it. Five minutes, then we have to start the chase again."

The smaller Merc shrugged, as though to indicate he was fine with the plan. His much larger companion continued to stare, glassy-eyed, at the ground, concentrating on resupplying his oxygen-starved body, yet he seemed not to hear the remark. Zarn turned away, shaking his head—he didn't want to admit defeat from three, puny humans because his oversized teammate couldn't hack it.

Finally, when the struggling Merc appeared to have recovered enough to stand up straight, Zarn tromped down the trail again, determined to win the race, chasing the quarry to ground. What he failed to understand was how the game changed—he may be a hunter, but Zarn and his team were also the prey.

When, and where would they intersect?

****

Grub sensed it before anyone else. First, a scent—a low growl. Kirv immediately stopped it from turning into barking by issuing a command in a low voice—they didn't want to tip off their presence on the trail.

Millie and Glade paused several yards behind him, waiting for his cue whether to continue south, or reverse course to put distance between them and whatever Grub discovered.

He stared down the relatively straight portion of the trail, struggling to see if there were visual evidence of Grub's unease. The dog remained crouched, hackles raised—that's when Kirv knew one type of creature was around.

Lizards.

Kirv shifted his gaze to the ground of the trail immediately in front of him. He was no tracker or professional hunter, but he'd been around the outdoors enough over the years to identify Lizard tracks heading south—the direction they wanted to go.

He didn't want to put his family in unnecessary danger, but there were inherent risks. *But what constitutes increased risk?* They were on the run from the conquering species who could pop up in any area, at any time. *Will we be safer or worse off by turning around, retracing our steps?*

His fight or flight instincts were at war with each other and what finally won out was the concept of Lizards on the trail heading south, focused on their mission. Perhaps their attention wouldn't be on where they just came from—the bastards were arrogant enough to believe any territory they passed through was secure.

Kirv glanced at his family, making eye contact with each. "There are Lizard tracks heading south—let's follow a distance to see what unfolds . . ."

Glade nodded to her husband. She didn't want to encounter those beasts, yet, she trusted Kirv's judgment.

They continued south.

\*\*\*\*

Since his encounter two days previous with the three Lizards tracking him, Devin was starting to loosen up a bit—hiding in the bush, waiting to be discovered, wasn't natural for him—instinctively, he was a man of action, especially since linking up with Tag and the girls, worlds ago.

He diverted onto an intersecting, southwest trail the day before—eventually, it turned due south, so he figured he was traveling parallel to his previous trail. Obviously, he had to pay attention to what may arise from all points of the compass—however, he was particularly attuned to the situation straight ahead.

His missing Claire didn't help matters, though . . .

\*\*\*\*

"Hold up!" The order came from the point man of Cletus's force. Halting was immediate, but it took awhile for everyone to come to a stop because they were strung out for quite a distance back up the trail. He approached, after Cletus's indicating to Nirva to stay with his second in command.

"What's up?" Cletus didn't like the look on his soldier's face.

Not taking his eyes off the trail, the soldier nodded toward the trail in front of them. "Sir, we have something lying in wait out there. I'm not sure exactly what, but it's there . . ."

"Lizards, or something else?"

"I can't be sure, but I'm thinking something else. It just doesn't feel like a Lizard situation . . ."

Cletus scanned the trail ahead. "We could send out flankers to flush out whatever's there . . ."

"Or, maybe I could go down a little farther on my own to have a better look."

Cletus glanced at the man. "I don't want you to get your ass fragged by screwing around."

The man chuckled. "I hear you, Sir—I don't plan on it."

"Alright—but keep in sight . . ."

The scout, Miller, inched cautiously along the trail, stopping to listen and soak in the environment—then he moved forward again to get closer to whatever was out there.

At seventy-five yards out, he once again became motionless concentrating on one particular location to his right. When he stopped, Miller had his Wave tech weapon activated, pointed in that direction. After about twenty seconds a voice called out from a concealed position in the thick bush. "For Pete's sake—don't use that alien ass kicker on us! I have no desire to be splattered all over the jungle!"

Miller didn't flinch. "Come on out—real slow."

Several seconds later, a thirty-something man emerged from hiding, accompanied by a wary, medium-sized dog.

"Who are you?" The Wave tech rifle never wavered from its position fixed on the man's torso.

"The name's Kirv—a farmer. Or, at least I used to be until the Lizard bastards started murdering and burning." Kirv turned to glance at his hiding place. "My wife and daughter are with me, back there." He nodded his head toward a thicket of bushes. "Is it safe for them to come out?"

Miller nodded. "Yeah, sure—Cletus told me about

you." He lowered his weapon, pointing it at the ground.

"Glade, you and Millie can come out. It's safe . . ." Kirv called to his wife before returning his attention to Miller. "Is Cletus here?"

"Yep—back up the trail, waiting for me to flush you out."

"Well, now that you've done that successfully, can I see him?"

"Sure—I guess." Miller turned to face up the trail, hand signaling the all clear. Two minutes later, Cletus and Kirv were enthusiastically shaking hands, the large Commander standing a head taller than the stocky farmer. He acknowledged other family members with a nod. "I'm pleased to see you got out in time—a lot of farm families didn't. It was a brutal display on the part of the Lizards—if they meant to quash the rebellion through fear tactics, all they ended up doing was pissing off survivors—some of whom we linked up with already. And, let me tell you—they're itching for payback, and then some . . ."

"Well, you can add us to that list—anything to cause the aliens a world of hurt so they wish they were anywhere but here . . ."

Cletus laughed. "That's the spirit! We welcome you into the ranks, if it's your desire to do so . . ."

Kirv looked at his wife and daughter—both nodded.

"You just got more conscripts, Cletus!"

"Outstanding! Morris over there is my second in command—we set things up on a military basis with the thinking precision and control are vital."

"Makes sense—we're in, Commander."

"Why don't you move over to the center of the column—introduce yourselves. There's one you'll already know . . ."

As they walked further back, Kirv spotted her. "Nirva! It's good to see you!" He always enjoyed the matter-of-fact woman who ran the slave kitchens, his dealings with her enjoyable.

"Kirv, how are you?" Her smile was always genuine.

"Good, thanks! Meet my family—Glade and Millie. The mangy critter beside me is Grub . . ."

"You're all welcome! Even you, Grub . . ." She reached down to give his ears a rub and a tug.

"I heard the Lizards went back to the camp to clean out any survivors . . ." He watched her reaction closely.

She nodded. "Yes—Cletus came for me just before they arrived. He and I are together now . . ."

Kirv laughed, which he hadn't done in a long time. "Well, good for you! It's about bloody time something joyful occurred around here!"

# Chapter Twenty

They arrived close to headquarters in three shuttlecraft airships, Regional Headquarters picking them up eight hundred miles out, the extreme range of their sensors. Notification quickly passed to Beal's office, and orders were issued to muster the remaining guard as well as prepare for a hot reception if things turned sour.

Now, it was a waiting game.

Each shuttle carried ten members of the elite Planetary Reserve Force—usually one hundred members strong—always used as an emergency stopgap for dire situations. Beal's scraped-together force numbered sixty-three if he counted the administrative staff who were handed a weapon and told to stand at attention. The rest of his troopers were out in the field, chasing human resistance fighters or neutralizing farming families who were helping the revolt—not promising since his troops were second rate, at best. The soon-arriving, elite force would be front-line fighters capable of handling any circumstance.

Not a good situation for him, at all.

Beal realized the Prime's force was likely ordered to arrest him and, undoubtedly, they would anticipate his objection and possible resistance to those orders. However, the leader of the group probably didn't think his landing force would enter into a trap ready to spring the instant they arrived. Beal initially considered shooting the airships down, but two issues stopped him—first, the airships would be armored, and there was no guarantee they could be knocked out of the air. Second—and, more important—once he wiped out the arriving troopers, he could use the airships for his own purposes.

He knew it seemed a ludicrous thing for Lizard to be fighting Lizard on a conquered world currently under revolt—but, there was no way in the universe Beal was going to let himself be arrested. If they took him, he knew the Prime would use him as a scapegoat, ordering his execution—anything to divert blame from the off-planet authorities governing him.

He turned to Vanc. "Is everything ready for our guests?"

The Sub-Commander smiled at the illusion of the approaching airships bearing guests.

"Yes, Commander, everyone has their orders. As soon as new arrivals completely disembark from their vehicles, they will be brought under fire from all quadrants."

"And, those sent out to greet them?"

"Dregs who are dressed up to suit the charade . . ."

"No loss then?"

"None."

"Excellent—carry out the directive as issued."

"Of course, Sir."

As Vanc turned to leave Beal's office, he was concerned if all of their troops would actually fire on fellow Lizards from High Command. If they didn't, it would be a short fight with a dismal result for them.

Not for the first time, he wondered if he were fighting for the right faction.

****

He was suspicious of the circumstances under which Sub-Commander Garoc apparently went missing—or, at the least, failed to communicate back to Planetary Headquarters. The more he thought about it, the more he knew something was rotten about the whole damned thing.

The Prime felt better sending Commander Quarn, head of the Planetary Reserve Force, into Beal's HQ to determine what happened to Garoc and his guards. Quarn was shrewd, and the Prime warned him of possible treachery, but that didn't bother him. The thirty elite troopers were some of the best fighters left on the planet. Hopefully, they should be able to handle whatever Beal threw at them.

As added insurance, The Prime had two more air shuttles on the way, fifteen minutes behind Quarn's initial strike force—which meant he had twenty elite fighters on standby. It seemed reasonable to take such a precaution—he had a strong feeling violence would break out once they reached Beal's headquarters. Why? He knew Commander Beal for many years—his character wouldn't submit to being arrested according to the order Quarn carried.

\*\*\*\*

He awoke sensing danger.

Gently, Tag reached over and shook each of the girls, squeezing their arms as a signal to be quiet, both instantly recognizing something was wrong.

"I think they caught up with us overnight," he whispered. "I feel as if they aren't very far away—grab your stuff, and let's move out . . ."

Within a minute, all three were moving onto the trail, heading south.

Tag had the girls ahead, moving as carefully and as fast as they could in the early morning light. He moved ten paces back, checking their six on a regular basis. Among them, they had a human-built rifle, a hand gun, a big-assed combat knife, and a few explosives courtesy of their friends on their last version of Earth. However, they would likely be useless against the Lizards' Wave tech equipment which they used for offense and defense. The stolen Wave tech weapon was in their possession, but Tag didn't want to expend its power because the whole purpose of the trip south was to get a functioning weapon into the hands of the human scientists.

In Tag's mind, there was nothing more important than their mission—the salvation of the planet for humans may depend upon it.

****

Even though they were making good time down the trail, he wasn't satisfied. If they stayed ahead, spending most of his time looking over his shoulder went against his basic nature of being in control of a situation. Eventually, something would happen—they'd be caught sleeping, or whatever—and a fight would ensue.

*Why not control the situation, and fight it out in a location of my choosing?* Tag could pick the ground suitable for an ambush and defense if the opposition proved too strong—what he didn't relish was being caught by surprise, forcing a disadvantage.

So, as he jogged down the trail with the girls still in front, he kept his eye out for a suitable location to make a stand. Over the past several months of firefights and ambushes, Tag knew how to pick a spot to pull it off.

Conceiving the idea of finding a place took a half an hour and, as he put the final touches on his plan, they came around a sharp curve in the trail, leaving them blind to what lay ahead. He slowed, calling ahead to the girls. "Hey—hold up for a minute . . ."

Rose and Claire stopped, waiting for him to catch up.

"I've been thinking . . ."

"That can be trouble!" No matter the situation, Claire couldn't resist her typical, smart-assed answer.

For once, Tag ignored her. "I'm getting tired of running all the time—maybe we should bring a fight to them on our terms . . ."

Claire asked the obvious. "So—we set up an ambush, wait it out, and around the bend comes way more than we can handle. Then what?"

"If they're too strong, let them pass—they won't even know we're here. When they blow by us, we wait until it's safe, then vamoose back the other way to find another trail. We've seen a few of them branch off in different directions on our way south, so far. . . ."

"Do you think we can outrun them," Rose asked.

"Possibly—however, they gained on us last night while we slept. They're tough enough to eventually wear us down, and they seem to follow our trail easily. The odds favor their catching us at some point—I don't want it to be when it's inconvenient."

"Okay," Claire commented, "so we set up and hunker down, waiting—how do we disappear, so they don't see where we went? Our tracks are pretty evident to someone who knows where to look . . ."

Tag didn't answer immediately as he considered the problem. In some types of terrain, they could simply move carefully off a pathway minimizing the disturbance on the ground to effectively cover their tracks. In their current location, the jungle floor presented a different challenge—it was softer and left a subtle, telltale imprint visible to a trained eye.

He turned a three-sixty, scanning everything around them. Then his gaze rose from the jungle floor to the trees above—interspersed were long vines, some of which dangled just off the jungle floor.

The girls followed his gaze. "The last time I ended up in a tree," Rose commented, "the bloody snake I encountered looked bigger than I. I'm not too keen on repeating the situation . . ."

Tag smiled. "But, we're technically not going to climb the trees—we're after the vines."

"So, our tracks suddenly disappear, and the Lizards aren't going to figure out what we did?" Claire was stunned by Tag's plan. "They're creeps of the first magnitude, but they aren't stupid!"

He smiled. "True—however, if we back down the trail while removing our tracks, then climb the vines and move to this location, they won't know exactly where we are. They'll have to search all points of the compass as they move from the spot of our last footprints, not knowing which way we went, or how far. That leaves a large area for them to cover."

"So?" Claire stood, arms crossed. "As they're stumbling around, off the trail searching and, if the odds are right, we spring the trap and get the drop on them. If not, we blend in and let them pass."

"That's about it . . ."

Did she have a better idea? Probably not. "Okay, Tarzan, lead on . . ."

\*\*\*\*

It was a long night of traipsing along the trail in the dark, trusting the prey wouldn't go to ground, or veer off onto another path in the dark. Luck was with them when first light showed evidence of where they'd slept, then took up their trek south again. It was, at least, some progress, and the Merc team kept at it, proving once again their legendary tenacity when hunting down the target.

By midmorning, Zarn suddenly called a halt just before a sharp bend in the trail, his team members appreciating the break. But, it wasn't for their benefit—he lost evidence of the targets. He warned his team about wandering around, spoiling the area until he had a chance to thoroughly canvass where they went.

"Damn! They disappeared suddenly, just like the single target before . . ."

He scanned the trees. The vines. Evidence of their travels. He was convinced they took to the trees or vines to escape detection—if that were the case, he could only guess which way they went, and where they descended from above.

Zarn hand-signaled his team forward. "Split up, and scan the area—they used the trees and vines." He paused, a quick flash of irritation evident in his eyes. "What's with these humans? They act like they're bloody monkeys!"

He stayed close to the humans' exit point as his two team members divided their search up and down the trail from his position. It was the smaller Lizard Merc who eventually rounded the sharp bend in the trail while searching—engrossed in his task, he didn't notice he was out of sight of his companions.

\*\*\*\*

The Lizard Merc hunters suddenly pulled up on the trail, appearing to be searching for something or someone. Where they stopped, Reese and Logan had an unobscured view of three Mercs, and Logan could tell by their behavior the Mercs were on the hunt. He was familiar enough with their sort because he'd seen Merc teams pass through, and meet with the Warder of the Wash Hunting Preserve. By the way they dressed as well as their demeanor, they were distinguishable from regular Lizard troopers or guards.

As they watched, the Merc team split into a search grid. The one in the middle—whom Logan suspected was the leader—kept looking up into the trees as if the target might have gone up into the jungle canopy.

Logan leaned over to Reese. "They're searching for whatever they've been hunting—the target must be close by. But, now they're split up and distracted—if you plan to strike, now would be an excellent opportunity."

Reese turned from studying the two Mercs separated, but still in sight. "Sure, why don't we add a little adventure to their day? I'll take the big one who's closest, if you can go for the one standing just before the bend in the trail . . ."

Logan nodded, then melted into the jungle as Reese vanished into the jungle on the opposite side of the trail.

Both were on the hunt.

## Chapter Twenty-one

One incident acted as the trip wire. Breelin, the smaller Lizard on the Merc team, rounded the sharp bend in the trail, moving slowly, searching for a trace of human prey.

They waited several minutes to see if another would appear before Tag leaned over to the girls. "I'm going to take out this one before more show up—I sense others are close by. Stay put and, when you see me in behind him, create a subtle diversion enough to distract him, but not the others."

Both nodded.

Tag moved stealthily making no sound, disturbing little in the surrounding foliage. It took several minutes to move into position behind the Merc engrossed in finding a telltale sign of the targets.

It must have been the Lizard's sixth-sense causing him to abruptly turn just as Tag moved to within several feet—the girls hadn't created the diversion yet!

The Merc's eyes widened at the sudden appearance of the human close behind him. He began to move, raising a hunting rifle into firing position—but, the brief lapse in reaction time was all it took. Tag leapt forward just before Breelin reacted. A pivot and a flying roundhouse kick knocked the rifle from the Merc's grip, sending it tumbling out of reach into the surrounding bushes.

The Merc shot a brief glance after the disappearing rifle, immediately giving up the idea of retrieving it. Instead, he drew a large—massive—combat knife, its upper edge curved and serrated. Brandishing it in the filtered sunlight, the highly-polished blade created a beautiful sight as light danced off its surface.

But, Tag wasn't interested in any of that. Focused on the knife's owner, he closed within striking range, inviting a retaliatory response from the Merc.

He got one.

Breelin was experienced in the use of the weapon, and he relished the sight of the human male moving into range of the large blade. It slashed out with a sweeping strike designed to disembowel the opponent, its cutting edge close to the midsection of the human who stepped back a half-pace at the last instant.

Once past his torso, Tag took an exaggerated hop forward to make up the distance between them, following through with momentum to create enough power for a right-handed strike to the Lizard's exposed throat. Fingers curled to his palm, Tag's knuckles created a knife-like edge that struck with enough force to crush

Breelin's throat. Gone was the objective of carving up his opponent as the Lizard Merc struggled to suck sufficient air into laboring lungs.

Tag stepped out of range of the knife—which was down at the Lizard's side—watching the realization on his opponent's face, knowing he was dying. As his eyes dimmed and rolled back, the Lizard's body began to collapse on the jungle trail. Just then, Zarn rounded the bend, stunned by the human standing over Breelin's body. With a roar, Zarn raised his weapon and commenced firing as the human disappeared into jungle cover.

Back around the corner, the large Merc, Assin, moved in the other direction searching for prey and, once the firing started, he lifted his weapon and turned toward the sound. Unknown to him, he offered a profile target to Reese who already had the Lizard lined up in his weapon sights. The sound of gunfire in the distance surprised Reese, but didn't delay his opening up on his target. The first few shots deflected harmlessly off Assin's armor, who turned, facing back down the trail. Good thing for Reese—Assin was now a full frontal target. Reese placed two shots into the Lizard's forehead, causing him to stagger and back up two steps before collapsing to the ground.

Around the corner of the trail, Zarn cursed as he missed the fast-moving human flitting in and out of view as it moved swiftly through the foliage. Out of ammo, Zarn expertly disengaged the expended clip, slamming a full one into place.

Just as he refocused on the moving target, bringing his rifle to bear, several high-velocity shots impacted his protective Wave tech armor, staggering him slightly. Without delay, he moved off the trail and into cover. Even though he could tell the shots emanated from a right rear, unknown source, there was nothing he could do but continue to move deeper through the jungle to give himself a little distance—he needed time and space to reassess. One thing he knew for sure—Breelin looked finished, so his team was down to him and, maybe, Assin. However, just before the shooter started firing at him, Zarn heard other shots up the trail indicating Assin was engaged with something. Or, someone. Since he didn't know the outcome of the shots, he figured it safe to assume there was only one survivor.

Him.

Once the firing stopped, Reese and Logan slowly emerged into the open, approaching the large, dead Lizard Merc. "Nice placement of the kill shots," Logan commented, referring to Reese's double tap to the forehead spaced millimeters apart.

"Thanks—yours appears to have gotten away."

"Yeah—he reacted faster than I've seen any Lizard move. He ducked into cover before I could do the same to him."

The two men stared at the body before them. "We need to be careful he doesn't circle back to try potshots at us."

"Agreed. Where is the third one? I didn't see him . . ."

A human voice called out from the brush to their left. "He's around the bend of the trail, rendered hors de combat."

Both men swiveled, weapons at the ready.

The voice called out again. "I'd rather you didn't do that—I've had enough shots coming my way today . . ."

"Come out, but first throw out your weapons," Reese ordered.

"I don't have any."

"Okay—come forward. Slowly . . ."

A rustling occurred as a young man emerged purposely making lots of noise for them to hear his complying. When he was fully on the path in front of them, he stopped and studied the pair of armed men.

"It's customary to come out with your hands up in these types of circumstances," Reese observed.

The young man stood calmly in front of them with his hands at his sides. "Seemed like a silly thing to do since we're both hunting Lizards . . ."

Reese smiled. "Yeah—I guess so. But, this is the part where I'm supposed to tell you to put your hands down. Where's the third Lizard?"

"As I said, he's around the corner, gone to the great Lizard land in the sky."

"We didn't hear anything before finishing this one and scaring the other off," Logan interjected. "I thought you said you were unarmed—did you leave your weapon behind?"

"Nope—never had one."

Logan's eyebrows shot up. "Are you saying you went up against a trained and, presumably, armed Merc Lizard without any weapons?"

"Well, yeah—he had a rifle and a big-assed knife."

Reese pressed him. "And, now he's dead. Done by

hand?"

"Yes, Sir."

Reese and Logan shared a look before turning back to the young man.

"What's your name, Son," Reese asked.

"Tag."

"You alone?" Logan wasn't sure of anything right about then, let alone a young man who just eighty-sixed a well-trained Merc Lizard by hand.

"Nope—I got me a couple of fine-lookin' women-folk hidin' in the bushes just around the corner . . ." Of course, he sounded as if he were from the Deep South—just for fun.

Both men looked at him in surprise before bursting into laughter. "Of course you do! I'm Logan, and this is Reese—why don't you lead on, and we can meet them?"

\*\*\*\*

Exhausted, he sacked out the previous night, sleeping until morning—he would've slept longer, but the noise of multiple footsteps awakened him. As he listened, he recognized it was a large group, but something was wrong. Something was off. What he heard wasn't the heavy tromp and odd gait of the Lizards. Were they humans? If that were the case, what were they doing so deep in the jungle?

Devin worked his way closer to the trail to check it without being seen and, moments later, he confirmed his suspicions. A straggling group of humans traipsed along the trail, and they weren't just fighters—multiple families and children were part of it. Some were unarmed, but most of the men and a few of the women carried rifles as well as assorted weapons.

Suddenly, he noticed several men carried Lizard Wave tech weapons, some of which were meant for war. As he watched and remained hidden, Devin couldn't believe who was part of the group—Kirv and his family, including Grub! He figured if Kirv's family were comfortable enough to travel with the group, he was, too!

But, there was a trick to making his presence known—startle one of them who carried a Wave tech weapon, and it could be a messy ending. "Kirv! It's Devin!" He hoped gently calling Kirv's name would attract the farmer's attention and, at first, he didn't think Kirv heard him—until Kirv paused and looked around to determine the source of the sound. Once he determined the location, Devin rose, offering a wave.

The farmer brightened, a huge smile stretching across his face. "Come on over! You're among friends here!"

Devin approached, then shook hands enthusiastically with the farmer. By that time, Glade and Millie dropped out of line and, when Glade recognized him, she wrapped him in a warm hug. Millie waved shyly, and Grub's tail wagged as he renewed greetings with a former human acquaintance.

"Where are your companions?" Kirv glanced around, expecting to see the rest of the Travelers.

"That's a hell of a good question—we successfully pulled off the mission to liberate the Wave tech stuff, but ran into Lizard troubles. Unfortunately, we were separated in the action, and I haven't seen them since. We had two imprecise rendezvous locations, but linking up didn't happen. So, I'm on my own, heading south to the last meeting place with the scientists."

"How do you know they're alright?"

Devin shrugged. "I don't know—I just do. After we separated, I skirted back to check the site where we had the last dustup, then followed the trail south. No trace—so I'm betting they're doing the same thing, heading south to get the technology in the hands of someone who can, hopefully, figure it out."

"Well, as you can see, we're heading in the same direction . . ."

Devin glanced at the line of humans moving down the trail. "What happened? Where did they all come from?"

"For the most part, they're ex-slaves from the work gangs, and quite a few are surviving farm families."

"What do you mean surviving farm families?"

Kirv paused, realizing the young man must've been out of touch while in the jungle—of course he didn't know what happened elsewhere. "After you and your friends left to steal the Wave tech, the Lizards started rampaging through the district, killing humans, and burning down farms. A lot of good people died . . ."

"Shit! Did we cause that?"

"No—it had more to do with a slave revolt, and grew from there. You and your friends had nothing to do with it."

"That's good--I'd hate to think we were responsible. Is there a leader for everyone here?"

"Indeed—Cletus. He's a former pre-invasion military officer from the headquarters planning staff when we had such a thing. He's a good man for the job . . ."

"How many are there?"

"I'm not sure, exactly—we keep coming across individuals like you or small groups who want to join us, although a few stayed out on their own." Kirv hesitated, trying to quickly crunch the numbers. "Three to four hundred would be my guess . . ."

"That's a hefty number—you can do some real damage to any Lizards you come across . . ."

"That's already happened a few times—we wiped out a couple of patrols, but we lost a lot of good folks . . ."

"Unfortunately, that tends to happen when they have you outgunned . . ."

Kirv nodded his agreement. "Why don't we find Cletus, and I'll introduce you. With some of the action you experienced in the last few months, I'm sure he'll have good use for you, if you're willing."

Devin grinned. "Sure! I don't expect to reap benefits from joining your group unless I'm willing to contribute my share to the cause. Lead on!"

\*\*\*\*

He seemed to vacillate with more ups and downs than a yo-yo, gnawing away at his normal upbeat, good humor. And, damn it, they had a wedding coming soon, and planning under a cloud of worry wasn't something she needed for such a special occasion. Of course, it wasn't his fault, or anyone's for that matter—the whole thing just sucked.

Jackie was frustrated by her inability to help him figure a way to get Tag back. Sure, she could support him until the cows come home, but the reality was not many people on the planet could work at a high level in Kyle's scientific field. To her, how to figure out the inner workings of a wormhole, then try to control it seemed to be something only in the imagination of comic book or science fiction writers.

Yet, Kyle attempted to accomplish the seemingly impossible feat on his own. No wonder he was down—some would go insane with such an impossible challenge.

\*\*\*\*

One moment, he and his team members were on the hunt, closing in on the prey, even though they took to the trees. The next moment, Breelin and Assin were down, and Zarn found himself on the run, completely surprised the humans attacked from both directions.

Something he didn't count on.

As Mercs, one of their options was not to use full battle shields which would have completely protected them from frontal attack. But, their decision made sense—with their fast-moving lifestyle, bulky equipment would be cumbersome, slowing them down unnecessarily. Besides, it was a mark of distinction for warriors of his ilk to forgo what regular battle troops used to protect themselves. Still, the trade-off ended the lives of his teammates, their vulnerabilities exploited by humans learning to take advantage.

In the end, the important thing was he survived the change in fortune. Zarn knew he could always recruit more Mercs to reconstitute a team because he did it before. But, what was his immediate goal? Admit defeat and wear a permanent mark of failure affecting his previously unblemished reputation? Completely unacceptable. That choice would ultimately affect future revenues chargeable to his customers.

Not a very satisfactory situation.

However, if the setback could be immediately avenged as well as corrected by recovering the missing tech items, perhaps the damage would be minimal. Nonetheless, if he chose that route, Zarn would need to go up against an unknown number of humans experienced in battle—on his own. The question was would he accept the challenge? His DNA and warrior background screamed out for him to choose the latter.

\*\*\*\*

"What do you mean there are two ships?"

"Sir, they were concealed by cloaking. They're only minutes behind . . ."

Beal's mind reeled at the thought. If the two new ships were fully loaded, the Prime's force could number up to fifty elite warriors, easily exceeding the ability of his people to resist effectively.

The circumstances flipped on him, and he had minutes to decide—he could try to knock shuttles out of the air to even the odds, or the ships could land, and they would take him. The problem with starting an air fight would be the airships— they had effective offensive weapons. With that option, his landing port would be in shambles, and some of his effectives would surely be killed. Clearly, Wave tech weaponry didn't leave much room for wounded to survive.

Beal glanced at the Sub-Commander who had the same worried expression on his face. Vanc knew the likelihood of his being included in the arrest order, as well as the ultimate outcome of that scenario. The thought of fleeing his headquarters flitted through his mind, but he couldn't realistically consider it—running and hiding weren't on his agenda, and the idea of being a fugitive wasn't appealing. Eventually, he'd be found and, in the meantime, spending his time looking over his shoulder. Besides, where could he go? Nowhere—especially with a restive human population actively revolting in his area.

He quickly determined his choice was to fight with

a slim chance of surviving, or submit and be executed. Beal knew he had many shortcomings, but being a coward wasn't one of them. He turned to Vanc. "Sub-Commander, have the landing port's air defenses take the first three airships under fire. They constitute a threat to this headquarters . . ."

Vanc hesitated while the ramifications of the order swirled in his brain. *This is going to be a terrible mess*, he thought, signaling to the technicians controlling the air defenses. "You heard the Commander—open fire and bring down those ships!"

At the same time, on board the ship carrying the strike force leader, Commander Quarn of the Planetary Reserve Force issued a similar order. "Beal's gone rogue—bring the landing area defenses under fire. We can't land until the hot zone is neutralized . . ."

It was then the conquering species went to war.

With each other.

\*\*\*\*

"This is Rose, and she's with me. And, that's Claire—her better half is wandering around these parts somewhere."

Reese smiled as he registered the delineation of relationships emphasized again by the intriguing young man. During his time in Special Forces Recon, Reese saw a lot of so-called warriors—many were pretenders, only a few were the real deal, and he was certain he had one of the latter standing before him. While there wasn't any swagger to him, he looked as if he'd seen his fair share of action. Obviously, from the barehanded elimination of a dangerous Lizard Merc, Tag knew how to handle himself—a situation he wouldn't want to be in himself.

"So, where is this friend of yours," Logan asked.

"His name is Devin," Claire responded. "We were separated in a fight with a Lizard patrol—unfortunately, we haven't been able to link up yet."

"What's your plan? The area has a few Lizard patrols still wandering around . . ."

Tag decided it was too early in the game to tell them about their mission. He glanced at each of the girls, hoping they would follow his lead. "We'll keep pushing south to see if we can link up with our friend . . ."

It was a topic Tag didn't want to discuss—at least not right then. It was always a tricky decision—if he told Reese about their arrival via the portal, Reese might not be receptive to the idea. If he didn't tell him, Tag was pretty sure Reese would suspect something.

Tag was right—Reese figured something else was going on, but decided to cut them some slack. "Which work camp were you in?"

A pause. "Actually, none of them. We've been traveling, trying to avoid anything that will keep us in this place . . ."

"You had to be somewhere—a camp, or a free farm?"

"I learned if we keep moving, it's possible to slip between the cracks of certain controlling forces. Perhaps, we should leave it at that . . ."

# Chapter Twenty-two

The introduction occurred during a rest stop for the long column of humans. Kirv sought out the leader, finding him sitting on a large rock talking with Nirva.

As he approached, Cletus looked up. "Hey, Kirv, how are you?" He directed his question at the ex-farmer, but the leader studied the tall, young man standing at his side.

"Good, Commander. This is Devin—we helped him and his companions before the slave revolt, and they stayed with us for a while. I can vouch for him . . ."

Cletus stood to shake hands with the new arrival. A tall man himself, Devin noticed the leader towered over him with an almost hulking presence. But, once he got past the leader's physical aspect, Devin noticed the bright, intelligent glint in the man's eyes. Clearly, he was much more than a large chunk of muscle.

"Glad to meet you—are you considering joining us?"

"I'd like to for a little while—I'm still searching for my friends. We saw some action, and were separated . . ."

"Any idea where they'll end up?"

"Nope—somewhere to the south. We set up a final rendezvous point, and I'm hoping we can link up there."

"Well, feel free to tag along. We're headed in that direction—at least for now."

Cletus noticed the flash of a smirk on the young man's face.

"Did I say something funny?"

"Sorry—to me it was. The leader of our traveling show is named Tag. It just struck me as funny you should express the invite that way . . ."

Cletus nodded. "I see the humor—what's going on down south?" He noticed the young man hesitate. "You don't have to tell me anything you don't want to or can't tell me. I know Kirv trusts you, and that's good enough for me . . ."

Devin glanced at Kirv standing to the side, who gave him a head motion indicating it would be alright to disclose their plan.

Again, he focused on Cletus. "Do you have a few minutes to go over some stuff?"

The Commander nodded.

"The seed of the idea came from Kirv who told us about a loose network of people keeping tabs on things behind the backs of the Lizard overlords. Apparently, there is still a collection of scientists down south who may be able to figure out the workings of the Wave tech weapons the Lizards use. That's the hope, anyway. If they can, maybe there's a way to neutralize the Lizards' tech advantage, making it easier to kick their asses..."

"Now, there's a worthy goal! How do you plan to go about it?"

"We're past the planning stage, and actually did it. We stole some of their technology, and were on our way south when we ran into a Lizard patrol—that's when we separated."

"Who has the liberated goods?"

"Tag, and the girls..."

"Girls?"

"Yeah—mine and his."

Cletus smiled. "Ahh, now I see the reason for your eagerness to link up with your friends."

Devin smiled and nodded.

"You probably noticed some members of our force are equipped with Lizard weapons..."

"I did—how did that happen?" Kirv supplied some background, but Devin wanted to hear the details from Cletus.

"It started with a revolt in a work camp I was in— the Lizard guards were overwhelmed and disposed of, but many humans lost their lives in achieving that goal. Slowly, our numbers increased, composed of many individuals with previous military experience—then, we started actively hunting Lizard patrols and other units. We had successes, losing many of ours along the way. Thankfully, we replenished diminishing numbers with people like you joining us . . ."

"So, now you have multiple weapons with Wave tech?"

"Yes—however, we don't know how to analyze what makes them work. We need the scientists to do that. So, your mission is still valid . . ." The Commander assessed the young man as they talked. "You look like you've seen some action. Ex-military?"

"Yes to the former, and no to the latter . . ."

"Where?"

"Actually, in quite a few places . . ." Devin didn't think it was the time to get into the interplanetary portal travel.

The Commander accepted his obvious reluctance for specifics. "Good—we can use your experience. Now, we're moving the main column of our people—but, once we stop to set up camp for the night, patrols will have to go out. Perhaps, you could join one . . ."

"Yes, Sir—glad to help out."

The Commander helped Nirva to her feet. "Good—carry on . . ." With that, Cletus guided her to the front of the line.

As they disappeared from view, Devin turned to Kirv. "He seems a confident sort—sensible, too."

"The Commander is highly intelligent and motivated. He tends to come across as casual, but everything he does is carefully calculated..."

"I'll keep that in mind..."

\*\*\*\*

"Ladies, you may exit from cover—we have company." Claire and Rose emerged from both sides of the trail, approaching the three males standing in the open on the path.

"Gentlemen, these are my friends. The tall, lovely one is Rose, and the diminutive, brainy one is the wonderful Claire." The girls smiled, not totally sure of the situation. "Meet Reese, and this is his trusty sidekick, Logan..." Introductions completed, Tag considered his mission accomplished, and everyone loosened up.

"What's your plan," Logan inquired.

Claire was first to respond. "We're heading south to link up with Devin who's wandering around the jungle somewhere..."

"Do you have a rendezvous point?"

"Yes..." She wasn't sure whether to elaborate, deciding in favor of providing minimal information until Tag indicated otherwise.

"What are you up to?" Tag figured it was time to

learn something about them.

"Up until recently," Logan commented, "I was a hunting guide for the Lizards on one of the preserves..."

"Preserves? I take it not of the fruit variety?"

Logan chuckled. "When the Lizards conquered Earth, they set up a series of hunting areas for entertaining guests to the planet. Pre-conquest, I was a guide and tracker for human hunters—so, when the Lizards found out about my background, they put me in the Wash Hunting Preserve because I was already familiar with the indigenous wildlife. The bastards then wanted me to track humans for their hunting pleasure..."

"You did that?" There was a tone of derision in Claire's voice.

"Hell, no! I pretended to lead them on a human hunt, when, in reality, they went everywhere but the direction of the human targets—if I knew their approximate locations. Occasionally, a person inadvertently popped out of cover, and was taken. Nothing I could do about chance..."

"Sorry about that—but the idea of hunting humans for sport shocked me..."

He nodded. "Although we don't talk about it much, most people know about these preserves. I understand they're set up all around the world—humans, by far, are the favored targets."

"What's your background," Tag asked Reese.

The ex-soldier noticed the cleaver diversion from their conversation, but decided to play along. "I was in the military, pre-conquest. I did all of the basic stuff, then ended up in Special Forces Recon for the last three years. My unit was in the thick of it when the Lizards hit us . . ."

"What area?"

"Just on the other side of the mountains—I was part of a twelve-man advance unit sent in to see what the hell was going on when they first landed. Before we knew it, they kicked the shit out of us—their Wave tech advantage made it real tough."

"How many of your unit made it out?"

Reese took a few moments before answering. "You're looking at him . . ."

Tag shook his head. "That's tough—I know the feeling."

"Yeah?"

He nodded. "We've been in some action, and I had people under my command. Some didn't make it back—it's never an easy thing . . ."

Reese started to reappraise the young man. *He can't be more than eighteen*, he thought. *What the hell have they been up to at his age to have that position of authority?* "Well, it got worse—I ended up in two more outfits before the end. Other than a few bumps, scrapes, and one shrapnel wound from a piece of flying rock, I came out unscathed, the sole survivor of three units sent into battle. Makes you ask the question, why me?"

Tag studied him carefully and saw the barely-contained rage underneath the professional demeanor. "I asked that same question more than once, but I never arrived at a satisfactory answer." Reese and Tag gave each other a long look, seeing a kindred spirit in the face of the other.

"If you folks are okay with it, Logan and I can travel along with you. It seems to me you have a mission of some sort, and I don't need the details unless you want to share. Maybe we can hunt Lizards along the way..."

\*\*\*\*

The landing platform and support facilities were in shambles, the last, fixed defensive weapon of the port completely destroyed. Other than portable guns held by staunch defenders, the port stood open for landing two remaining ships. The problem facing Commander Quarn of the Planetary Reserve Force, however, was finding a large enough area clear of debris to set down his last airships.

Defenders proved adept at targeting crossfire from multiple guns—they had sufficient numbers to defeat the protective armor and technology designed to keep them flying in battle conditions. Twenty elite shock troops and their airship crews were blasted out of the air.

No survivors.

The pilot of Quarn's command ship announced the mess on the platform, allowing only one airship at a time to land—the initial group of ten fighters would have to hold until two other ships took their turns. "Order in the first ship, and get boots on the ground," he commanded as Quarn watched the airship. It approached, quickly flaring at the last moment, allowing ten seconds for troops to disembark and lift off again, making room for the second ship.

Ten elite fighters spread out to protect the area for arriving reinforcements as small arms fire struck around them, taking down only one fighter, his remains splattered against the side of a support beam. The team didn't carry full battle shields—fluid movement was more important.

The second airship swooped in and landed, off-loading passengers, its fighters dispersed in a preset defensive pattern. The Sub-Commander on the ground signaled for the nineteen fighters to move forward to clear the area of defensive fire before the command ship appeared for a landing—at least that was the plan. At the moment he stood to lead his warriors, the landing platform disappeared in a massive explosion and, before they knew what hit them, the attackers and defenders were obliterated. The second airship—still in the process of pulling away—was caught in the inferno, exploding once it was engulfed in flames.

Commander Beal and Sub-Commander Vanc were in rear positions controlling the platform defense and headquarters. As expected, the elite attacking force finally overwhelmed his defensive front line, but Beal was encouraged by the destruction of two airships before their combat teams had a chance to land. His strategy was to enact a two-stage withdrawal plan when the massive explosion occurred.

Beal and Vanc were far enough back to survive, but

the force of the blast knocked them and surrounding troops to the ground. "What happened," the Commander asked Vanc as he regained his feet.

"I don't know, Sir—this wasn't our doing. Maybe a stray shot hit something, but I don't know what that could be." Both Lizards watched as the remains of the structures burned.

In the command airship, Quarn looked down at an inferno where, moments before, his attack force was advancing. Pieces of the airship caught in the explosion lay strewn across a wide swath of ground, and it suddenly occurred to the Commander he had only sixty specialized warriors of the Planetary Reserve Force to cover other contingencies for the whole planet. Within the last several minutes, he witnessed the loss of forty percent of his pre-battle force as his remaining airships circled the scene, waiting for his orders.

Unknown to Lizard opponents on either side of the shattered landing platform, there was a third force—the Sapper team sent by Commander Cletus did an exemplary job of carrying out its mission.

****

He tracked them easily—there were five altogether, more than enough to leave multiple evidence on the jungle trail. Zarn hid in deep cover, watching two male humans link up with a third. They moved past Breelin's body, joining two female humans who emerged from cover on each side of the trail.

The group headed south.

He followed at a distance, careful to remain out of sight, and it was a question of being patient. Eventually, an opportunity would arise where he could move in, pick off one or two, and winnow down their numbers—trying to take on all five would be too risky. Hunting was what he did for a living, and Zarn was good at it—and, he intended to avenge the loss of his dead teammates. Now, it was more than a contract—it was personal.

# Chapter Twenty-Three

Well, he made progress. There were at least ten different ways he explored that didn't bloody work. All he could do was cross them off a list containing hundreds of thousands of possibilities.

Kyle knew his effort to find Tag was causing tension between Jackie and him, but what could he do? Give up trying just because it was tremendously hard? Tag was his younger brother—he couldn't just up and quit, writing him off.

Tag wouldn't settle for that if the roles were reversed.

So, the solution was to create a situation where he could balance both needs. Continue to look for a way to get his brother back while, at the same time, keeping Jackie happy.

****

"Sir?" It was the second time the captain tried to get his attention. He was torn between making his report, and respecting the Prime's privacy. But, after a few moments, the highest authority governing the planet turned, acknowledging his subordinate with a subtle nod.

The captain recognized the signal to present his report. "Prime, we have the initial report from Commander Quarn."

"Yes . . ."

The officer hesitated.

"Proceed!"

"Yes, Prime. The Commander reports the loss of three of his ships as well as forty members of the Planetary Reserve Force, plus air crews."

With that news, he had the Prime's full attention. "How's that possible? Three ships down, and forty fighters lost?"

The captain explained everything.

"What about the remaining attack force?"

"They diverted to a nearby clearing, and landed their battle teams. Commander Quarn attacked their headquarters and took control after a brief fight. Apparently, the large explosion wiping out the landing port complex as well as most of the defenders was enough to dishearten the survivors."

"Beal?"

"No reports of his capture—or, that of Sub-Commander Vanc."

"Thank you, Captain, you may leave . . ."

"Yes, Prime . . ."

After the officer left, the Prime turned to the window, considering ramifications of the losses incurred in the attack on Beal's headquarters. It severely weakened his ability to respond to other problems which may arise, and he realized things were slowly drifting out of control. If he reported the true situation to Off-Planet Command, he would forfeit his and his family's lives—they didn't take kindly to failure. *Perhaps,* he thought, *I can rescue the situation before it slides to that conclusion. What do I have to lose?*

\*\*\*\*

The four-vehicle convoy slowly made its way down the jungle trail barely wide enough to accommodate it. A few hundred yards in the lead, a scout vehicle assessed their situation—so far, they appeared to have made a clean break from his captured headquarters.

Beal figured with the Planetary Reserve Force's losses, they wouldn't have enough personnel in their vicinity to mount a serious hunt for them—at least not yet. Still, it was critical to put distance between him and the destroyed base. In all, he escaped with twelve troops and Sub-Commander Vanc, who currently commanded the rearguard vehicle. Not much of a force, especially when he was being hunted by his own kind, not to mention rogue groups of humans wandering around loose seeking to inflict harm on their former masters.

\*\*\*\*

Finally, the majority of people in the column grabbed a quick meal, then bedded down for the night as daylight vanished under the jungle's canopy. He stood at the outer edge of the small group of fighters listening to Cletus's briefing. "I'd like everyone to keep your wits about you, and not wander off on your own. This patrol is small—ten people—so pair up, and stick with your partner. Don't initiate confrontations—simply scout the area. Try to return just after midnight because you're going to need some rest—we have a good trek tomorrow, and I'd like to start early. Push out on the trail we plan to take in the morning—I have a five-man patrol scouting the trail we already covered to make sure our six is clear." Cletus paused. "Any questions?"

None.

"There's a new man, Devin, who's joining you, so make him feel welcome—he's been around the block, and will be helpful." He waited a moment before issuing his final order. "Okay, head out and keep your heads up. Remember, it's not just Lizards who are a threat—there are plenty of things living in this jungle, and we're in their house. Please tread carefully . . ." As the patrol took to the trail, the leader counted off pairings of the members.

An hour later, Devin and his assigned partner, Harris, were on the side of an adjacent trail lying in a prone position, listening to the activities of animals obviously on the hunt. "We're downwind," Harris commented, "so it should be relatively safe here—be ready to move if they catch our scent." But, it ended up the pack caught something and started to feed, ignoring or not noticing the two humans.

Two hours later, they completed their circuit without incident, arriving back at the rendezvous point. Several pairs of members were there already with the rest filtering in within the next half hour. The patrol leader was just about to direct them back to camp when the night was shattered by the roaring sound from the discharge of several Wave tech weapons fired simultaneously. One moment the leader was standing in front of them and, a second later, his remains were scattered throughout the jungle. One team member met the same fate, spraying in another direction.

"Move!"

The exchange of rifle fire and Wave tech discharges continued for a full two minutes. Members of the two different species involved took losses, but humans suffered the most—they didn't have protective armor to ward off the effects of a hit.

When the rate of fire diminished, Devin found himself behind trees thirty yards from the epicenter of the firefight. Harris was glued to his side, moving with him as the last shots rang out.

"What the hell," Harris whispered.

Quiet for a few moments, Devin listened in the darkness. "A night ambush, and we foolishly walked right into it . . ."

"What do we do now? The patrol leader is dead . . ."

"If you want to survive, keep quiet and follow my lead—I think we're out of the center of it now. Let's wait until the enemy makes a move, then we'll hammer their asses. Go for head shots only . . ."

"Okay . . ." Harris didn't sound too certain.

After five minutes of intense listening, Harris whispered again. "I can't see crap out here . . ."

Devin sighed quietly. "Close your eyes if you have to, and listen—open up your other senses to feel the jungle. It will come to you. And, stop talking! We have to wait the bastards out . . ."

"Got it . . ."

During the next few hours, they heard the odd rustling of something moving close by, then settling again. Only the first glimpse of light revealed the faint outlines of things their opponents disturbed. They watched as the vague shapes of five Lizards emerged from cover, appearing in the center of the small clearing where, hours ago, humans died.

Harris flinched slightly, then started to shift position. Devin reached over and placed a hand on his arm, shaking his head, motioning him to stay still. Then Devin lifted his rifle and mimed shooting, pointing to his own head to remind Harris to take head shots.

His team member indicated he understood.

As they waited, the light quality improved, and they could see their enemies who conveniently stood grouped together, talking. The muffled sounds of their grunting drifted to the humans and, considering the situation favorable, Devin indicated to Harris to get ready.

Lifting his own weapon into firing position, he drew a bead on the largest of the Lizards who happened to be facing him—Harris, too, prepared to fire.

Just as it appeared the targets were winding up their conversation, Devin took a breath and, while exhaling, squeezed the trigger. The semi-automatic deposited a ring of three shots into the Lizard's forehead, spinning and dropping him where he stood. Beside him, Harris managed to clip one of the Lizards in the cheek, but it was hard to know if it were a kill shot as the Target lurched into the trees.

The three remaining Lizards readied their weapons into firing positions, trying to trace the origin of the shots. Before they could locate the source, one of them spun away clutching his head where he'd been hit—a shot originating from behind. Clearly, Devin and Harris weren't the only humans involved in the firefight.

The two remaining Lizards scattered in different directions.

After a few minutes, a voice called out. "I think they're gone . . ."

Carefully, two night patrol members emerged from the other side of the clearing, and Devin motioned for Harris to follow him, the four of them joining in the middle. "We shouldn't stand exposed," Devin advised. "Let's make sure the three who were hit are finished off, and head back to camp."

The Lizard Devin shot was obviously dead, and they found the other two in jungle cover, one dead and the other close to it. The current war between the species wasn't one where prisoners were taken—it was a matter of dead or alive, and wounded didn't count.

The Lizard wasn't alive for long.

\*\*\*\*

They traveled together for a day and a half and, as they headed south, Reese and Logan learned the full story of the Travelers attempting to get the Wave tech weapons to the scientists, as well as how they traveled to and from different versions of Earth via portals.

"That's quite the tale . . ." Before spending time with them, Logan probably wouldn't have believed it. But, as trust blossomed, he knew Tag and the girls weren't the types to embellish.

Tag nodded. "It is—some people would think I was

on drugs, drunk, bullshitting, or all of the above to come up with that story!"

"I see now where all of your combat experiences happened—that's a lot of action to pack into a few months." Reese wondered how Tag acquired his quasi-military acumen, and once he heard the stories, it all made sense.

Tag took a moment to answer. "Some of it seems to have flown by while, other times, things seem to move in slow motion. Weird, huh?"

"I get it—thinking back to the post-invasion action, there are bits I can't sort out from other events. Kind of a sensory overload situation, I guess . . ."

"Must be the way our minds work to protect us from going nuts."

"Makes sense—with this portal thing, how do you know when it's coming?"

"We don't—no control. No warning. The trick is we never know where the hell we'll end up."

"Did you ever have one of the enemy follow you through it?"

"Nope—usually they're close, but not close enough before it winks out. Plus, I don't think many of them have the balls to jump in . . ."

"That doesn't surprise me—did you ever have a chance to get word back home?"

Tag paused, thinking about Kyle, the portal, and the tube with a message from home. "Yes . . ."

"How'd that work?"

Tag explained the tube containing a message from his brother that made it through behind them on one of their portal trips.

"Did your message make it back?"

"I don't know . . ."

"Interesting—so, portal travel doesn't involve an element of time travel?"

"We don't think so—most of the trips land us in a new version of Earth. We can verify it's the same day and time, minus however long the portal trip takes, which is measured in minutes. In the primitive world, there wasn't a way to confirm a date—but, I see no reason to suspect it was any different from the other trips plunking us down on the same day in another place."

"How disorienting was that?" Tag's story should've been one Logan didn't believe—but he did.

Tag chuckled as he recalled his departure. "On the first trip and arrival, I was a bit overwhelmed . . ."

Rose laughed, recalling her first encounter with him. "Not a bit overwhelmed—in total shock is more like it! He had trouble remembering his own name!"

"Yeah, I was out of it." He glanced at Rose. "Thanks for pointing out my shortcoming . . ."

"You're welcome!"

Reese smiled as he witnessed their loving banter. "Do you suffer any ill effects from the portal travel? Anything long-lasting?"

"Well—I've traveled the most and, other than feeling weird and out of sorts for a few minutes, once I dismount from the portal, everything is fine . . ."

"Is there a link as far as progressing from one world to another? A pattern of some sort?"

"Nope—it's totally random." Tag paused for a few seconds to reconsider the question. "Hold on—now that I think about it, there might be something . . ."

"Such as?"

Tag looked at the girls before responding. "The first version of Earth I ended up on after the portal travel was Rose's and Claire's home world. I quickly learned they had an oppressive society—step out of line, and they came down hard. The next world we visited was in societal collapse—random violence, and law and order were breaking down. That one was much worse than the first . . ."

"Then," Claire added, "we ended up in the primitive version of Earth. We were chased by big aliens, and had a skirmish or two with them—after a while, though, we became friends. Then, we met an indigenous species who were guardians of the environment and animals—they were invaded by a swarming, ultra-violent species that we helped fend off."

Rose picked it up from there. "Then, the portal deposited us in the middle of a generational civil war on the next iteration of Earth."

Tag's turn to finish the story. "Finally, we ended up here—a slave planet conquered by a miserable alien race, and the humans are actively revolting . . ."

"It seems to me," Reese pointed out, "you're being subjected to increasingly complex, violent scenarios. If this were a training exercise, I'd say you were being tested to see how you measure up . . ."

The Travelers were stunned!

****

"I want every group of them within a day's travel operating here."

"Sir, how will we entice all of them to join?"

"Promise them anything they want, just get them in place. We need to rectify this situation quickly . . ." He turned back to the picture window.

The officer bowed to his superior's back, then quietly left the office. How exactly he would fulfill the Prime's directive was going to present a challenge. They tended to be highly independent and resistant to authoritative measures, which is why they were so efficient. But, even if he could persuade the Mercs within range to congregate on Beal's territory, it still might not be enough to rebalance the critical situation.

****

A frustrated Commander Quarn paced back and forth in Commander Beal's office—well, his ex-office. He wanted nothing more at the moment than to chase down and apprehend Beal, but, the reality was he had only a few troops left, most of them currently occupied in an effort to staunch the multiple incidents of minor explosions occurring in the area. After the major blast that wiped out the landing area of the headquarters, numerous smaller explosions were wrecking important infrastructure components supporting the base.

So far, Quarn realized, his elite battle troops were always a step behind the hit-and-run tactics of whoever was active in the campaign to eliminate the base as a functional headquarters.

*It's bloody maddening!*

\*\*\*\*

"Pull over."

"But, Commander—we haven't reached the safe zone you wanted."

"I know that. Pull over—I need to find a tree."

"Oh—yes, Sir. Of course . . ."

When the vehicle stopped, it effectively blocked the narrow trail they were following, and getting out of the door without having a branch end up in his ear proved a challenge. But, he managed to do his business, then head back to his vehicle.

Unfortunately, he didn't see or hear it coming.

Within five steps of the passenger's door, a Wave tech projectile struck his reactive armor and, as he hurried to open the door, two more struck the backside of the armor. Beal barely made it inside in one piece. "Get us out of here!"

The driver punched the accelerator, headed over a small rise, and promptly slammed into a fallen tree across the trail. A scout vehicle lay turned over on the other side, and whatever took it out happened before the tree dropped to block the trail. In other words, a classic ambush maneuver. In a flash, it crossed Beal's mind another tree would be dropping behind their small column, effectively trapping them.

"Get out! Everyone into defensive positions in the treeline—form a perimeter covering all directions."

His radio operator relayed the order to the other vehicles, but as troopers exited their vehicles, gunfire ripped through the jungle and trimmed leaves, branches raining down on the jungle floor.

Two of Beal's troopers went down with headshots.

Once in cover at the base of two large trees growing out of the same trunk, Beal paused to consider the situation—not bloody good. They were stopped in their tracks and forced out of their vehicles, surrounded by an enemy of unknown size.

It suddenly struck Beal he wasn't aware of the enemy's identity.

Were they human, or his own kind?

# Chapter Twenty-four

"You nailed three of the bastards?"

"Yes, Sir."

"Outstanding! While you were on patrol, we received word the Lizards are now fighting among themselves. Apparently, small fighting airships attacked Beal's headquarters, and they ended up losing several of them, plus a few squads of troops on both sides. Then the platform blew up, taking out another airship, and the remainder of them within range on the ground."

"It blew up?"

Cletus grinned. "Yep—I left behind a Sapper team who managed to blow up the sucker right in the middle of the Lizards' battle between themselves. Classic—absolutely classic!"

Devin never saw such a broad grin—especially from Commander Cletus, and he could have sworn it made the man look ten years younger. "This is great! Let them do our work for us!"

"Absolutely! I spoke with surviving members of the patrol you were on and, when the leader was killed, I heard you took the initiative when needed. That's good leadership—I'd like to make it official . . ."

"Sir?"

"I'd like you to take over command of the patrol as a replacement for the lost man."

Comfortable with previous command experience on other versions of Earth, Devin didn't hesitate. "If that'll help out Commander, I can do that."

"Thanks. We need the column to proceed carefully further south—we don't want a repeat of last night. With the amount of people we have strung out over a narrow trail, it's a tempting, easy target."

"Commander, if you can have someone watch our backside, I can take out a reinforced patrol ahead of the column to sniff out any problems."

Cletus slapped the young man on the shoulder. "You do that, Son—much appreciated!"

****

Devin sent Dwight ahead as a lightening rod—apparently, others in the reinforced patrol were unanimous when vouching for him as the best tracker within Commander Cletus's forces.

And, he just proved it to his superior.

Strung out twenty-five yards behind him, Dwight signaled the patrol to halt. Everyone at the front watched as he knelt and studied the trail, taking his time between what he saw on the ground, and observing the jungle growth on both sides of the trail ahead. Devin watched as he cocked his head several times, listening to jungle sounds.

Eventually, he made his way back to the patrol.

"What's up?" Devin figured Dwight saw or heard something.

The tracker nodded toward the trail ahead. "They're close, waiting . . ."

"What did you see and hear?"

"It's what I didn't hear—it's too quiet up there with not enough jungle sounds to suit me. And, the ground on both sides of the trail shows a clumsy attempt to hide footprints. It's too perfect . . ."

"Any idea of how many?"

"Not really—but, I'm leaning toward not too many. A large group would have left more evidence of trying to melt into the undergrowth.

"On both sides of the trail?"

"Not unless they want to shoot each other—I'd set it up on one side, and cap it at the front when the action starts. Wait until the head of our column reaches the end of the line, then let loose."

"Makes sense—do they know we're here?"

"Probably—but I stopped short of their being able to spring the trap."

Devin thought for a few moments. "Okay—we have twenty of us, and we need to remove this threat. The main column is half an hour behind, and the way needs to be clear. Since we don't know for sure which side they're on, you take four fighters and penetrate behind on the left, and I'll send another group in behind on the right. Try to flush them out onto the path ahead, but don't enter it. I'll have the balance of our force set to fire down the trail." He paused, looking at the path in front of them. "Thankfully, it's relatively straight here. Stay back at least ten yards from the trail at all times—we'll be shooting at anything entering the kill zone, so stay clear. We don't want to shoot your asses—only the Lizards."

"Roger that . . ."

"Select your fighters and head out . . ."

The process took twenty-five minutes of waiting quietly and patiently. Devin dispersed his group in a narrow, cone shape on the edges of each side of the trail—some lying down, others kneeling, and the remainder standing in such a way that everyone's line of fire was directed toward the open trail ahead. Just as a precaution, two fighters—a man and a woman—were twenty yards back up the trail just in case the Lizards got behind them. After all, with both sides operating in the thick jungle, anything was possible.

The peaceful atmosphere was suddenly shattered by sounds of several rifles firing from the right, followed by peculiar whooshing of a Wave tech weapon. For the next few minutes, the jungle reverberated with sounds of gunfire—it seemed longer, though, since both sides were out of view, jockeying for position. Several times, the firing was punctuated by screams of someone's being hit.

Devin clearly explained to the shooters in his group not to fire until his command. And, when they cut loose, go only for headshots—more difficult, but they would circumvent the Wave tech protective armor.

Suddenly, there was movement ahead! Three Lizards burst onto the trail, running south, away from them. He was about to give the order to open fire, when two more entered the pathway, facing toward them. *Better yet,* he thought.

"Commence fire!"

The two Lizards facing them were immediately cut down in the hail of bullets, both taking headshots. Then, Devin's fighters aimed at the three running south—two fell. The third made a desperate attempt to retreat from the line of fire by diverting back into the jungle on the left side. Slowly, the gunfire stopped—no one was in sight.

Nothing but silence.

Thirty seconds later, a three-round burst from a human's long gun rang out, followed a few moments later by Dwight's voice. "We got all the bastards! We're coming out, so if anyone fires, I'll kick their ass . . ."

Devin chuckled, as did the fighters with him. "Put your weapons on safety—we don't want any mishaps." Devin glanced quickly at his patrol, making certain they complied. As they prepared to continue their trek, the two groups sent into the jungle to flush out the enemy rejoined the patrol.

"Good job of getting the buggers out of cover and defeating their ambush attempt!" Devin wanted to make sure they knew he was proud of them.

"Yes—but we lost two of ours doing it . . ." Dwight pointed out.

Devin shook his head. "I noticed . . ."

He turned, selecting a female fighter from his group. "Head back the way we came, find the main column, and advise Commander Cletus about what went on here. The way should be clear—but, proceed cautiously since more of them could slip in behind us after we pass. We'll continue south, trying to keep things clear . . ."

As the woman nodded and headed off, Devin turned back to his reconstituted patrol group. "Let's pave the way, shall we?"

\*\*\*\*

"Tested?"

"That's what it seems like to me—you know, to see what you're made of, and how you handle adversity in increasingly difficult circumstances. It's a classic training tool—no magic to it."

Tag considered Reese's observations, meeting the stares of Rose and Claire who seemed shocked by the suggestion.

"But," Claire commented, "it seems so random. It never occurred to me there could be a Controller manipulating things."

"Hey, I'm not saying there is—it's just the way the pattern unfolded for the three of you. Maybe it's something else—it's only one scenario..."

Rose glanced at Claire. "I prefer the random concept rather than the thought of someone's or something's controlling what happens to me in some sort of galactic experiment..."

"Amen to that..."

Tag was quiet as they walked down the trail.

Claire elbowed Rose. "I can hear the wheels turning."

He snorted. "I heard that!" He turned, walking backwards beside Reese. "So—what if there's some master planner guy controlling where we go. Is there some way to contact him—or, it—to influence where we want to go?"

"To your home planet..."

"Exactly..."

Claire stared at both of them. "Well, then—how would you go about it? Waving your hands in front of the opening to get the portal guy's attention? That might work..."

Tag smiled. "However, think about the music I heard coming through the portal—all songs I know. Then we had the message tube from Kyle come through—maybe it had a little help along the way..."

"But, why?"

"Maybe it's all part of the experience . . ."

Rose shook her head. "This is starting to weird me out—thinking of something watching us in the portal."

"Who said it has to be confined only to the time of portal travel," Claire pointed out.

"What! You mean it could be looking at us right now?"

"Sure—why not? If it controls the portal, maybe the Controller built the damn thing. And, if it's that far advanced, then why not take a peek at anyone, anywhere in the universe whenever it feels like it?"

Rose balked at the thought. "That's downright creepy! Maybe I should give it the finger just in case it's watching now . . ."

Logan walked behind the girls, following the conversation. "Have at it—tell it what you really think!"

Reese smiled. "Let's not get too carried away on that theme—it was only a suggestion of one, potential possibility."

"On that note," Logan advised, "I need to find a tree—I'll catch up with you . . ." He stopped, watching the group continue down the path. Then he turned, walking five yards into the jungle off the trail. Suitably out of sight, he went about his business and, as he finished and started to turn back to the trail, he noticed a shadow across his line of sight.

Instinct, the will to live, a sixth sense. Maybe the fight or flight dynamic—whatever it was, it kicked in immediately and, as he stepped back, the blade of a large combat knife cut through the air precisely where his throat had been an instant before. *Shit! That was close!*

Logan felt naked, standing empty-handed without a weapon. His rifle was leaning against a tree, conveniently located behind the Lizard, and totally out of reach.

The Lizard recovered from the missed attack, and started to move toward him.

*Great—now what do I do?*

\*\*\*\*

Tag walked, half listening to the girls' conversation, when he stopped abruptly in his tracks—Rose, while looking at Claire, didn't notice, bumped into the back of him, and bounced off.

"Hey! Signal when you're going to stop . . ."

He didn't answer.

"Tag?"

She walked around to face him, but he turned to face the way they came.

"That's rude!"

"Shh..."

"What?"

"Quiet, please..." He concentrated up trail.

Both girls and Reese stared at him, but all heeded his request.

"Logan's in trouble—we have to go back! Now!" Without waiting for a response, Tag broke into a flat-out run back up the trail. Reese reacted immediately, running after him, followed by the girls.

As Tag pounded the trail, he had the sinking feeling he wouldn't arrive in time. Reaching the spot where he noted Logan's leaving the trail, he veered into the jungle without breaking stride, Reese following five yards behind.

Swerving around a massive tree trunk, Tag didn't take time to pull his weapon from behind his back. Instead, he launched himself into the fray as Reese rounded the tree, watching Tag take two large steps forward. Tag planted his left foot and leapt forward, spinning around with his right leg, whipping his foot into the back of the Lizard's knee joint as he prepared to eviscerate Logan. On a human, the impact force would have shattered the back of the joint—but, with the heavily-built Lizard frame, it crumpled the right leg forward, sending the Lizard off balance and falling to his right.

Something struck him hard, collapsing his leg, causing him to fall, but, somehow, Zarn managed to keep from being totally laid out on the jungle floor by landing on his knees. He struggled to get up, the right leg not performing as it should to take its share of his weight.

He saw two human males, the younger one closest to

him. Still clutching his large combat knife, Zarn focused on the one in front of him who apparently caused him the problem. *It's time to teach the young one a lesson . . .*

Lurching forward he raised the weapon, intent on slicing the target in half, but without success. The young one easily moved out of range, and Zarn was having difficulty getting closer. He decided to forgo the pleasure of using the knife, sheathing it as he drew the Wave tech weapon off of his shoulder. But, before he could get it into firing position, a single shot rang out, and he could feel something running down his face.

Blood.

He'd been shot.

He looked at the young human standing calmly just out of range, then refocused past the young male. An older human male stood behind and to the side of the young one, his rifle mounted at his shoulder prepared to fire another shot, if needed.

Well, Zarn knew enough about hunting prey to know the enemy wouldn't need another shot. Legs weakening, he started to pitch forward, trying to use his weapon for support, but his body felt heavy—all he wanted was to rest on the ground. When the Lizard was finally down, Reese approached, kicked the Wave tech weapon away, studying the Lizard who wasn't in good condition.

Tag stood beside him. "Thanks for the assist . . ."

Reese focused on the young man. "You're welcome—but, I'm thinking there's a bit of disappointment in you that I interfered."

Tag shrugged. "Not really—as long as he's down. That's the important thing."

Reese looked back at the Lizard lying on the jungle floor, laboring to stay alive. "He's not a guard or regular trooper, and he's dressed like a Merc. Those bastards hunt us down for hire . . ."

Tag stared at the Lizard. "I'm afraid this one won't be hunting anything for a while—it's going to be touch and go if he lives . . ."

They watched as life slowly faded from the massive body, neither knowing the Lizard's end.

The two men stood in silence.

*I wonder what his mission was?*

## Chapter Twenty-Five

They were at dinner, the three of them—Kyle, Jackie, and Lego. "I never considered the hazards of distance eating," Jackie announced. "Maybe, if my fork were longer, I could actually get a decent load on it. At this rate, effectively, I'm on a diet . . ." Lego's large frame blocked her from tucking her chair under the table.

Kyle chuckled. "I could put him out in the backyard, if you like." Of course, he was referring to Lego.

"Don't you dare—he's often a sparkling dinner companion compared to you."

"Ouch! Coming in second behind the dog—isn't that a little harsh?"

"Does the truth hurt? Maybe it will prompt you to

try harder . . ."

"Geez, tromping on my feelings is hardly romantic, don't you think?"

She smiled sweetly. "A good relationship is something needing constant attention and fine tuning."

"Ha, so this is your version of tuning me up?"

"In the long run, it's for your own good . . ." She laughed, enjoying the repartee with the man she loved so much. It was good to have him out of the doldrums—for a while.

\*\*\*\*

It was early evening, darker than one would expect due to the heavy canopy of trees shrouding the jungle floor. The column stopped to bivouac for the night at several small clearings to each side of the trail, accommodating a good portion of the human contingent—the rest were left to find their own resting spots.

Devin's patrol arrived as the main group dispersed within their camp, soon locating Commander Cletus who was talking with several of his subordinate leaders. Nirva was close by, supervising some of the families as they got comfortable for the night. With the number of people traveling in the column, everyone was responsible for feeding themselves, helping those close by if they were short of provisions.

Cletus noticed Devin's approach. "How did it go?"

"Fine, Sir. I sent a fighter back to report an encounter with the enemy . . ."

"Yes—she arrived, and informed me. Any other issues?"

"Not that we could tell. However, it's not a blanket endorsement everything will be peachy by morning."

"Understood—anything can change in the next few hours. It's a fluid situation with Lizard and human groups moving through the jungle hunting one another—not to mention the infighting of the Lizards among themselves. That's a bonus . . ."

In the failing light, Cletus noticed weariness etched on Devin's face. "Why don't you tell your patrol members to get something to eat, and bunk in for the night? I'll send out another patrol group for tonight's recon . . ."

"Sounds good, Commander."

After passing the word to his patrol members, Devin sought out his own spot to bunk for the night. As it happened, Kirv and his family were close by. "Hey Kirv! How are you?"

The ex-farmer looked up, and smiled. "Devin—hi! We're doing fine. How was the patrol?"

"Interesting—there are random, small units of Lizards skulking around in the jungle. So, as we move along tomorrow in column, please be aware some of them may get past our sweep, or slide behind us and attack the main body."

"Roger that—I have a rifle, and so do Glade and Millie. We'll be ready to take them on, if needed."

Devin thought of the skirmishes in the jungle. "A rifle is a good weapon—just keep in mind it won't do anything against their Wave tech body armor. You'll have to go only for headshots. It's harder to hit than their torso—although, thankfully, their heads are a hell of a lot bigger than ours."

Kirv smiled. "It's kind of funny how something like an oversized head in another species works to our advantage."

Devin lowered his voice so only Kirv could hear him. "How are Glade and Millie holding up?"

"Thankfully, very well. Both are healthy and strong from all the work around the farm . . ." He stopped, considering the loss of his home and livelihood.

Devin figured Kirv was thinking about the shattering experience of losing everything his family spent years building. "Hey, if it's any consolation, all of you escaped in good shape—many didn't."

"I know—as bad as it was, it could have been far worse since some farm families ceased to exist. For that, one day, I want to be part of the payback."

Devin put a hand on the man's shoulder. "And, you will. Maybe sooner than you think . . ."

****

"Sir, we managed to insert four groups into the territory immediately south of the headquarters site. So far, they turned up little in the way of leads."

"Only four? Where are the others?"

"They're the only ones answering the summons..."

The Prime considered the failure to collect enough Merc teams a hindrance when putting a halt to the constant sabotage of guerrilla warfare occurring in Beal's former command region. "Those blasted Mercs aren't responding to the call. What makes them valuable—their independent action—is also maddening. The fools haven't realized if this situation worsens, our grip will slip on controlling this planet—then they're in the same shitpile with the rest of us."

The officer was shocked by the lengthy response from the usually taciturn, concise leader. Cultured beyond anything the officer ever hoped to achieve, the use of the base comment was something he never heard uttered from the Prime's mouth. Obviously, he was flustered more than he showed—something deeply worrying the captain.

Perhaps, the situation was far worse than he imagined.

\*\*\*\*

He couldn't stand the concept of working with undisciplined Mercs. As potential saviors of their deteriorating situation, it was repugnant to him as a highly trained, indoctrinated Commander of the Planetary Reserve Force.

Quarn glanced at his subordinate. "Sub-Commander Klinit—take a squad to find out who's damaging my headquarters while there's still something left standing. I'm tired of waiting for the next thing to blow up in this facility—we can't be shown up by Merc teams hired by the Prime. It's unseemly . . ."

"Sir," the Sub-Commander pointed out, "we have so few elite troopers left. If I take a full patrol, it'll only leave ten remaining to guard you."

"Klinit—if we can't catch those responsible, then I'm not worth protecting. In any event, I'd like to believe I can still defend myself, if necessary. Get to it . . ."

"Yes, Commander—I'll do it immediately." He turned and headed to the door, stopping at the sound of his Commander's voice. "Don't return until you achieve success in your mission . . ."

Klinit paused for a few seconds. "Of course, Sir . . ."

In his gut, Quarn knew there was a limited amount his small force could do. The region was large with too many places for sabotage perpetrators to secret themselves as well as their explosive devices.

Not for the first time on his mission, Quarn wished

he were back in a more familiar circumstance, leading a phalanx of troopers into a planetary conquest campaign.

Then, everything was straightforward, and out in the open.

****

An hour later, there was an extensive amount of surrounding jungle turned into a smashed jumble of broken branches—and bodies.

Lizard and human.

Beal found it disconcerting to have humans using Wave tech firepower against the creators of such fearsome weapons. Most of his troops were blown apart with such force, bits and pieces hung from low-slung branches. Substantially smaller, the humans made less of a mess. At least he felt they eliminated the enemy in the violent skirmish—if there were human survivors, they appeared to vanish into jungle cover.

Beal's two troopers and Sub-Commander Vanc were all who were left. In a stroke of luck, Vanc was only hit by a human-designed rifle, clipping off his right ear, leaving a large dent in the side of his head.

Beal turned to Vanc. "Can you function?"

"Of course, Commander . . ."

"Good. Get a trooper over here, and blow apart this fallen tree so we can pass . . ."

As the two walked far enough away to be clear of the soldier using the Wave tech weapon, Beal turned to Vanc. "Who imagined a few weeks ago our secure, easy-occupation mission would turn so quickly into this piss-pot situation where I'm a fugitive in my own command territory? Not to mention my own kind and human slime are hunting me. What a mess . . ."

"Commander . . ."

Beal glanced over at Vanc when he didn't continue.

"They're hunting me, too."

The Commander was so egocentric he hadn't stopped to contemplate how their situation may affect Vanc, and the surviving troopers. Of course, they wanted to cover their own tails, possibly abandoning Beal in the process if they came under attack again. *I'll have to watch them carefully*, he thought.

"Of course, Vanc. I was thinking in terms of all of us."

The Commander looked away quickly after uttering the statement, and Vanc knew he was bullshitting to save face. He figured if it hit the fan again, the Commander could look after his own tail because Vanc would be in full self-protection mode.

Things were getting too dangerous.

On the Edge of Now: Book V—Jagged Edge

****

He couldn't see out of his left eye. His head pounded with jackhammer force. He was sick to his stomach. All from a bullet to the head—yet, he still breathed and, in between spasms of pain, he could think.

Before, he and his team would easily catch and defeat the humans they hunted—hardly a sporting outing. Why, with this group of humans, was it so different? He lost his teammates, and now he lay, perhaps, mortally wounded—he wasn't sure. The worst part was they hadn't inflicted so much as a scratch on any member of the three-male, and two-female group.

Zarn decided if he survived the encounter—which was highly unlikely—his occupation as Merc hunter would end. However, the question which really plagued him was why they let him live? He was aware of the human enemy standing over his prone form, helpless. They had a conversation, some of which he managed to focus on despite severe bouts of pain, and it would've been easy to finish him off—a blessing, really. But, they didn't. Why?

Part of him wanted to lie there and expire—somehow, it seemed like the thing to do. Yet, another part of him obeyed the genetic blueprint for survival. With a massive groan, he rolled over, struggling to reach a kneeling position. Resting for a minute in the awkward stance, he slowly rose to a partial stand, leaning against a tree for support. Waves of nausea assaulted him, forcing him to be violently ill again—once that passed, he felt slightly better.

It took him a full ten minutes to gain the wherewithal to stand upright, taking a few tentative first steps. Then the realization struck him—survival was possible.

It was all a question of personal will.

And, stubbornness.

\*\*\*\*

Unconsciously, everyone in the group picked up the pace. The encounter in the jungle with the Lizard Merc spooked them, especially Logan. They expected random patrols of the enemy, especially since there were rogue Mercs wandering about. Even though only a single threat, the idea of individual Lizards skulking in the jungle, waiting in ambush, made it harder to detect their presence and avoid surprise.

Everyone was unsettled.

"We've come a fair distance from Beal's headquarters," Tag commented to Reese. "You'd think we'd be clear of his reach by now . . ."

The former Special Forces Recon warrior nodded. "Beal's territory was extensive, and we're on the southern periphery now. He may have enlisted the help of this region's Commander—if that's the case, they'll pick up where Beal's troops leave off . . ."

"Does one Commander allow another's soldiers to

encroach on his turf?"

"To my knowledge, not ever—these buggers are highly territorial and power hungry. They'd probably get in a fight over someone else's stepping over the line of demarcation. Cooperation isn't big on their agenda . . ."

Tag agreed. "Kind of makes you wonder how they got their shit together enough to conquer this world in the first place."

Reese chuckled. "I hear you—however, when they sent their A-Team into the invasion, it was a whole different thing. They've obviously done this on many occasions before—their timing, integration of forces, and Wave tech weapons contributed to blowing through our defenses almost as though we didn't have any. I think they save those guys as the planet busters, and then ship them out for the next planetary target. The bozos we're dealing with are third rate, at best . . ."

Tag chewed on that information for a moment. "If we find the scientists and get the technology in their hands—and, if they can decipher how it works—then leveling the playing field and overthrowing the occupation forces on this planet is only a beginning."

Reese glanced at him. "Yes . . ." He wanted to see if the young man followed through on the thought.

"Then, if it starts to slip from them . . ."

"When it does . . ."

Tag smiled. "Yes, thinking positively—when it does, the occupation command here, wherever they're located, has to call for off-planet reinforcements. Then, you're back to facing the top dogs again if they have the guts to reinvade . . ."

Reese gave the young man a check mark for following the thread. "Exactly—we cycle the same scenario. The only way is to break the pattern." He waited to see if Tag followed up with question or comment.

He wasn't disappointed. "How did they get here in the first place, and how long was the trip?"

"I've heard rumors the initial trip from their home planet took many years."

"So, if you kick them off your rock, you have a breather for quite a while to prepare a welcoming party if they decide to return..."

Reese nodded. "Maybe..." He waited, understanding Tag was a bright young man who could analyze situations in logical fashion. "Unless they happen to have closer spacecraft, or occupy another close-by planet..."

"Well—that would definitely suck."

"Big time—but, we can't worry about that now. We need to be successful with the first step, and get them off our world first."

****

Since the night patrol ambush and counterambush, they were on the trail south for a week and a half. Of course, there was the odd brief encounter with the enemy, although when the Lizards saw the size of the human column, they disappeared into the jungle to let them pass. Even the aggressive, superior-minded Vicalla knew when to back off.

Devin led several patrols, alternating with another leader, Prac, and his crew. After each venture out, the two leaders got together, sharing intel—any scrap of information could turn a potentially dangerous situation into something more positive.

That night, it was Devin's turn, and Commander Cletus called him over for a briefing regarding the evening's mission.

"Is your crew ready to go?"

"Yes, Sir—locked and loaded."

"Just keep it a regular recon, and your nose tucked out of trouble—the usual drill."

"Will do, Commander." Normally, Devin would hustle out as soon as he could. That evening, however, he remained in front of the Commander.

"Is there an issue, Devin?"

"I'd like to ask a question, Sir."

"Of course..."

The younger man looked around to see if anyone else were within earshot. "It's kind of embarrassing—it involves my girl."

"You're not going to ask me for dating advice, are you?"

Devin looked startled. "No, Sir—I have that part

figured out."

"Excellent—well, what is it?"

"I'm to link up with her and her friends, as I told you before..."

"I remember."

"Well, here's the thing—I have a rough description of the location, but I'm not so good with distances. I don't know if we're getting close or not—so, I'm wondering if you could help me figure it out."

The big man laughed. "And I thought you had some dire news. Of course! When you get back, grab some chow, sack out, then come see me—we'll find your long-lost love for you!"

\*\*\*\*

Thankfully, nothing noteworthy happened on the night shift, and Devin's patrol members made it back in one piece. He finished breakfast with Kirv and his family, appreciating the fact they took him under their wing when it came to meals and housekeeping.

Afterward, he found the Commander walking with Nirva. Devin started to turn away, not wanting to intrude, until Cletus called to the young patrol leader. "How did it go last night?"

"Clear, as far as we could tell, Sir."

"Good. About our discussion last evening—I took the liberty of mentioning it to Nirva, enlisting her help. She was raised in this region, and her knowledge of the geography in these parts is considerably better than mine."

Devin hesitated slightly before responding. "That's fine, Sir."

Recognizing his embarrassment, she took Devin by the arm. "I'm going to walk with this delightful individual, and we'll discuss things. Cletus, you can run off to find someone else to command . . ."

With that, she wandered off with Devin in tow.

The Commander stood there, shaking his head and chuckling. *She's right*, he thought. *Devin can use a gentler touch . . .*

When they were away from everyone, Nirva glanced at Devin. "Tell me about her."

"Well, Claire's short where I'm tall, she's athletically built, not petite at all, wavy honey-brown hair that's goes a little crazy. Cute . . ."

"That's how she looks—tell me about her."

He nodded. "Okay—she's wicked smart, sassy, and don't even think of getting into a one-liner, zinger contest with her. But, behind the brazen exterior, Claire's thoughtful and caring. She'd go to the wall for a friend. Her eyes will suck you in—the raw intelligence and wisdom in there are amazing for one so young."

"Perhaps, she's an old soul. Now, that tells me

something about her—thank you. Now, explain the link up plan with your friends, and we'll see if I can help."

"That's the thing—there wasn't much time to formulate a detailed plan. We had a dustup with the Lizards, and had to separate. I tried to find them at two predetermined spots, but it was a no go . . ."

Devin hesitated a few moments, and Nirva picked up on his reluctance. "And . . ."

"Well, I kind of have this little problem with figuring out distances. It sounds weird, but I can't tell if I trekked five miles or twenty, and I relied on the others to figure out stuff like that, and I followed along."

She smiled. "It's nothing to be ashamed of—we all have our weaknesses and failings. Describe to me what you're looking for . . ."

"Apparently, there's an enclave of surviving scientists located approximately two hundred and twenty miles from Kirv's farm—so, it would be about the same from the work camp you were in. That's the ultimate destination, and Claire, Rose, and Tag should be heading for the same spot."

Nirva picked up on Devin's wondering if his fellow Travelers would make it. "I'm sure all of us are moving toward it—are there any landmarks to delineate where it is?"

"Apparently, there's a valley which has a decent-sized river in it, as well as an island with a large rock outcropping. Viewed from the north side, it's supposed to resemble a bear's head."

He noticed a large grin expand on her face.

"What?"

Nirva laughed. "I know the place—I used to go there with my father when he fished the river. I've seen the island, and the bear's head before!"

"Do you remember how to get there?"

"Of course! Are the scientists supposed to be on the island? It's not very big . . ."

"I'm not sure—it's probably a point of reference for wherever they are in the neighborhood."

"Hmm . . ."

"What?"

"If they're in that area and as valuable as you seem to think, they may well be secreted and not amenable to revealing their hiding place. I wouldn't be surprised if they are well guarded, and any efforts to find them may well be discouraged. Perhaps, vigorously . . ."

Devin thought about that for a moment. "Well, if we do link up with the others, then I guess we'll have to do something about getting them to bring out the welcome wagon. We can't allow this opportunity to be missed because someone decides to be shy . . ."

# CHAPTER TWENTY-SIX

The door creaked a little, but, for the most part, silence prevailed as an officer or other functionary stood waiting to be acknowledged. *Let them wait,* he thought. *I have problems on a planetary scale to contend with—being polite to an underling holds no priority!* Minutes passed as he gazed out the window, his mind crammed with permutations of how to extricate himself from such a planetary mess. Finally, he tired of the litany of useless choices, then turned to the officer standing at ramrod attention.

Acknowledging the cue, the captain began. "Sir, Commander Quarn sent a letter stating his patrol liquidated several humans who were around the headquarters center."

"So? What's your point? Are they the perpetrators

of the attacks, or simply random humans in the wrong place at the wrong time?"

"I'm not sure, Sir."

A long stare. "Perhaps it will be better for you to find these things out first, then advise me."

"Yes, Sir . . ." The scolded captain tried to leave the office with some dignity intact.

Rubbing his brow with concern, the Prime wondered what became of the four Merc teams he hired to eliminate the problem.

****

"Get over to the other side before we're surrounded!"

It was hard to hear the command over the crashing sound of Wave tech weapons ripping the jungle apart—branches fell and tree trunks split, interspersed with rifles' echoing cracks.

Larnk was no stranger to firefights—no surprise since his chosen occupation was a Merc team leader. But, this shitshow was a topper—his five-man Lizard team was currently pinned in place, most likely by the same humans they were to hunt down and eliminate.

Somehow, there was a perverse humor in the

situation.

Whomever they were, he considered them good. His team traipsed down the trail busily looking for signs to track and, now, he cowered behind a large tree trying desperately to keep his team alive—a nice turn of events by the opposition.

Another thing he discovered—which was entirely different from previous hunts—the prey was packing Wave tech weapons, making him realize it wasn't much fun having his own kind's destructive weapons discharged in his direction. But, just when he thought there was no way out, the other side's rate of fire slackened. Within thirty seconds, the jungle fell eerily quiet, contrasting sharply with the barrage of previous noise.

"What's going on?" He called to his team members, hoping they had a handle on everything.

They didn't.

"Stay put—it could be a trap to draw us into the open."

Several minutes passed before he heard a voice call out in his own language, yet it was one he didn't recognize. "It's clear to come out—that's if you can let go from clinging to the tree for shelter." His teammates' laughter echoed through the jungle.

Larnk peered around the tree trunk, cursing—it was a squad of troopers from the Planetary Reserve Force. He bashed his head against the tree trunk in frustration—being rescued by them was worse than being pinned by the human contingent. There was no love lost between Mercs and Reserve Forces—in fact, they hated each other and, sometimes, it was difficult to restrain his team from actively fighting with them using their weapons on full power.

Once word got around about the fiasco, Larnk's reputation would be permanently tarnished, which would directly affect the viability of future employment as well as the value of his contracts.

Slowly, he moved into the open, dreading the coming contact, his team members following his lead, revealing themselves.

The squad leader snorted. "Five of you, and a group of puny humans had control of the situation—pathetic."

Larnk barked an order, quashing the movement of one of his team members' reacting to the insult. "Sure, they had the upper hand, but, you wouldn't be so cocky if those Wave tech weapons were targeted on you—and, they know how to use them effectively."

The other Lizard bristled at the suggestion, his troopers stirring at Larnk's comment. He growled a command, ordering them to settle down. "How large was their force?"

"I admit I have no idea—they hit us so fast, we simply took cover. There must have been at least a dozen, given the amount of firepower directed at us . . ."

The squad leader indicated he needed to speak with Larnk privately, and they moved far enough down the trail in order to engage in private conversation. "I'm tasked with finding the human team of saboteurs—do you think they're the ones who ambushed you?"

"Maybe—however, they didn't use explosives, which they could have. Only weapons fire, which was plenty. So, I'm not sure . . ."

The squad leader thought for a few moments. "This whole situation of thousands of humans, armed and roaming the region, is getting critical. If this spreads to other regional command areas, the viability of holding this planet in slavery is going to be tricky—unless Off-Planet Command sends fresh forces to support us. If not, all of us may be in jeopardy."

Larnk never heard such an admission from regular troop members, let alone from a Special Reserve leader. Suddenly, he appreciated the gravity of the situation.

They could lose.

\*\*\*\*

"By my estimate, we must be getting close . . ."

Reese turned, looking back at Logan who was tromping directly behind. "Okay—where are we?"

"According to the description of what Tag's crew is looking for, it seems we should be seeing some of the landmarks pretty damned soon. The topography is starting to match, and the river over there could be the one. I've never seen the Bear's Head island before, but it sounds distinctive enough to pick it out if we stumble upon it."

"To me, the distance is about right . . ."

Walking behind the men with Rose, Claire interrupted. "If you want to hold the discussion and look around, perhaps you might see something revealing . . ."

The three men stopped walking, and looked at Claire, waiting for her to expand on the comment. Instead, she gestured, inviting them to examine their surroundings.

It didn't take long.

"Son of a bitch! There it is!" Reese shook his head and smiled. They'd been so involved in the discussion of where they wanted to be, no one was carefully studying where they were at the moment. Approaching from north of the small island, it was fairly easy to recognize the large rock resembling a bear's head.

"We're here!" Rose elbowed Claire a well done.

Once he saw the obvious landmark, Tag turned slowly to examine the surrounding area. Nothing indicated where a human group would be, but, if it were the place and the scientists were being protected, it made sense they'd be well hidden. "Okay—now what?"

Reese scanned the area before answering. "We wait—I suggest we scope out an area to camp far enough off the trail so we don't attract attention from anyone hiking by. If this is the location, let's play it cool to see if the locals make themselves known. We don't want to appear as a threat, so I suggest being armed for protection—we don't want to actively hunt the Lizards."

"Sounds reasonable . . ."

Reese turned to Rose and Claire. "I suggest none of us wander too far on our own—there may be Lizards passing through, and the locals might not be friendly. Especially if they feel our presence is compromising their security . . ."

Watching them and overhearing the conversation, the Observer nodded agreement to the last statement. *What are you doing here, and why do you want to involve us in whatever it is you're seeking?*

She pulled back quietly with extraordinary care learned over the years guarding their home. The Protector needed to learn immediately of their new neighbors, and she anticipated his displeasure at the surprise development.

\*\*\*\*

Difficult as it was, he managed to hike south for two miles down the trail, but the speed of his progress was a fraction of his normal gait. *This damned injury is slowing me down . . .* His left eye was useless. Focusing with the right one combined with periodic nausea made it difficult to concentrate on where he was—and the recurring vertigo didn't help, either.

Just as he stopped at the side of the trail to quell another bout of nausea, Zarn managed to distinguish the sound of an approaching vehicle coming from behind. He lumbered off the trail into the trees to find cover—with humans in possession of Wave tech weapons, it wasn't a stretch to imagine some of them liberating Lizard vehicles as the next step in their rebellion.

As the vehicle approached, he noticed its proceeding slowly down the path. Upon closer inspection, he observed battle damage, causing him to wonder how the vehicle made it to his location given its poor state. As he watched, he could see the front-seat occupants were his kind and, normally self-reliant, Zarn knew in his present physical condition he wouldn't get far on his own.

When the vehicle was almost to his position, he stepped onto the path, and the driver swerved in an attempt to avoid hitting him. In the front passenger seat, Beal swore loudly as the damaged vehicle groaned under the strain of the impromptu stop. Facing them was a sorry sight—a disheveled and obviously wounded Lizard stood swaying before them, clearly trying not to collapse. "Find out who this is, and what's going on," Beal ordered one of the troopers in the rear seat.

A second trooper also exited the vehicle, taking position to cover the trooper tasked with approaching the wounded Lizard. Beal watched from the vehicle as his soldier spoke with the stranger and, after a brief conversation, his trooper returned to report. "He's a Merc who lost the rest of his team in an encounter with a small human group—they left him for dead. The poor bastard's got an eye shot out—he says his name is Zarn, and you hired him to catch humans— obviously, they got the drop on his team. In his condition, I don't know how he made it this far . . ."

With all the turmoil Beal had been through with the firefight at his headquarters as well as the ambush on the trail, he completely forgot about the Merc team he hired to track the stolen Wave tech equipment. Given the state of the slave revolt and the quantity of weapons—and, other equipment in the hands of the humans—it seemed the original mission was trivial by comparison. "There's no point in leaving the Merc for the next human group to come along and finish him off. Get him into the back of the vehicle, and let's move out—I don't like sitting stationary on this open trail."

Beal really didn't care what would happen to Zarn. He figured even in poor condition, the Merc's presence added another gun to the mix if they got into another tangle with a human force.

\*\*\*\*

Thinking over the last several months since Tag's disappearance, Kyle reviewed the steps he took to unravel the questions surrounding the event. One, it was almost a given Tag left by portal travel—the physical evidence at the site confirmed the finding. Two—call it intuition or a sixth sense—he could sometimes feel his brother's situation. He was still alive, dramatic happenings occurred with regularity, and he had companions with him. And, even though his colleagues would challenge him to properly describe how he knew such things, he would still defend their validity.

Three—he couldn't bring himself to conceptualize the death of his younger brother, and Kyle willed the survival of Tag to be true. On the other hand, he still beat himself up over the question of having done enough to sleuth out the workings of the portal system. How could he help to get Tag back?

For months, he strove endlessly to achieve progress toward that goal. His regular work suffered to the point he had to approach the company with which he contracted to request an extension to finish his project. Thankfully, they recognized his past exemplary work, and accepted his 'personal reasons' excuse at face value. Their understanding freed Kyle to concentrate on the portal question—however, the burning issue remained. Was it possible to figure out enough of the portal phenomenon's intricacies to aid in his brother's return?

There was no question his health suffered as he drove himself to learn more, and Jackie pointed it out regularly. Physically and mentally, he was often drained by the challenge, but, he rarely lost focus on the quest. It was something he could never let go until either Tag returned, or Kyle was convinced of his demise.

Tag had to make it home.

## Chapter Twenty-seven

He walked down the trail with Prac, the other patrol leader, comparing notes for the patrol's scheduled nighttime watch. At the head of the extensive column of humans freed from Vicalla's enslavement, their total count numbered over five hundred, most armed with weapons or devices presenting a considerable force.

Four days passed without Lizards ambushing them, and scouts didn't catch a glimpse of the enemy. Speculation ranged from the Lizards' running short of troops, their being pulled back for a counteroffensive, or the human column was traveling between Lizard administrative regions. In any event, it was a welcomed relief to have a few days in a row without conflict.

"Well, young man, I think I have some good news for you," Nirva interrupted as she approached.

Devin gave her a warm smile. "What good news is that?"

She chuckled. "We're here . . ."

"Here?"

"Yes—near the Bear's Head . . ."

"Really? How far?"

"If I remember correctly, it should be just around the bend in the trail up ahead. If you take a left, there should be a small lookout point where you can view the island and river from above. Further along, a small trail branches off from this one, heading down to the water's edge."

"Excellent! I'll ask the Commander's permission to range ahead, and check it out . . ."

Nirva laughed at Devin's excitement, knowing he couldn't wait to see Claire. "Don't bother—I already told him you're off seeking romantic bliss in the wild, and don't expect you to be patrolling tonight. You're free to go—but, take some fighters with you for security purposes."

He gave her a quick hug before dashing off to round up a few volunteers to accompany him. Nirva smiled and shook her head as he disappeared on the side trail branching off from the main path.

The trail was steep and, once they reached the bottom, Devin stopped to consider which way to go. From the valley floor, the Bear's Head wasn't quite as obvious, and he realized Nirva's assessment was correct—the island's size probably discounted it as a sanctuary for the scientists they were seeking. More likely, it stood as a sign post for those acting as sentinels, alerting the powers that be they were in the vicinity. Acutely aware the area may be guarded, Devin figured caution was prudent, although it may be difficult knowing Claire was in the area. So, without specific reason, he struck off heading along the river's edge in a southwestern direction. Head on a swivel, it was challenging to keep all the scouting techniques learned over the past few months at the forefront of his mind when he kept focusing on finding his friends.

His only worry was what if his fellow Travelers hadn't made it there yet—worse, what if something drastic happened to them? In the end, however, his search was short and ended unexpectedly. As he picked his way along the river's shoreline, his security detail behind him, Devin heard a familiar and welcomed voice. "Hey, Sailor—going my way?"

He stopped, and soon spotted Claire standing on the edge of the small ridge overlooking part of the river valley. His five companions halted by the side of the river, amused as they watched his scrambling attempt to climb the steep bank to reach the young lady cheering him on.

"What took you so long," she teased as he reached her, scooping her up in a giant bear hug.

And, there they stood, wrapped in each other's arms, with no intention of letting go anytime soon.

****

"What?"

"Initially, there was a group of five—now there are hundreds streaming into the area . . ." He remained silent, grappling with the concept of so many suddenly descending upon their quiet, secluded life—they guarded one of the last vestiges of their scientific community which almost ceased to exist after the conquest.

The thirty-year-old female Observer remained silent, watching emotions register on the Protector's face. He was ultimately responsible for all matters relating to the care, secrecy, and security of the small, but thriving community of intellectuals.

Eventually, he came to a decision. "We can't reveal ourselves with so many sitting on our doorstep—pull in all but a few observers to watch what they do. I want to limit the chance of any interaction . . ."

She hesitated to correct him, since he always took criticism badly—however, in such a situation it was important they didn't make mistakes.

"Protector—the column appears to be well organized on a military-like basis with advanced scouts, security details interspersed at regular intervals among them, and a carefully-guarded supply train. It seems they're led by someone with a strong military background—the group seems subject to a chain of command structure."

It was the most detailed report he ever heard from the Observer—normally, she was accurate, yet concise, and he'd learned to pay attention when she spoke. "I understand. Still, I want to be low key and invisible until we determine their intentions. I'm hoping they're simply passing through—if they decide to stay, that'll pose a difficult problem . . ."

"Sir, there's no logical reason for them to stay here as a choice over anywhere else along the trail. Chances are much greater they'll move along . . ."

"Let's hope so. Dismissed . . ."

She saluted, then left him to his own thoughts.

The precious group of brain power was well hidden from prying eyes—yet, if the intruders decided to stay for any length of time, exploring the area, chances were good the secret would be revealed.

He couldn't allow that to happen.

\*\*\*\*

"Excuse me, Sir . . ."

"Yes?"

"We heard from Commander Quarn."

"And?"

"He reports two of the Merc teams were dispatched."

A pause. "As in sent somewhere?"

A hesitation. "No, Sir—they were eliminated."

"The other two?"

"One team was rescued by a Reserve Force squad. No word from the other . . ."

"Not a very satisfactory state of affairs."

"No, Sir."

"Is there anything else?"

"Not at this time, Sir."

"Very well . . ."

"Thank you, Prime . . ."

As the officer left quietly, the leading authority on the conquered world knew they were one step closer to calling in reinforcements from Off-Planet Command. The trick was to gain back control with the forces at hand without tipping off his superiors—they couldn't lose their grip, leaving it too late to recover even with off-planet help.

****

"So—you lost your team?"

Never known for his diplomacy, the cutting remark started the injured Merc thinking of ways to cause harm to the arrogant ex-regional leader—perhaps the knife would cut both ways.

"At least all I lost were two, easily replaceable team members compared to your losing most of your troop force, headquarters, and regional command. By comparison, I find my failings trivial." Sitting in the rear seat, he could see Beal's anger kick in. *Good*, Zarn thought. *It suits the situation to have the loudmouth enraged and embarrassed at the same time.* Over the years, the former Commander insulted and degraded Zarn and his team members at every turn. It was nice to finally be in a position to return the favor.

"I could have you shot for that remark!"

The Merc actually chuckled out loud. "I've already been shot and left for dead—your threat has no effect on me. Besides, you need me to help save your precious tail since there seems to be a current scarcity of others available to perform that function."

Beal seethed in the front seat of the damaged military vehicle, knowing the Merc was correct on each point. Besides, the conversation was going nowhere other than upsetting him.

Time for a different tact. "We're trying to get to the headquarters of the Regional Commander immediately south of here and, undoubtedly, you contracted work from him—what's Talak like? I've never met him . . ."

"A right bastard most of the time—however, he's smart enough to listen when it involves matters of security and guarding his own interests. Then he becomes sly, and it's time to watch him carefully . . ."

"Will he help?"

"He'll get involved only so far as it furthers his position— bring him something of value, and you'll have his attention. Otherwise, you and your few survivors are only a pain in his tail, and he might not be amenable to providing assistance."

****

Without letting go completely, he pulled back enough to see her face. "I missed you, a lot . . ."

Claire smiled. "I know—me, too."

"Where are the others? Are they with you?"

"They're close by—I stepped out to scout the area and to stretch my legs when I spotted you traipsing along the river bank."

"Is everyone okay?"

"They are—who are the people with you, and why are you leaving them standing around down at the river?"

"Oh—right. Let me talk to them . . ." Devin let her go, and walked closer to the ledge overlooking the river. Five faces stared up at him, two smirking, and three attempting to suppress grins.

"I found her!"

"No shit," one muttered.

Devin ignored the jibe. "One of you head back to Commander Cletus, and tell him what happened. The rest of you might as well climb up here . . ."

As his troop made its way to him, he returned his attention to Claire. "Is Tag still on the mission?"

"They're all good—and, yes, he's motivated to complete what we started. By the way, we picked up some new friends—just a heads up before you meet them."

"Lead on—just don't get out of my reach for a while, okay?"

Claire smiled. "No chance of that happening!"

They hiked for ten minutes to reach the small camp situated deep in the jungle, well off the main trail. "Hey! Look who I found!"

Attention turned to Claire as Devin came into view behind her. Tag and Rose got up to enthusiastically greet their missing companion while Reese and Logan held back, each taking in the new arrival rejoining his friends. Obviously, the affection between the four friends was genuine and heartfelt.

Reese shifted his attention to the four armed individuals—three men and a young woman—who stood back while the reunion continued. They were taking turns watching the reunited friends as well as eyeballing Reese and Logan. Figuring on welcoming them rather than having them stand awkwardly, he walked over and introduced himself to each, while carefully examining them from a military standpoint. Each measured up.

Finally, Claire guided Devin to Reese and Logan for introductions. "This is Devin . . ." She slipped her arm around his waist. "Devin—these two gentlemen were kind enough to join us for part of our trek south. We've been through a skirmish or two along the way . . ."

The men shook hands, each appraising the other. Reese noted he looked directly in the eyes of the new arrival—it felt strange because he was used to standing taller than most people he met.

After the intros were over, Devin turned his attention to his friends. "Did you see the Bear's Head?"

"Yep," Tag responded. "That's why we're hanging out here—this seems to be the spot, but, so far, nothing. Although, I get the sense we're under observation . . ."

"And, you're letting them check you out in the hope that none of you look too frightening, and they'll come forward and reveal themselves . . ."

"Bingo . . ."

"How long have you been here?"

"For almost two days now without a glimpse of anyone—but, we're keeping it low key. Although, as I said, I feel strongly we're being observed, and probably sized up." Tag rubbed his chin. "If doing nothing overt doesn't work, then we may have to start scouring the area for signs of where they're hiding. It's well done—nothing is obvious. Someone could come through here, and not have a clue there's some sort of habitat."

Devin nodded. "I've been part of a large column of people moving south—in fact, they should be passing on the main trail, as we speak. That, of course, may spook the locals . . ."

"How many?"

"North of five hundred, at least . . ."

Tag arched an eyebrow. "That's a lot of people . . ."

"Yep—and most have a weapon of some sort, and a fair number are sporting Wave tech arms taken in a few dustups along the way." Devin was quiet for a moment before continuing. "And, they know how to use them . . ."

"Really—it would require some serious Lizard firepower to take on a group that size."

"Well, we've gone four days now without challenge, so I think you're right. Oh, by the way, Kirv and his family are with the column—they had to flee when the Lizards started wiping out farm families helping with the human slave revolt."

"How widespread is the revolt?"

"Massive—the whole region is in chaos with human and Lizard groups battling it out. Apparently, Beal, the Regional Commander, was ousted, and his troops and others were fighting among themselves. Kind of saves us the trouble . . ."

Tag allowed Devin's information to sink in. "This is the time to strike back when things are in the crapper for our Vicalla friends, and the mission to get this technology to the scientists is more important than ever. We need to take advantage as soon as possible while the enemy is still in disarray. If they reinforce from off-planet, the opportunity may be gone."

"I hear you . . ."

"Perhaps, we need to accelerate our timetable and

instigate contact with the locals."

"Agreed."

"Okay—let's discuss a plan of action."

Reese and Logan listened to the two young men and, as a former military man, Reese was impressed by their quick analysis and can-do attitude. Obviously, the four Travelers had been around the block a few times.

## Chapter Twenty-eight

Prac was reporting to the Commander when the soldier Devin sent arrived to provide his update. Once the night patrol leader had his orders and departed, Cletus noticed the male fighter standing, waiting his turn. Giving a hand motion to come forward, he waited for the man to stand in front of him.

"What's up?"

"Devin sent me to report, Sir..."

"Roger that—how's he doing?"

"Well, he found the female..."

Cletus smiled. "Good for him! Nirva will be delighted to hear—she was rooting for him."

"He asked if you need him to come back..."

"Good Lord, why? He just found what he was searching for."

"Sir, I must say he was real happy to see her."

The Commander laughed. "I bet he was!"

"He didn't spell it out, but, I think he feels he has a commitment to you."

"Well, you can return to tell him there are no strings attached. He did an excellent job for us, and we welcome him and his friends any time. Speaking of which, did you meet them?"

"No, Sir. I was ordered to report to you before he linked up with the rest of them. I just saw the girl . . ."

"What's she like? Nirva sure as hell is going to ask, and I better have the answer."

"Well, I didn't get to meet her—I just saw her from ten yards away, standing on the bank above us. She's short, powerfully built, wavy blonde-brown hair, and kind of sassy."

"How did you come to that conclusion if you never met her?"

The man chuckled. "Sir, it was her attitude toward Devin—obviously, she's fond of him, but it were as though she were telling him to get his butt up the bank to see her, without her actually saying as much."

"I see—and, did he?"

"Yes, Sir. It was amusing to watch . . ."

Cletus chuckled at the mental image. "Okay—why don't you head back to tell him he's free to do whatever he wants. He provided good and valuable service to us while he was here—and, any volunteers who wish to remain with him are welcome to do so. If not, head back to us. The column will be moving south for another hour or two, then we'll camp for the night. If Devin and his friends need further assistance, come back to let me know."

"Yes, Sir . . ."

\*\*\*\*

The moving column was only a short distance away, so it took the man only twenty minutes to find Devin. He did note for the last fifty yards there were several weapons pointed in his direction, some of which were aimed by other volunteers who accompanied his leader. Once they recognized him, they lowered their weapons, and he approached the small camp.

"Well?" Devin waved to the soldier to join him.

"The Commander was happy you found what you were looking for . . ." The man briefly shifted his gaze to Claire sitting beside Devin, and she offered a quick smile. "Commander Cletus says you're clear—if you and your friends need anything, just let him know."

"That's gracious of him—I guess you and the rest of the volunteers should be heading back to join him . . ."

"Well—there's the thing. The Commander left it up to each of us—he figures you were a big help to him, so if any of us want to stick around and pitch in if you need it, then it's okay with him."

That was a surprise! Devin glanced at Tag, whose shrug indicated it was up to Devin.

"I'm embarrassed to admit I don't know your name," Devin confessed. "Sorry—but, you weren't on any of my usual night patrols."

"That's alright, Sir. There's no reason you should know me. I was walking by when you called for volunteers and I heard good things about you—so, I figured what the hell? Why not? I might as well give it a go. The name is Bodine . . ."

"First or last?"

"Last, Sir. My given name is Ebenezer . . ."

Devin smiled. "So, you and everyone else prefer to keep it strictly Bodine . . ."

"Pretty much, Sir."

"Okay, Bodine—what do you want to do?"

"If it's alright, I figure I'll hang out with you, Sir."

"Well, that's okay with me on the condition you stop calling me 'Sir'—my name is Devin."

After a brief pause, Bodine nodded. "Yes . . . Devin."

Devin glanced around the campsite. "Okay—I guess it's time for the rest of you to decide what you want to do. It's perfectly fine if you want to head back to the main column—there's certainly strength in numbers, which counts for a lot, especially these days."

No one made a move to leave.

"If you're joining up with Commander Cletus," Devin prodded, "you should probably head out now before it gets dark..."

Again, no one moved, each looking at Devin with a nod or a smile.

"Well, I guess we're in this together! Tag and I have important business in this location, so we'll probably need the help. So--thanks for staying..."

Claire leaned over to Rose. "'Devin's Devil Squad' is born," she whispered.

****

Taking the most direct route, they moved toward Commander Talak's headquarters. On the way, Beal and Zarn maintained an uneasy peace between them, spending time discussing the most effective method of convincing Talak to provide protection and support for them. It boiled down to what was in it for the Southern Regional Commander.

They decided to tell him the survival of his position

and command depended on counteracting the spread of the human slave revolt into his territory before it got out of hand. If he ignored it, his fate would be the same as Beal's command.

Hours later, they arrived at Southern Regional Command's HQ, which included what was formerly the Southwestern United States on their version of Earth.

The guards were skeptical about admitting them given the damaged condition of their vehicle, but one of the gatekeepers recognized Zarn, and let them in. Once they pulled to a stop inside the compound and cut the engine, it gave a groan as if appreciating not making it go any further.

The officer in charge motioned for them to exit their vehicle.

Beal protested from the front seat. "As though I need this lackey to tell me when I have to get out of my own vehicle . . ."

"You better control your temper and mind what you say—we're striving to be accepted as guests. You'll defeat that objective by running your mouth . . ." Zarn expressed his suggestion in stern terms, hoping the arrogant Commander would heed his advice.

Mumbling expletives, Beal exited the vehicle with the rest of his Command—two troopers, a wounded Sub-Commander Vanc, and a one-eyed, ornery Merc. It occurred to him how the sorry crew must look, and the Commander realized he had nothing left to show for all the years of service in the Vicalla military.

It was a sobering experience.

The officer in charge of the gate crew took note

of the epaulettes on the Commander's shoulders, not concealing his surprise.

Beal cringed at their pitying gazes.

Zarn took in the scene and smiled. *It's about time you were humbled, Commander . . .*

"What are you doing here?" The officer spoke directly to Beal.

"We came to see Commander Talak—to warn him." Beal kept eye contact with the officer to make sure he knew they were serious about the request.

"I see. I'll have to ask if the Commander is available—it may be some time . . ."

Beal grunted. "It better not be if he wants to keep all of this . . ."

Zarn winced at the lack of diplomacy, however true the statement might be. Talak better wake up to the fact a wave of human rebellion was at his doorstep.

\*\*\*\*

She decided to stay with the small group rather than follow the parade of humans moving down the trail. There were more people passing in front of her in the last ten minutes than she had seen in the last eight years since the conquest.

When she took on the role of Observer, it meant staying in a remote area of the jungle hidden from the invading Vicalla—the rest of humanity, too, except for a security detachment and the protected group. She hoped it was a sacrifice for a worthy cause. Eight years, and nothing happened to justify the sacrifice of seclusion. Although, the alternative was to be in the general population as a slave. Pre-conquest, Breeze had a husband and son—both died in the invasion, as did millions of others.

The first few years following that event were incredibly difficult for her—pain was daily, its edges starting to dull with time. Lately, Breeze fostered a dim hope of, one day, starting another family—she was still young enough. Unfortunately, the pool of likely candidates was small and unappealing to her, rendering her hope nothing more than a dream.

Lack of movement caught her attention, and she refocused on the scene in front of her. The last of the human column passed down the trail and was out of sight, leaving her with the task of monitoring the small group camped in the same location for the past three days.

Obviously, the small sub-group decided to forgo traveling with the human column. If they stayed put for any length of time, it would hamper the already restricted lives of those she and her companions protected.

She watched, trying to figure out how she could learn more about them—perhaps, drawing nearer would allow her to overhear their conversations, possibly learning why they were there. The Protector always wanted maximum information in such circumstances, especially when the security system's integrity was at risk.

Breeze spent the better part of an hour carefully making her way within earshot of the small campsite occupied by eleven individuals. They were actively working on expanding their living area to accommodate the addition of the six latest arrivals and, from her perch to the southwest of the camp, she had a good view as well as an easy time hearing the conversation in progress.

The youngest male in the group seated at the fire was addressing the group. "Since Beal's former territory is in total chaos from the Lizards' perspective, one might assume they have to be calling in reinforcements from other planet regions, off-planet sources, or both. If that happens, current progress may be suddenly reversed—the last thing humans want is to go back to the way things were. And, other considerations are acts of human reprisals—from what I've seen since we arrived on this version of Earth, these planet conquerors are big on having their own way. Now? Their grip is loosened and, if they tighten it again, they'll make someone pay. That's the human component of the equation."

A lean, tall, older man nodded. "I agree with your assessment. The local planet authority will try to keep a lid on it by having forces on hand deal with the current human problem. However, at a certain point, the rebellion's successes will work against us when the Vicalla realize they lost control—that will force them to bring in off-planet help. If they reinvade, we can't stand up to them unless we solve their Wave tech advantage. Cancel that out, and it levels the playing field. A lot . . ."

Two things startled Breeze—one, the revelation by the younger man's reference to his arrival on 'this version of Earth'. What did that mean? Was it, in fact, a true statement he came from another Earth somewhere? Two, the older man mentioned overcoming the Vicalla's Wave tech advantage. Overhearing bits and pieces of information from the scientists throughout the years, she knew they worked on the same problem at the time of the invasion. Somehow, however, the research stalled due to a lack of working weapons at their disposal for study.

She could see captured Vicalla weapons openly in view. If they were functional, the science group would certainly want to get their hands on them.

Breeze instantly decided the Protector needed to hear about the developments immediately. She carefully withdrew from her overwatch position and, when far enough away, she hurried to report her findings.

****

"Did the Watcher hear enough," Reese asked.

Tag nodded. "Yep—we definitely piqued interest."

Logan was a little doubtful. "How can you be sure anyone was there?"

"You can never be sure about these things until you see for yourself, but I sensed someone listening.

Hopefully, they understood the implications of what we were saying. Better yet, they'll report our conversation to someone in authority." Tag paused, thinking about their ultimate mission. "That's our best scenario."

****

They called a halt before dusk—with the amount of people to manage, everything took longer to accomplish. Campfires were being lit, and the prospect of a cooked meal was attractive to most—eating on the fly as they traversed the trail limited their culinary choices.

Cletus looked for Nirva once he finished issuing orders for Prac's night patrol. It came to him as he walked through the extended camp—he missed Devin. He didn't realize how much he looked forward to talking with the young man who was bright, experienced, and not afraid to make suggestions. *Refreshing*, he thought as he spied Nirva.

He watched as she helped set up a campsite and fire for a large family of ten, instructing three of the younger children to do simple chores which made the family more efficient in housekeeping. It struck him she would be a fantastic mother—and he wanted to be a fantastic father. It was an urge he never experienced before, and he could feel its becoming an imperative.

Nirva looked up, noticing him. "What's up," she asked as he crossed to her.

He leaned back and studied her face before answering. "I'd like to make you my wife, if you'll have me . . ."

She laughed. "Of course! It'll be an honor to be your wife!"

"Kids?"

"I always wanted to have children, but not as a slave—it's not fair to bring them into that misery. Now, we're free, and we can make our own decisions about where our lives are going . . ."

He held her tightly for a long time, relishing her answers.

## Chapter Twenty-Nine

"Excuse me?" A tone of incredulity hung in the air. "You must have misheard . . ." The Protector had a hard time believing the Observer's report—how could it be?

Slightly annoyed, she tamped down her anger, approaching the subject again. "No, Protector—I was close enough to see body language and hear the speakers' tone. They were serious . . ." Breeze didn't know whether voicing a suspicion she harbored would be counterproductive, but, suddenly, she decided it might lend credibility to what she overheard. "The younger one had an air of authority about him, as though he might be the leader, and I had the distinct feeling he knew I was close by. In a way, he directed his comments to me . . ."

"Your approach was careless?"

"Not at all—I used all of my stealth techniques. Still, he seemed to sense my being there."

The Protector thought for a moment. "They have Vicalla Wave tech weaponry?"

"Yes—I saw three."

"Working weapons?"

"I'm not sure because I didn't see them in use. However, why would they carry Vicalla weapons if they were completely expended and useless to them?"

After considering the information for a few seconds, the Protector nodded. "You're right—we need to get our hands on at least one of them . . ."

The room contained eight people involved with the security of their small community, and the Protector directed his next comment to them. "Perhaps, a night action—we can slip in to liberate what we need while avoiding conflict . . ." Several nodded their heads in agreement.

But, Breeze wasn't convinced by the Protector's proposal. His idea troubled her for some reason, and it seemed the wrong thing to do. "With respect, Sir, this is the opposite of what we should be doing . . ."

He gave her a hard stare, not entirely thrilled with her open disagreement in front of the others. Her candid comments were usually voiced in a private meeting between the two of them. "Explain . . ."

Ignoring others in the room, she focused solely on the Protector. "Nothing is certain—however, I get the impression the group, at least the five who originally set up camp here, have been waiting for us to reveal ourselves. I firmly believe they'll be our friends, and we'll work toward a common goal."

"That's a huge risk for us to take on the whim of your feelings . . ."

She offered a slight smile. "These are changing times according to slave revolt rumors—perhaps, this is the exact situation we've been waiting for since the occupation eight years ago." Breeze paused. "Protector—if not now, when?"

He pondered her question—what she suggested was contrary to all of their efforts to keep their small community safe. Finally, however, he swallowed hard with a nod of agreement.

It was time to take a risk.

\*\*\*\*

Just as arrogant as his counterpart sitting across the desk from him, he couldn't help smirking about the depths to which the other had fallen. By nature, the Vicalla were egotistical and tiresome, but those who rose to positions of authority magnified the characteristics. "So," he began, "you managed to lose your territory as well as the bulk of your command?"

"That's correct—things did not go well, at all. The same could happen here, and soon."

Talak couldn't refrain from a smirk and haughty laugh. "I think not."

It was Beal's turn to smirk. "You know nothing of what's coming your way. We passed a large body of armed humans on a parallel trail—and, guess what? They're aimed right at the north end of your territory—and, if they kept moving from the last time we spotted them, they should be well into your region. Even now, some of your forces may be coming into contact with them."

Talak didn't respond immediately, but the sudden look of concern on his face illustrated the impact of Beal's words.

"They shredded Vicalla squads and Merc teams sent to oppose them," Beal continued. "They have growing numbers, and appear to be well led—survivors report well-placed ambushes and excellent field tactics." He paused, making sure he made the most of his next words. "You should be worried, Talak . . ."

The Commander of the Southern Regional District couldn't help squirming in his chair.

Delighting in the obvious discomfort of the other Commander, Beal inserted the knife, and twisted. "Oh, by the way—the humans have possession of fully functional Wave tech weapons. I witnessed some of my own troopers' remains dripping from tree branches—not an attractive sight."

If Lizard physiology would have allowed them to turn pale, Talak's complexion should have been chalk white. Instead, he visibly flinched in his chair. "Humans with Wave tech?" His voice wavered in a slightly higher pitch than normal.

"A nasty thought, isn't it?"

"How?"

Beal admitted, "Obviously, the human animal hasn't quite learned to stay conquered, yet."

\*\*\*\*

At first light, most of them gathered around the revived campfire. Two volunteers, Bodine and the woman, were scouting the perimeter, one in each direction, and it was the woman, Drey, who made first contact. She was moving carefully through the thick underbrush when an unknown female stepped out from behind cover in front of her. Drey's immediate reaction was to bring her rifle to bear on the potential target.

The woman held her hands out, palms up, indicating she held no weapon.

Drey nodded. "Good—let's keep it that way. Who are you?"

"My name is Breeze—I live here."

"Alone?"

"No, there are others . . ."

"You purposely revealed yourself when you could have stayed hidden in thick brush—I would have gone by without seeing you. Why?"

"We needed to meet."

"Why?"

"You ask a lot of questions . . ."

"Yeah—I do. It comes from being naturally curious."

Breeze smiled at the woman standing in front of her. "I would like to address all of you, if possible."

Drey sized her up and liked what she saw—a tall, thirty-something, dark-haired woman who had a natural commanding presence. "Follow me . . ."

When everyone collected around the campfire, Breeze addressed Reese because he was the senior man in the group, but he deferred to Tag. "It's his show, so talk to the man."

As she previously suspected when spying on the group, the youngest male of the group was the leader. Close up, he appeared even younger than she expected, although, from the look on his face, he'd seen his share of action. "My name is Breeze—I spied on you earlier." She paused, and smiled. "But, you knew that . . ."

Tag nodded.

"There's a small community of people who reside here," she advised, "and I think you may have a common interest with some of them." Using the oblique reference, she didn't give much away.

He smiled. "My name is Tag—we definitely have an interest in your scientists..."

Breeze still approached the subject carefully. "Your people have Wave tech weaponry. Are they functional?"

"Of course—many Lizards learned that lesson, much to their detriment."

She paused for a moment, thinking. "We have those who will relish the opportunity to study what you possess. Will you permit it?"

He chuckled at her request. "Absolutely! It's why we came so far to find you! We need your scientists to finish figuring out how to defeat the Lizards, so we can kick their asses, and get them off your planet!"

\*\*\*\*

"So, how many people are we having at this shindig?"

Jackie toiled over a guest list during the past week, his advice only occasionally requested. As he watched her frustration in figuring out the details of their wedding, Kyle suddenly saw the raw appeal of elopement.

"I think no more than thirty," she commented. "Close friends and family mostly..."

Yep—eloping sounded pretty good.

****

The Prime thought for several minutes before answering. "I agree—a serious level of action has to be taken to counter this trend."

"I have your permission to cross Regional Boundaries?"

"You may take whatever action, wherever, required to fix this mess . . ."

"The plan is to hit them hard with almost the full compliment of my force."

"Prudent—but, Talak, I have a suggestion . . ."

"Yes, Prime?"

"Please coordinate your efforts with your eastern counterpart by joining in the attack from multiple directions. You should be able to catch the main body of the enemy in a vise, squeezing them until they break apart."

"Excellent suggestion—however, I must be in control of the action since it's my idea."

"There's plenty of glory to go around when you defeat them, but I'll advise Grel you're in overall, nominal command. You won't be popular, so tread lightly—you know what she's like if her tail gets in a knot."

A barking laugh from Talak terminated the conversation, and he got what he wanted. Now he could attend to the upstart humans who dared to think they would, once again, be free . . .

****

They arranged the meeting in the open, a safe distance from their secret living quarters. The new arrivals may profess to be in concert with efforts to sort out the Wave tech problem, but the Protector rightly pointed out they didn't know them well enough to trust yet—no sense in revealing everything.

Breeze, the Protector, and ten armed fighters fleshed out their security detail for the encounter, giving them twelve, armed individuals to counter anything the visitors could dish out. By midafternoon on a hot day, they only had to wait a few minutes before the other group arrived right on time, emerging from jungle cover.

"The young one in the middle," Breeze told the Protector, "is the leader. Don't take his youth lightly—he's bright, and misses nothing."

Nodding, the Protector took her point and focused his attention on their leader.

When the visitors were within a few yards, they halted. Each group eyeballed the other, the leaders ignoring everyone but each other.

Tag smiled and stepped forward, hand extended. "I'm Tag Townsend, Sir. I'm very pleased to have found you—we came a long way."

The Protector found himself automatically grasping the other in a handshake, matching the smile of his counterpart.

"You're welcome here—I understand we possess a common interest . . ."

"Yes, very much so. We bring you several operational Vicalla Wave tech weapons. Our hope is your scientists can solve their mysteries, so we can cancel the advantage they give our common enemy. Then, it's time to kick them off your planet . . ."

The Protector favored him with a broad smile. "A noble quest, and an excellent idea! Tell me, please—where are you from? Is there news from the outside world? You're clearly a smart man—as you may have already guessed, we're very secluded here . . ."

"Yes, Sir, it'll be my pleasure . . ."

"Terrific! And, Tag—can the 'Sir' bit. We're equals—my name is Aaron."

\*\*\*\*

Cletus stood on the low ridge, scanning the magnificent valley below, determining it was long enough to house the large group of people he now commanded. It provided some exposure to the south and east, and the other two directions were protected by steep cliffs—if forces were deployed properly, the area was defensible.

*This has to be it,* he thought as he surveyed the land. They traveled far enough to deserve the luck of finding such a place for their use as a new home, as well as a base of operations for engagements against the Vicalla.

He turned to Morris, standing at his side. "Well—what do you think?"

"It looks good to me, Sir—good ground, and a nice stream flowing through the bottom for a ready water source. If this is it, I'd set up on the north side and layer defensive belts spreading south and east . . ."

Cletus nodded. "Of course, you understand the flip side of this arrangement?"

"Sir, what makes it good for defensive purposes also makes it a trap with no exit—especially if the perimeter is breached . . ."

"Exactly—so, the trick is not to be found. And, if we're discovered, fight like hell to keep them out."

"Your orders, Sir?"

"Pass the word—we're home."

## Chapter Thirty

Two days later the offensive started, and the Vicalla struck back with a vengeance—anyone in the way perished unless they could successfully disappear before the onslaught caught them in a classic pincer move. Armored vehicles and airships swept aside all opposition as several medium sized human fighting groups made their stand and inflicted punishment—they quickly died where they fought.

There was no doubt—it was interspecies genocide, and the last one standing won.

An important element to their success was intelligence regarding where the human opposition congregated. Find them, surround their position, and crush them was the mantra of the Vicalla offensive—once they rolled over the opposition, secondary forces mopped up what was left.

The Vicalla were invincible.

\*\*\*\*

It happened by accident. A scout airship turned on the wrong vector and, before correcting the error, it flew over Cletus's new home. Hundreds of human workers were preparing defensive positions, and many were out in the open—of course, an eagle-eyed spotter noticed, and made a full report.

Several scouts ran to the Commander to report, but, as it turned out, Cletus noticed the Vicalla airship, watching it turn to make a lower pass over their new valley home. He called for Morris, who appeared in a matter of minutes from supervising defensive installations on the other side of the narrow valley. "Did you hear," Cletus asked.

"Yes, Sir. What do we do?"

Cletus rubbed his chin. Earlier in the day, they heard Vicalla offensive activities were chewing up everything in their path. "We chose this ground to live in and defend, if necessary—unfortunately, it appears conflict has come a little earlier than we hoped. I don't see a reason to change anything—I think we should try to break them here. They're defeating separate human groups, rolling them up one at a time." He thought for a moment. "It may take their land forces some time to get here, so we should put out the word, and spread our scouts further out to collect all fighters who want to make a stand with us . . ."

"I hear you, Sir—but reports indicate two, sizable, well-equipped Vicalla forces working together in the field. That's a tough nut to crack."

Cletus nodded. "Of course, you're correct—nonetheless, we need to be the rock their wave crashes on, breaking them apart. We can defeat them if we can draw them in on our terms. You know—sucker them by teasing the beast . . ."

"It's a big risk."

"A huge risk—if we fight them in the open, they'll roll over us. Fighting on home ground of our choosing from preset defensive positions helps balance the odds."

"Yes, Sir—but, speaking of balance, they'll have a hell of a lot more Wave tech weapons than we will. Then there's the defensive side of it, of which we have none . . ."

Cletus grimaced. "Morris—you wanted it to be a challenge didn't you?"

"Well, not quite that much, Sir . . ."

"Okay—let's get the word out they're coming, and we need to get as ready as we can before it hits the fan. We probably have two—maybe three—days, tops, before they arrive. Anyone who doesn't want to be part of this better clear out pronto . . ."

\*\*\*\*

It was three days. Midafternoon.

Lead elements of the eastern Vicalla force stumbled upon the furthest-out contingent of Force Cletus—which his fighters unanimously dubbed themselves—and human scouts ranged in front of their outermost defensive positions. The engagement was small, but brutal—savagery on both sides was at its most elemental.

By design—after giving the approaching enemy enough of a bloody nose—the surviving human scouts passed through their outer lines, taking a breather. Their initial part of the plan was done.

The Vicalla drew confidence from the remaining humans receding into the jungle in apparent retreat. The Sub-Commander in charge of the point element ordered an immediate pursuit to clean up the survivors.

A poor decision.

As the Vicalla encountered the first of the outer defensive positions, their roll forward came to an abrupt halt when the humans let loose with everything they had, including captured Wave tech heavy weapons—not good for the Vicalla. The few survivors retreated out of range, reporting in the heavy resistance.

Then—a substantial pause. Force Cletus brought up fresh fighters, rotating back one layer in the defensive ring of individuals who just saw action. For that, there were several reasons—Cletus wanted as many fighters to be 'blooded' in action as soon as possible. Plus, he was trying to avoid individuals' being quickly traumatized by the brutality of the action. Those dropping back already experienced action, and knew what to expect when the Vicalla pushed through each defensive belt—something they would do early in the battle.

On the Lizards' side of things, the unexpected, sharp resistance stopped their lead elements in their tracks. Further back, heavier units needed time to come up and deploy into attack formations, supported by available airpower. Even so, a huge edge went to the Vicalla who could reconnoiter or attack from the air, at will, unopposed.

The early action occurred on the eastern side of their perimeter. Cletus was careful not to shift fighters to the currently threatened side which would leave his western flank too weak. The approach of the other Vicalla force would likely be from the west—but, the actual attack would have to come from the southern, open end of the valley. Certainly, Vicalla elements could set up on the edge of the western cliffs, taking potshots at the humans in the valley. However, they'd be hampered by the dense cover of jungle—it would be tough to spot a target.

Cletus ordered scouts to range out, looking for Vicalla coming in from the west, splitting the attention of the defenders. It was something he would certainly do if the situation were reversed. The pause in the action allowed his people to catch their breath, also affording still-struggling individuals to finish off the last of inner defensive positions—they needed time to complete as much work as possible before intense action descended upon them.

\*\*\*\*

For several days, the scientists immersed themselves, studying the inner workings and theory of the Wave tech weapons provided by Tag's group. Three working models were donated for the cause—two were lighter hand weapons, one was a heavier rifle.

Word arrived progress was being made, albeit slowly. Several scientists worked on the specific problem eight years ago at the time of the conquest by the Vicalla—luckily, they managed to escape with their research records intact. In other words, they picked up where they left off.

Reports of the impending Vicalla offensive coming their way filtered through and, two days prior, a scout from Force Cletus communicated to several of Tag's volunteers about what was going on. When they reported in, he called a meeting with everyone, including Devin's crew, as well as the security elements of the Protector's team.

Aaron was first to get things going. "The whereabouts of our home base with the scientific contingent must remain hidden. We can't take any risks . . ."

Tag agreed, but he felt he needed to add to Aaron's thought. "I get that—however, the important thing is to break the secrets of the Vicalla Wave tech advantage, so those fighting and dying have a better chance of success. There's nothing more important to your planet right now." Tag paused, eyeing everyone in the meeting. "I agree they must be protected at all costs for their contribution to a higher purpose. However, if they're going to crack those secrets, we need it now—there's no time for leisurely, scientific protocols and study. This is a life and death fight for humans on this planet, and the opportunity to take advantage of the Vicalla's being off-balance may not come again. Now is the time—those you protect must understand this completely."

"We'll make certain they do . . ."

****

There were five scientists in all—three men, and two women. Work continued around the clock and, as one team member stepped aside, exhausted, the others stayed at it, tackling problems with working models they could reverse engineer.

In the late morning of the third day, the lead scientist found Aaron who was speaking with Tag. Both men looked up when she walked in, the weariness of non-stop work etched on her face.

"Can we get you anything, Doctor? Please sit down before you fall down . . ." Aaron pulled out a chair from their table.

Miriam sat. "Thank you. Well—we did it! We cracked the Vicalla technology. In the end, it proved unique, but not all that complex. My team is almost ready to test a prototype device to neutralize their Wave tech weapons. Of course, ours is rudimentary since time is of the essence—however, it should work effectively. If it's successful, we can build simple, hand-carried devices quickly, but we'll need the help of your security people for assembly under supervision of our staff."

"Don't forget, Doctor," Tag added, "you have our people, too. Just tell us how we can help, and we'll do it. Claire is exceedingly bright, so it might be effective if you give her a crash course on what to do—then you'll have another supervisor. Do you have sufficient materials to produce enough devices?"

"I think so—we have quite a supply in the storehouse that should work. When it was near the end for us at the time of the conquest, the planners of this complex had the foresight to scavenge potentially useful material to stockpile. It's the manpower and the time crunch to get the components together that present the challenge." The doctor hesitated for a moment. " I understand there's fighting going on now—true?"

"Yes—the Vicalla began a major offensive to crush us before the rebellion spreads to more of their territories. The situation will become dire soon. Your breakthrough must be put into the hands of as many humans as possible, while there's still time to make a difference . . ."

"If this works," Aaron asked, "how long will it take to assemble each device?"

She paused to consider the question. "If a suitably-trained individual knows what to do, and we divide the work into specialized areas of assembly so each person does only one thing, I think total assembly time would be about half an hour per unit. With enough people involved, ten units hourly isn't an unrealistic target—a lot of what we'll use will be preassembled components put together for different intended purposes. We just need to configure them into what we need, and tweak them a bit . . ."

"What kind of range will they have?" Tag needed to know if it were possible to cancel out the enemy's Wave tech weapons from a distance.

"These should work within a half-mile radius. But, keep in mind they'll neutralize your captured Vicalla weapons, too."

Tag nodded. "I think that's okay—it'll affect them considerably more than us. What about their defensive Wave tech hand-held battle shields? And, the protective shields on their vehicles and airships?"

"There's no reason to assume our devices won't be useful to neutralize those enhancements, as well. As long as they're in range, the Vicalla won't have an advantage."

"Actually, the advantage shifts to us—most of their weaponry is predicated on the Wave tech model. Remove that in effective fighting range, and all they have left is using their guns as clubs, as well as other non-Wave tech weapons such as bladed devices . . ."

Aaron nodded and agreed. "This has huge potential—the limiting factor is producing enough devices in time."

"And," Tag commented, "we need to get them into the hands of the fighting groups quickly, before they're overwhelmed by the Vicalla juggernaut. Don't forget that problem . . ."

The meeting ended with the doctor's returning to the lab to oversee the test, as well as coordinate with the other scientists in setting up the assembly process.

Aaron stood. "I'll advise my people and get them ready."

Tag nodded. "Let's hope this works . . ."

\*\*\*\*

Tag gathered everyone together. "Okay—the good news first. The scientists solved the Wave tech system, and have a prototype device to cancel it out. If it works, we need to put a production team together—Claire, will you find the lead scientist, Miriam, and get a crash course in what she needs? You'll be instructing the rest of us later . . ."

Claire was up and moving to the complex as soon as he asked his request.

"Rose—organize everyone but three volunteers into production teams, and get them to the complex in the next half an hour. I need three volunteers to go out and find wherever Cletus and his group ended up—they need to get word of what we're putting together. Then, it's a question of getting the devices to them. Have him send back ten individuals with you—they can learn how the new devices work, and transport them back for use in the field. And, whoever goes out, if you find other human groups, let them know what's going on. Any excess devices we have, they can use . . ."

Bodine and two others were already on their feet, receiving a nod of acknowledgment from Tag.

The scout team was selected.

"Wouldn't Logan and I be better suited to find Cletus," Reese asked.

Tag nodded. "Probably, but we don't have time for introductions and a getting-to-know-you process. Cletus knows these people, and they'll be immediately accepted, no questions asked."

"Sounds reasonable . . ."

"What you and Logan can be invaluable doing," Tag continued, "is to find where the Vicalla are, and if they're headed this way. If they are, distract and divert them elsewhere . . ."

Reese smiled. "Now you're talkin'!" He glanced at Logan, receiving a thumbs up about the coming mission.

Tag made the first move. "Okay, people—let's get moving. We have a lot to do, and little time in which to get it done."

# Chapter Thirty-one

"First reports are encouraging, Prime..." There was always an amount of trepidation when reporting to the supreme authority whether it were good news, or bad.

"Continue..."

"Commanders Talak and Grel advanced, sweeping all human groups aside, and their resistance seems to be faltering. Now, we have reports of humans streaming away from the battle sites as well as the advancing vectors."

Silent for a few ticks, he looked directly at the captain standing before him. "Have the Commanders encountered large, human fighting units yet?"

"No, Sir."

"Well, when they do, that will be the true test of whether they can crush this rebellion."

Another officer hovered at the doorway.

The captain motioned him in, extending his hand for the written communication the officer held. Scanning its contents, his eyebrows failed to conceal his surprise.

The Prime noticed. "What is it?"

"Sir—this is a preliminary report from Commander Grel's force. They encountered a heavy concentration of entrenched human fighters, and have been thrown back. The Commander is assembling heavy elements supporting land vehicles, as well as airships to coordinate a massive push."

"Did Commander Talak engage them from the other direction?"

"Apparently, his force isn't up yet—it'll take another half a day before he can commit . . ."

The Prime stood, thinking. If this were indeed the large human group they heard about, now was the time to commit all resources to breaking it. If their biggest unit were vanquished, the rest of the human fighting troops should lose heart. "'Should' being the operative word . . .

"Contact Commander Talak," the Prime ordered, "and order him to engage quickly from the west. Also, get me Commander Quarn—he just returned, and I want the balance of the Planetary Reserve Force airships on the way to the battle site within the next hour . . ."

"Of course, Sir—it will be done."

After the captain left to fulfill his orders, the Prime turned back to his window. *The oncoming collision,* he thought, *will be the high tide of the rebellion.*

*It's time to finish this . . .*

\*\*\*\*

'Intense pressure' described it pretty well.

Kirv was on the current frontline which, two hours ago, was a defensive belt behind the units locked in combat. That line disintegrated under the Vicalla onslaught, although superior numbers weren't the deciding factors—rather, the quantity and quality of the weapons the Vicalla used. The Lizard groups simply blew apart defensive positions, sometimes taking human defenders with them.

Where human fighters were equipped with like weapons, they could do similar damage—unfortunately, they had too few to really make an impact. Vicalla using battle shields tended to defeat Wave tech weapons, unless they were heavy-duty. Occasional Lizards brazen enough to proceed into the open without shields were soon cut down by multiple headshots from human snipers frustrated with being otherwise ineffective.

It was the small victories keeping spirits up on the

human side.

Kirv was in the thick of it—several defensive locations to his right ceased to exist, and Vicalla ground troops supported by three vehicles were moving directly at his position. A handful of fighters attempted to halt the advance.

Next to him in a foxhole, a Sapper prepared an explosive charge, its destiny the destruction of one or more approaching vehicles. Humans wielded Vicalla weapons, yet they were hard-pressed to make a dent in the Lizards' Wave tech armor. Still, they hoped the vehicle would pass over the charge, its explosive force taking out the underbelly, immobilizing it.

A woman looked up at Kirv and nodded, indicating the device was ready to go.

"Okay—when the Lizard vehicle on the left goes around the small grove of trees, they'll be out of sight for a minute. Dart out and plant your charge where you think they'll appear, and get your ass back here. I'll lay down suppressing fire on the infantry to the right." Kirv paused, as if he forgot something. "Just out of interest—how do you detonate that thing?"

She held up a hand-held remote trigger.

Both refocused on the front. The moment the vehicle swerved to avoid the trees, the woman sprinted toward the target zone while Kirv fired to the right, drawing the attention of the four Vicalla troopers. Using short bursts to conserve ammunition, he kept peeking to the left to track her progress. She made it to the trees, and dug rapidly with her small shovel, creating a shallow indentation for the charge—the last thing they wanted was to have it sticking up above ground! However, on her way back, a Vicalla spotted her and opened fire—the first shot landed next to her, blowing her leg to smithereens.

She lay in the short ferns growing close to the ground.

When he saw she wasn't moving, Kirv half stood up and yelled over the cracks of gunfire and Wave tech weapons to the troopers next to him. "Cover me! I'm going for the trigger!"

Not waiting for an answer, he ran as fast as he could in a crouched position. When he got to her, he could see the trigger device still clutched in her hand and, from the look of it, she wouldn't be using it anytime soon.

He didn't even know her name.

Kirv pried the trigger from her hand, then started his sprint to the foxhole when the Vicalla vehicle appeared from behind the trees. Just as he hit the ground, Vicalla fire zoomed over his head!

He lay there, waiting. It seemed two things could happen—one, the Lizard vehicle would drive over the charge. Two—he could be wiped out by a Vicalla weapon. Luckily, it was the former—when he saw it drive right over the hole, he squeezed the trigger and, a moment later, the Vicalla vehicle disappeared in a mixed cloud of dirt, smoke, and flames.

Kirv wasted no time getting back to cover, and it was a good thing, too--an enemy shot blew up the side of his position. He lay stunned and covered in dirt—vaguely, he heard crashes of explosions and weapons' discharges before passing out.

****

Back at the center of the defensive rings, Commander Cletus directed the battle as best he could. Reports came in from the eastern vector they were being pressed backward, but, there was a cost to the Vicalla advance. The enemy swept aside the skirmishers, penetrating the first two outer defensive layers—to be expected, really, considering the powerful Vicalla force. The good news was the continued strong resistance by his people—his force, thankfully, didn't collapse, and they were paying out ground at a desirable rate. They would either wear down the Vicalla—who might give up before they reached the center—or, he would run out of fighters left to defend their camp.

Most worrisome was the Vicalla's appearing from the west—but, if he could deal with the Vicalla on the east side and defeat them, they may have a chance. However, if the other Vicalla force engaged soon, they would be stretched too thin to defend in depth.

Again, timing was everything.

****

Bodine stood on a hill two ridgelines over from the action. From his higher position, he observed the battle action for ten minutes, although jungle cover interfered with part of his view. But, from what he could see, it was apparent the defenders on the eastern side of the human defensive perimeter were getting the shit kicked out of them.

Suddenly, something in the far distance caught his attention. He could see over the top of the valley system Cletus occupied—from the west, vehicles were advancing his way.

The second Vicalla force was on-scene.

Bodine realized he wouldn't be able to get past the battle lines to see Cletus, advise him of the situation, and bring out individuals to transport back the Wave tech canceling devices. Even though they were sorely needed, that plan was in the crapper, and it was obvious Cletus would need every last fighter available just to hold on.

He turned, and started running at a good distance-eating pace—he needed an hour to arrive back at camp and the science complex.

*It's gonna be close*, he thought as his feet pounded the ground. *It's gonna be close* . . .

\*\*\*\*

"Okay, people—production is lagging, and we need eight more of these things put together. I'm offering a prize to whoever gets the most done correctly in the next hour—if it doesn't work, it doesn't count..."

A tall, blond haired security man leaned over to a coworker. "I wonder what the prize will be? I know what I'd like it to be..."

The short woman at the end of the room looked up from assembling the parts in front of her, locking eyes with the fellow who just made the comment. "No, it's not what you think, Cretin—the prize is an evening of scintillating conversation with me..."

Claire was relieved to hear the group still had a sense of humor after hours of intense concentration on building the anti-Wave tech devices. The prototype worked as it should after the science team made a few tweaks, and they immediately jumped into production for as many units as they could manage within the time constraints.

Twenty-two working devices were stacked at the end of the room, and eight more would reach the target of thirty—however, that number may be unworkable since they were starting to run short of parts. The science team was currently scrambling to find what else they could substitute for the missing items.

Fifteen minutes later, Aaron came into the large production room, asking for everyone's attention. "We just learned a major battle is happening now with Cletus's group—a Vicalla force is attacking him from the east. When Bodine left the site to report here, a second enemy force was approaching from the west. It's safe to assume they're likely engaged by now. Cletus and his people are trapped in a pincer, and under severe pressure—we can't wait any longer to finish the last of the devices. Completed devices have to make it to the front lines—now."

"We almost have two more ready," Claire called out.

The Protector nodded. "Very well—you have ten minutes. Anything not done by then gets left behind. I want everyone here—excluding the science team—assembled outside at the fifteen-minute mark, and everyone carries at least one finished device as well as whatever equipment you have to arm yourselves. Where we're going is a hot zone, and we'll need to fight our way through to distribute the devices." He paused, quickly scanning everyone in the room. "Not everyone here is going to make it—some will die trying to get through. Is there anyone here who thinks the effort isn't worth it?"

Silence.

"Good. I'll meet you outside in fifteen, and then we're on our way. Tag and Devin, please organize everyone here into teams of three which can operate independently. The Vicalla can't catch us as one big group—multiple small units have a greater chance of getting through. See you up top . . ."

The Protector left the room.

Everyone remained still, considering the task.

Then, nothing but motion.

****

Unbelievably, the injured streamed back into the central part of the camp. A direct hit by a Vicalla Wave tech weapon usually guaranteed body parts would be redistributed in all directions, and people brought in were victims of nearby hits causing injury by concussive force, or flying debris.

Glade and Millie worked the infirmary—they had one doctor for the whole camp, and two people with partial nurse's training. Glade had a first-aid background, plus experience working around the farm tending to sick, injured, and pregnant farm animals—so, it was no surprise when the doctor appointed her as his go-to triage person.

The doctor and nurses were fully occupied treating the wounded, while Millie pitched in bringing supplies, fresh water, and helping the injured—it was, in fact, a field hospital.

The sounds of the battle reverberated through the valley where the camp stood. Previously, the echo of gunfire was more distant, emanating from the eastern side only. Now, it was much closer—as far as they could tell, action was on the eastern and southern perimeters.

There were at least a dozen fighters—men, women, and a few young ones in their early teens lying in wait for Glade. But, it was the seventh person in line who caused her to gasp. In front of her, Kirv lay quietly—almost peacefully, as if asleep.

Recovering quickly from the shock of seeing him, Glade knelt and checked him over—there were no apparent, superficial wounds. His breathing and heart beat were regular, so she gently slapped him on each side of the face to see if she could bring him around.

No luck.

Obviously, something happened to knock him unconscious, but he didn't seem to be in apparent distress. Relieved to discover his situation wasn't dire, she glanced up and down the line of the injured, some of whom she already checked, others still waiting for her attention. The dilemma she faced was the urge to put her husband, father of her child, at the top of the list to be treated next by the doctor—but, there were obviously more serious cases needing immediate attention. As hard as it was for her to do, Glade put her hand on his face and leaned over to kiss him. "Sorry—you'll have to wait, my love. You'd tell me to move on to the more serious if you could talk right now—hopefully, you can sleep this off, and I'll see you later. I love you . . ."

She moved on to the next person who had a broken leg and arm. But, try as she might, it was difficult to get Kirv out of her mind enough to focus completely on the injured as she moved down the line. As it happened, however, a mere ten minutes after Glade left him, Millie came down the line of wounded waiting for their turn to be treated. She was checking everyone to see if she could get them something to ease their suffering. When she saw her father lying on the ground it was, surprisingly, less of a shock to her than her mother. Millie knew her father was fighting on the front lines, and she resigned herself to the real-life fact chances were she would never see him alive again.

Maybe, all of them would perish.

Then, she recalled a time back on the farm when she had to douse her father with water when he passed out from too much moonshine—maybe it were the same thing. Millie spotted a full bucket of water she fetched from the river, leaving it for the wounded if they needed a drink.

Well—she dumped it on him.

He came to suddenly, sitting up and sputtering to clear the water from his nose. Kirv was conscious, looking at his daughter standing over him, bucket in hand.

# Chapter Thirty-two

Force Cletus was fully engaged on their eastern and southern fronts, their defensive rings penetrated and reduced to the last fully defensible perimeter. It forced shifting last reserves—which weren't many—to and from each front, joining them to form a semi-circle. If that line failed to hold, they would be facing total collapse and annihilation.

Several days prior scouts swept a wide area, collecting small groups of humans who agreed to join the larger force, increasing numbers in excess of eight hundred souls, of which six hundred and fifty could be counted on as fighters.

Cletus reviewed their current situation, and there was no disguising it—his numbers were probably down to less than two hundred. Of course, that number was an estimate—casualties were heavy, and it was difficult to determine exact numbers, especially since casualties mounted by the minute.

Cletus understood the end would be near if the Vicalla made one more determined push. His people fought valiantly, many dying horrible deaths, but, if things went south in the next hour, some might claim their passing was in vain. He never would, however, because they fought for their freedom and the right to live. On top of that, his reserve force was down to thirty fighters, almost half of which suffered injury, but they refused to step away—Cletus needed them to plug a hole in the defensive line if punched through by relentless Vicalla.

There was no doubt the humans inflicted losses on the enemy, but not enough to hold them back—the Wave tech advantage, especially on the defensive side, weighed heavily in favor of the attacking force. Human weapons and captured light Vicalla weapons couldn't effectively penetrate their protective armor, and explosives were the only way to defeat them—a problem because the humans were running woefully short of munitions.

As he struggled to find something he could do to save them, there was a huge shout to the left of the defensive ring as the Vicalla poured through a hole punched in the perilously thin line of defenders.

Cletus turned and shouted at his reserve force of fighters standing behind him.

"This is it—everyone into the breach! If we don't stop them, we're done!"

With a mighty roar they followed him, throwing themselves into the fight. Frustrated because their weapons couldn't fire through battle shields, some human fighters leapt on the Vicalla infantry soldiers, pulling down their battle shields while a teammate fired directly into the faces of the Lizard warriors. Others engaged in hand-to-hand combat with the much larger foe, trying to get close enough so the Vicalla couldn't use their Wave tech weapons.

In less than a minute, they were down to eight fighters, and Cletus. The Vicalla were falling too, but more struggled to open the plugged hole again. Cletus—the tallest human defender—could see over the action as a fresh unit of Lizard warriors moved into position directly behind the weakest part of the perimeter where the fighting was heaviest. With a sinking feeling, he knew they couldn't hold the additional pressure.

There was no one left to help.

\*\*\*\*

"Shit! Look at that mess!" With Tag and Rose, one of Aaron's security contingent looked down on the battle raging in the valley below. From his many fighting engagements during the last few months, Tag could tell at a glance the battle was almost won—not by his side.

"Okay—let's move! There's no time to observe—each of you go down the hill another fifty yards, spreading out another fifty yards from me. I'll be in the middle. Deploy your devices—however, we may already be too late."

Within the next minute, three anti-Wave tech devices pointed into the valley.

At first, the three humans on the hill couldn't see any change, a sick feeling permeating each of them as they believed their efforts failed. Slowly, however, something shifted as multiple Vicalla stopped the advance, checking their weapons and defensive systems for malfunctions. The thin line of human defenders immediately pressed the attack as they realized something was wrong with the Vicalla—they were suddenly defenseless except for non-Wave tech weapons! Lizards started to fall in mounting numbers, prompting a retreat away from the humans who charged and fired at will, mixing into the Vicalla units, striking out in all directions at anything with a tail.

\*\*\*\*

Hours later, Tag met up with Cletus—the two knew of each other, but hadn't met. "Well done, Commander," Tag praised as he shook the large man's hand. "The stand your people made was among the best I've ever seen—they should be proud."

"Thanks for the cleanup . . ."

"It was nothing compared to what happened here." He rendered a brief smile. "We were happy to help . . ."

"I heard there was a little more involved, but, thanks again—we were on the brink, and those devices saved us."

"Glad it made a difference, Sir . . ."

Cletus eyeballed Tag. "Young man, you commanded fighters in battle many times—we're brothers in arms to that extent. Please call me Cletus . . ."

"Yes, Sir, Cletus!"

Both men smiled.

"I have to tell Nirva," Cletus commented, "I still have all of my working parts—and, how everything is looking up from here. I'm sure we'll meet again . . ."

With that, Tag watched the massive man walk away amidst the destruction of battle, understanding Cletus had the chops to take back what was formerly their own.

\*\*\*\*

The junior officers rebelled against the idea, so it fell to the captain to report. He approached the open door to the large office with a mixture of curiosity and trepidation—it wasn't every day he had the opportunity to observe the highest authority figure on a planetary conquest humbled by events on his watch.

"Yes . . ."

"I have a report, Sir . . ."

A pause. "You hesitate to present it?"

The captain moved into the room. "It's an after-action report from Commander Talak . . ."

"Continue."

If the Lizard anatomy had lips, the captain would have licked them to cover his nervousness. "The report outlines the attack on the large human contingent by Commanders Talak and Grel. The battle was intense, involving a great loss of life to both sides. Talak's command was forced to retreat."

"I see—and, Commander Grel?"

A hesitation. "Commander Grel as well as virtually all of her force were eliminated—however, there are unconfirmed reports of a few scattered survivors. Her command was the most involved in the combat, and Talak's group came into action later in the battle."

"What about the human force?"

"So far, they appear to be staying put. Their losses were extremely high . . ."

"So, they don't present a threat to invade any other regions?"

"Not at the moment." The captain avoided giving the worst news—however, he had no choice. "Sir—there's a critical problem that overshadows this defeat..."

The Prime finally turned to look at the officer. "How can anything be worse?"

"The humans—somehow, they managed to design a countermeasure to our Wave tech advantage. In essence, they cancel it out..."

It took a few moments for the information to register its full effect. Apparently, what allowed a minimal Vicalla presence to control millions of humans on the conquered planet was now gone.

The Prime struggled through the tumbling thought process of what to do next, until he concentrated on something familiar. "Bring Commander Quarn to me..."

"Ahhh... Sir, the Commander did not return from the battle. None of the Reserve Force sent in came back."

That was it then—he had no Planetary Reserve Force left. There were a few headquarters guards, the officers attached to HQ, and some administrators—and, he had only eight more Regional Commanders and their contingents scattered across the planet. Their numbers couldn't be more than a few thousand, at best. Surrounded by multiple millions of humans and the Vicalla now without their best weapons, it wouldn't be long before the human rebellion spread worldwide. There wasn't anything to do about it, and the decision he delayed making now couldn't be avoided.

"Captain, contact Off-Planet Command. Send a message requesting immediate reinforcements—otherwise, this world will be lost to us." Deep in thought, he didn't register the officer's leaving him to comply with his order.

****

They sat in the headquarters commissary sharing a drink, mulling over a decidedly bad situation. Things went horribly wrong, and neither Zarn nor Beal had a definitive solution to the problem. Even though they were attempting to make the best of a dire situation, they figured it was better to work together rather than be at odds.

"Do you feel better now?"

"How so?"

"Well, the cocky Commander Talak is about to join you in losing his job."

Beal stared at the one-eyed Merc, and shrugged. "Not really—now we have to worry about the issue of when the humans will attack this headquarters—and, they certainly will."

"True. In the meantime, though, it's time to plan where to go to avoid that unpleasantness . . ."

"That's only a temporary reprieve, Zarn. It won't be long before there's nowhere left to hide—there are too many humans left alive . . ."

"Won't we bring in reinforcements, or reinvade?"

"I don't know—I heard we're spread pretty thin in this quadrant. Too many worlds were conquered, and not enough of us to manage things properly."

His statement was more than sobering, and the former Merc team leader considered the Regional Commander's comments. "So—how do we get off this shithole?"

# Chapter Thirty-three

"It's a good thing you have a thick skull." For a moment, the patient looked as if he might be offended, but it was just his slow thought processes trying to connect the dots. Once that happened, he laughed. Glade and Millie, of course, thought it was hilarious—they could laugh now because it was clear the patient dodged serious injury.

Tag smiled at Kirv. "It's really good to see you're on the mend . . ."

It was three days after the battle. The defeated Vicalla survivors vanished from the area, and the western force withdrew. The eastern contingent in the thick of battle was shattered—few made it home to their headquarters.

Now it was time to clean up the valley as best they could. Burials—mostly body parts due to Wave tech weapons—took the better part of the three days, the human toll much higher than the Lizards'. Finally, however, it was done—the following day, they could start getting the valley back into shape by removing downed trees, cleaning up debris, and filling in shell holes. Thankfully, the fighting never reached the inner core of their camp, so shelters and the supply train weren't touched.

But, even in the midst of such destruction, they discovered something quite interesting—while salvaging the Wave tech weapons as well as turned off canceling devices, it turned out exposed Vicalla weapons were permanently affected. Something in the canceling wave fried the components, rendering them useless. The unexpected effect was a huge advantage to the human side—something Cletus should know, Tag figured. So, he set off, finally locating the giant man walking with Nirva at the riverbank—a peaceful scene after their hard-fought victory.

Cletus suddenly realized Tag and Nirva hadn't met. "Tag, I'd like you to meet Nirva—we're engaged to be married!"

"That's great news! Congratulations!" Tag grinned at both of them. "We need good things to start happening for all of you!"

"Agreed—but we have a small technical issue . . ."

"Which is?"

"There's no one here with authority to marry us."

"Hmm . . . I see. Well—you're the ranking military authority in this community."

"Yes . . ."

"Given the circumstances of the recent battle as well as the serious situation in general, I think a declaration of marshal law would be in order."

The Commander started to smile as he figured out Tag's plan.

"And," Tag continued, "with such authority, you're within your rights to appoint a designated civilian member to conduct business as necessary for the well-being of your community—including the ability to conduct wedding ceremonies."

By the time he finished, Cletus and Nirva were beaming back at him. "I can see the logic of his proposition," Cletus agreed, grinning at Nirva.

"Perhaps, you should name him!" She laughed, her delight obvious.

"Yes! How about Administrator Tag, Chief Civil Authority of these parts?"

"I appreciate it, but my friends and I may be leaving in the near future—if things go our way . . ."

"We know—still, the idea is a good one!" Cletus thought for a moment. "We only need to pick the right candidate—doing so will free me up to continue the military end of things. We have a long way to go before this fight is over . . ."

"What about Kirv," Nirva prompted. "He's a man of the land, and a solid family man. He's well connected with the farming community, many of whom came with us—and, his operation always produced well, and my dealings with him were honest and straightforward."

Cletus rubbed his chin considering the notion. He

looked over at Tag who nodded his agreement.

"Works for me! I'll talk with him after my meeting with Tag . . ."

Nirva gave him a hug, and a wink to Tag. "I'll leave you gentlemen to it . . ."

As Nirva left, the two men walked along the riverbank. "There truly is a long way to go to win back our world," Cletus commented. "What happened here in the last few days is only a beginning . . ."

"True—but what a hell of a beginning! A revolt and moving firefights, culminating in a set piece battle? It's classic, really."

"If we can only repeat it . . ."

"Agreed—that's the trick."

Tag stopped, looking at Cletus. "Get this—the canceling devices have an added benefit rendering the Vicalla weapons permanently neutered." He paused, thinking of what he was about to say. "This changes your whole approach—don't fight the big battle, trying to cancel out their weapons on the field when engaging them. Instead, send out special teams to covertly approach Vicalla strongholds and forces in the field. Get close enough and zap their weapons systems—while they're attempting to figure out what the hell is going on, they'll start to panic. Then you move in—that way, you'll keep your losses down to a fraction of what they've been so far . . ."

Cletus examined him closely. "I approve—when do you go in on the first attempt?"

"Whoa! I'm just strategizing here, that's all!"

"No—you planned a perfect covert mission. So, that makes you the lead on the first one. A test, as it were . . ."

"Clearly," Tag mumbled, "I need to learn to keep my mouth shut!"

\*\*\*\*

"You did what?"

"Well, it kind of happened by accident . . ."

"Yeah, sure . . ."

"No, really—I simply proposed using a different tactic, and before I knew it, I'm to lead a sortie to test it out. It's not my fault . . ."

"Right." Devin shot the 'don't get me involved' look in Tag's direction.

Claire sat, watching him squirm as he tried to justify his mission to Rose, who was a tad upset. "Look," Rose pointed out, "we've been low key in this world, not getting our noses too deep into things—at least until the end of the battle. And, we survived—now, you virtually volunteered for a mission which has a high risk factor?"

"Yes, I agree—it's been a different kind of experience from the last world. Here, I feel we helped to do our share—but, Cletus would like me to try this new move on the Lizards and, if it works, then a tremendous amount of humans will be saved to achieve success. There are more territories and Vicalla to deal with—and, if they bring in more troops from off-planet, they need techniques to deal with that."

She stared at him for a bit, enough to make him start to feel more uncomfortable. "Okay—describe the mission."

He took heart from the fact she wanted details. Perhaps, there would be progress. "The idea is to take a team as well as several anti-Wave tech canceling devices—the group should be small enough to minimize the chances of detection, yet large enough to provide security if we encounter a smaller enemy unit. But, the idea isn't confrontation—rather a totally covert operation. Sneak in, turn on the devices, zap their weapons, then get out of there. If the Vicalla never knew we were even there, bonus points . . ."

"What's the target?"

"Cletus figured it should be the headquarters of the western force involved in the battle. They suffered fewer losses, yet they were hurt in the fight. The weapons they had in the field should already be toast, so it makes sense to go after their base. We'll neutralize their other weapons while they're weakened, then Force Cletus can go in and mop up survivors."

"Is the intent to penetrate their headquarters, or sit outside and flip a switch?"

Tag hesitated, but he had to be honest. "That's the thing—we know in the open the devices work well with an effective range of half a mile. However, this is a test to see what happens when the target weapons and defensive equipment are behind cover—an armory, for example. Will the walls shield the weapons from the device? Obviously, we don't have structures with thick walls here to test it. That said, the scientists in Aaron's compound found the underground complex shortens the range of the devices, but they still work. We're not sure what happens with walls built of various materials . . ."

Silence.

"Who'll go on the mission?"

"The Commander told me to pick my own team, and set up whatever parameters for the mission I feel are appropriate."

Again, silence.

Tag figured it was lucky for Cletus he wasn't standing there at the moment, or else he'd have some explaining to do. "I had quite a few volunteers—it'll be a chore to select, and keep the numbers down . . ."

By the steely look in Rose's eyes, Tag figured maybe it wasn't a good idea to have spoken to others first. "Sorry—I needed to see if there were enough people willing to go. I want individuals to decide for themselves, not be told to go. Everyone here has gone through a traumatic time in the recent battle, and it's hard to tell who will be up for another potential go around with the Vicalla so soon after the last one." His explanation seemed to mollify her a bit, so he hurried to answer her original question. "Reese, Logan, Bodine, and Drey volunteered, as well as Breeze from Aaron's security detachment—they'll observe the results, and report back to the scientists. Cletus suggested his man, Miller, who was a former Special Forces Recon scout, and who operates well on point."

No one said anything until Devin took the reins. "So— while you're seeing the sights at the Vicalla resort, what am I supposed to be doing?" There was a bit of an edge to his tone.

Not insensitive to the issue of leaving him out, Tag explained. "I didn't want to take you for granted—it's something I was going to discuss."

"Which we are doing at the moment—if you go on your own, Rose will have my ass. I'd rather face the Vicalla . . ."

He glanced at Rose who smiled sweetly, confirming he did the right thing by having Tag's back. Devin was reluctant to look at Claire, but, after a few seconds, he felt her tucking her arm into his, giving it a squeeze.

Tag looked at each of the girls. "I'll appreciate your staying in camp to help out—I'm trying to keep the numbers down on this mission."

Each of them nodded, although he figured there might be a private discussion with Rose in the offing.

"You might consider one more," Devin suggested. "I'll have to talk to him first—Prac was the other nighttime patrol leader when I was with Cletus's people on the way down here. He's very good, plus I can see his leading future missions. It'll be helpful for him to see what's up on this test run . . ."

"Sounds reasonable—will you ask him?"

"Check—when is this shindig happening?"

"I'm thinking tomorrow night. I understand it's about a five-hour trip to the target, so if we leave in the late afternoon and get close just as it's turning dark, then we can reconnoiter before we take action."

Devin scratched his head. "I have a question . . ."

"What?"

"How do we know if this is going to work on the Wave tech stuff inside their headquarters? I mean, we need to test it for success, right?"

Tag hesitated. He hoped to discuss the issue on the trail. "Well, that's the trick—someone will have to go inside."

Rose's voice went up an octave from normal. "Tag!"

# Chapter Thirty-four

"Are you entirely sure you're talking to the right person? I'm just a farmer . . ." Kirv questioned why he was the right person for Tag's plan.

"There's nothing the matter with that kind of background—in fact, it's helpful. You know from years of experience what it takes to start a process to see it all the way through to create something, then share it with others. Not everyone can do those sorts of things . . ."

At first, he eyeballed the Commander standing in front of him, then shifted his gaze to Glade who smiled back and gave him a nod of encouragement. Then he glanced at Millie who was slightly wide-eyed at the prospect of her father's being someone of authority over more than just her.

Focusing again on Cletus, he finally shrugged. "Well,

if you truly think this is going to work, I'll give it a shot."

"Outstanding!" The Commander beamed at the farmer's response. "I'd like to gather everyone together tonight to make the announcement. It's time I address all of our people to talk about what they achieved together in the battle, as well as where we go from here . . ."

\*\*\*\*

While it was still light, the night patrol readied to leave after everyone's evening meal. There was an open area large enough to accommodate the surviving community's depleted population at the bottom of the valley next to the river, but, even though new people joined since the battle, they were still short of their original numbers.

Cletus mounted a large rock outcropping half-buried in the ground so he could survey his people, making it easier for them to see him. In the foreground, he spotted his intended wife, and next to her were Tag, Devin, Rose, and Claire. On the other side, Kirv and his family stood looking up at him.

"We've been on a journey together," he began. "A short time ago, most of us were slaves tasked with doing whatever the tyrannical Vicalla wanted since their conquest of our planet—you joined me in throwing off that burden by fighting back. We traveled a great distance to get to this beautiful place, to make it our new home. Many people joined us along the way, and we made a common cause together in our mission to remain free like all of us were eight years ago." He paused to let his words sink in.

"In the last several days, we were called upon to make a choice—run away, or stand to defend our new home. To fight against the oppression. A great many of us died for that purpose, yet none of those deaths were in vain. Today, survivors stand free, ready to continue the struggle to rid ourselves of the Vicalla. We honor those who fell in that cause—now, however, is the time to move against the enemy while they're weakened. We must be relentless in the fight against them, letting them know they'll pay in blood for every wrong action they took against us . . ."

He had everyone's undivided attention.

"We're planning the next steps by taking action against the Vicalla, and I encourage new arrivals to join us to increase our numbers. As a means to bring further order to our community and, after consulting with a few people I respect greatly, we determined it will be beneficial for us to have a civilian authority to oversee us while I focus solely on military matters. Therefore, with the authority I have as your Commander, I appointed an Administrator—he will possess the same level of authority as mine, only on the civic side of things."

He looked down and smiled.

"I ask Kirv Lingar to come up, and join me . . ."

He waited while the farmer mounted the rock, and

stood beside him.

"Kirv agreed to take on the role of Administrator, and I expect all of you to provide the same level of respect and support as you have given to me. Knowing we have a good, responsible person governing our community allows me peace of mind—and, with your help, I'll direct my full attention to liberating more of our territory."

"Let's be thankful we survived, able to build a new home for ourselves. There's a long way to go to defeat the Vicalla, but I'm confident—if we set a high standard here and conduct ourselves with dignity—others in our world will join us. Together, we will eventually overcome what the Vicalla did to us. It's only a question of determination to see it through." He paused, taking a moment to survey his people. "Are you ready to join Kirv and me?"

An affirmative shout resounded through the valley. "Alright! Time to move!"

He and Kirv climbed down from the rock, greeted at the bottom by family and friends, and Tag shook hands with both. "Well done, Cletus—your people are behind you." He turned to Kirv who stood with his arm around Glade. "I'll miss the old Kirv," he admitted. "Now, it's 'Grand Pooba' and genuflecting whenever I'm in your esteemed presence."

Tag could have sworn he saw a flush creeping up Kirv's neck. "I'm kidding—you'll make a great leader. People are naturally drawn to you, and they'll listen to what you have to say. That's all anyone can ask . . ."

Kirv nodded his thanks and opened his mouth to respond before Glade cut him off. "All of this is fine," she commented, "as long as he understands who the real boss is on the home front!"

****

By early evening, light shining through the jungle began to fail, and the team stayed just within the perimeter of cover as they surveyed the target. The Southern Regional Vicalla headquarters was extensive, although smaller than they expected. Observing the comings and goings for the last hour, it was obvious the Lizards' numbers were substantially reduced from battle losses.

Thinking of all possible cover positions in the approach to the HQ, Tag moved further into the jungle with his team. Once everyone formed a semi-circle around him, he took time to meet the eyes of the other eight individuals on the mission with him. "Okay—as you know, we have three devices with us. Now that I've seen the layout of the Vicalla headquarters compound, here's what we're going to do—we divide into three, two-person teams. Three teams will consist of an operator of a Wave tech canceling device, accompanied by another fighter for security. We need the devices set up within two hundred yards of the perimeter wall of the compound, so let's cover the near side and each flank. We'll leave the far side alone. The fourth team will have three members . . ."

"What's the fourth team doing," Reese asked.

"Well, other than slacking off while the rest of you are working, they'll approach the headquarters perimeter, penetrate it, then monitor the effects of the Wave tech canceling devices."

"How exactly," Prac asked, "will that team monitor the effects? The only way would be for a Lizard to try using his weapon to see if it works . . ."

Tag smiled. "Exactly. Team Four will have to pick a fight with a Vicalla to see if they get blown away . . ."

That said it all.

Everyone understood where the real danger lay in their current mission.

"Alright—here's how it works. The three teams with the devices are as follows—Team One is Logan and Drey, and they'll take the left side of the compound. Team Two is Bodine and Breeze—you'll be on the right. Team Three consists of Devin and Prac to cover the center." Tag saved Reese and Miller—both former Special Forces Recon soldiers—to accompany him into the compound where the action would start.

He continued. "The first three teams can sort out between themselves who will be the device operator, and who will be the security person. Each of you will be armed, and you'll need to review how the devices work should one of you go down. It'll be dark when we leave jungle cover, so I want you to go back to the edge, scoping out the route you plan to take. Once in position, turn on each device—that part doesn't require any coordination since, at that stage, the Lizards won't know anything is going on . . ."

"Once Team Four is inside the Vicalla perimeter, we'll set up a situation to instigate a confrontation. This is where it'll get interesting—if all goes well, Lizards will be cursing non-functioning weapons as we beat a hasty retreat. If, on the other hand, the devices don't penetrate the compound walls, then yours truly and my two amigos are in for a nasty time of it."

He again made eye contact with each member of the

first three teams. "Once you hear the action start inside the compound, each team is to turn off their devices and return to this rally point—unless Vicalla response prevents you from doing so. Then proceed back home as best you can—don't wait for the others. If the enemy isn't pressing outside of their compound, wait only fifteen minutes for Team Four to arrive. If we don't, then leave ASAP—and don't stop until you're home." Tag paused. "Any questions?"

None.

"Okay—go up and have another look, and we'll jump off as soon as it's completely dark. Everyone do a weapons and gear check, and give the devices a once-over. We want everything ready to go. Good luck . . ."

\*\*\*\*

"They must be in position by now." Tag's voice was nothing more than a whisper.

"Agreed . . ."

"Okay, then—let's breach this sucker!"

By design, Miller led. His previous job in Special Forces Recon was scout and point man, and he knew his business. Tag figured if he had someone with that kind of expertise, it would be foolish not to use him to the fullest extent. And, where they were about to enter, they'd need experience and luck.

Tag went next with Reese bringing up the rear to cover their six. Although he saw plenty of action within the last several months on several versions of Earth, it was nice to be in the company of two former professional soldiers who had highly-specialized training for action in the field.

The outer wall was fifteen feet high, a gate anchoring each of the four directions, and their approach in the dark was uneventful as Miller led them to the southwest corner of the perimeter. Equipped with a rope and small grappling hook, once they determined an unoccupied area of the wall, the scout cast the rope, successfully catching an edge of the stone wall—seconds later, he scrambled up and disappeared over the top. Within a few moments, he gave the rope a tug, indicating the way was clear for the other two members of the team to join him. Tag was next, then Reese—when they reached the top, each stayed low to minimize their silhouettes.

The top of the wall was about four feet wide, providing a walkway for patrol guards. Understanding one of the Lizards could pass by at any time, they drew up the scaling rope, not wanting to leave evidence of their arrival. To negotiate their descent on the interior side into the compound, Tag and Reese hand-lowered Miller as far as they could, allowing him drop to the ground—his landing made minimal noise, and didn't seem to attract attention. By then, they were fifty yards away from the nearest structure which was dimly outlined by an exterior light in one corner.

A strong man, Reese could handle lowering Tag to the point of letting him go, and he landed lightly with knees slightly bent to absorb the impact. Two men on the ground, Miller and Tag waited for Reese, each scanning a quadrant from their position. Crouched in the shadows, they were essentially invisible to anyone without a light source.

They heard Reese land with a grunt and a stifled expletive.

"You okay?" Tag's voice was barely a whisper.

"Yeah—I just twisted my ankle. I'll be fine—lead on!"

Tag tapped Miller on the shoulder. "Let's try for the closest building—if we can isolate one of the Lizards and take him out, we can test the weapon."

Without a word, Miller moved out with Tag following, and Reese trailing.

\*\*\*\*

The alarm shrieked, immediately drawing the attention of one of two security guards stationed in the control room. He checked the appropriate camera, adjusting the angle and sensor frequency to determine if a small animal were triggering it. The infrared indicated three larger forms with bipedal movement in the southwest corner of the compound, and the guard signaled the officer of the night watch—a breach occurred.

Within seconds, alarms blared outside the buildings as high intensity searchlights switched on—suddenly, the dark corners of the compound were revealed.

The trio of humans reached the edge of the nearest building when everything cut loose, each flattening himself against the wall, observing the Vicalla response. With no need for quiet, Tag yelled to be heard over the alarm. "As we suspected, the place is rigged for detecting intrusions—we should be seeing Lizards coming to investigate . . ."

Sure enough within a minute of the alarm, four Vicalla guards emerged, two from each side.

"Here goes your test," Reese yelled. "I'll take the ones on the right . . ."

Tag and Miller focused on the guards to the left.

\*\*\*\*

Outside the walls, human Teams One through Three heard the racket inside, each thankful their roles consisted of simply firing up the canceling devices and pointing them at the headquarters compound. Outside lights directed beyond the walled complex came on, but Teams One and Three had sufficient natural cover to remain undetected.

Team Two sat exposed on flat ground with a portion of one light cone partially illuminating their position. Bodine and Breeze tried shrinking down to ground level to minimize their outlines, but a careful check by one of the enemy would likely spot them. Breeze put the device down in front of her and drew her weapon, joining Bodine in scanning the area in front of them.

In an unexpected turn, the outside team received first enemy action—a guard on the wall spotted what he thought were intruders. He raised his weapon, pulling the trigger to discharge a surge from the Wave tech rifle. Nothing. He checked to see if the charge magazine were empty—it appeared to be full, yet the weapon wouldn't discharge. He tried to fire it again, without effect.

That was as far as he got.

Bodine noticed the guard's efforts, and decided to take him out. A good marksman, Bodine had little trouble drawing a bead on the guard standing on the wall, backlit by lights from the compound's interior.

His first shot was all it took.

\*\*\*\*

He saw both guards aim their weapons, attempting to fire at him with no effect. In one motion, Reese turned and fired. The Lizard on his left went down and, before he could line up the second one, the guard crashed into him knocking Reese over on his bad ankle. The guard continued forward, ready to take on the other two humans facing away from him.

Tag was engaged with one of the Lizards struggling with his weapon, the Lizard rounding the corner so quick Tag didn't get a chance to fire a shot. Now, the beast was trying to bludgeon him with his weapon, wielding it as a club. Tag dodged both blows and was preparing to connect with a roundhouse kick, when he suddenly dropped to the ground—call it a sixth sense. Coming from behind him, the blade from the enormous Lizard's combat knife cut through the air where his head was a moment before!

He swiveled on the ground, kicked out, and connected from behind into the attacker's left leg, causing the Lizard to lose his balance. Fortunately, the move catapulted him into the original guard accosting Tag from the front. While the two Lizards attempted to disentangle themselves, Tag quickly gained his feet—but, he couldn't find his weapon in the shadows.

That meant hand-to-hand combat.

The two Lizards disengaged from each other, turning to face Tag. Luckily, the attacker from behind was closer, moving independently from the other, giving Tag the opportunity to engage them separately for at least a few seconds.

The beast lunged again with the spear-like knife. Fortunately, the benefits of being huge compared to his human opponent were counterbalanced by his slowness, and the point of the knife sliced through nothing but air. The human abruptly moved out of the way with incredible agility before the guard could retract his weapon—then the human leapt in the air in a spinning maneuver and, with his right leg trailing, whipped his foot into the chin of the Lizard. Rocked by the impact, the stunned guard wobbled for a few moments before a second leg strike to one of his knees caused him to collapse.

The attack by the first guard—now on the ground—conveniently blocked the advance of the second guard. Still wielding his inoperable Wave tech rifle as a club, he took an ineffectual swing at the human who easily moved out of the way. But, Tag knew he didn't have long before more of them started arriving, and his team would be overwhelmed. In his peripheral vision, he could tell Miller was still upright and engaged with his Vicalla opponent, but he didn't have time to check out what happened to Reese.

Tag avoided another swing at his head, and the guard's follow-through caused him to slam the end of his rifle into the side of the building. His exposed right side gave Tag an easy opportunity to land a kick which only elicited a grunt. On the recoil, as the guard turned to face his smaller opponent, another kick landed in the middle of his torso with little effect—it was the guard's misfortune he decided to stop and laugh.

The Lizard saw the young human male nod his head. Then, with dizzying speed, Tag spun to his right, whipping a leg kick to the side of the Lizard's left knee followed by another whipping kick to the exact same spot. The knee joint failed, and the Lizard toppled over, landing on his left side, his face partially on the ground. Struggling to get up, three successive strikes to the neck caused the Lizard to lose consciousness.

Tag turned to see Miller still upright, but pinned against the wall about to be struck by the massive hand of his opponent. But, before Tag could intervene, a shot rang out, staggering the guard.

A second shot put him down.

Tag turned to see Reese lower his rifle, and hobble over to them.

"Well," Reese observed, "at least we know the canceling devices work. Can we go home now?"

Tag grinned. "How's the ankle?"

"When the dirtbag Lizard ran me over, I twisted it again. I'm not sure if it's a sprain, or I busted something—either way, I'm not going anywhere fast on my own."

"Miller, help me get him over to the outside wall, and let's get the hell out of here!"

# Chapter Thirty-five

Awakened by something going on in the compound, Commander Talak tried getting through to the Security Detachment Office—the fools weren't answering. Swearing, he slammed down the communicator, got out of bed, walked to the anteroom outside of his quarters, and started yelling down the corridor.

Finally, a junior officer came running, halting in front of him.

"Well?"

"There's been a breach into the complex, Sir."

"And?"

"I'm not sure, Sir."

"Find out, and report back. Call out all the guards and troop detachments and, whatever it is, stop it!"

"Yes, Sir!" The officer scrambled down the corridor to comply with the order.

Talak dressed quickly and grabbed a weapon from the rack outside his office, then made his way downstairs to the building entrance. Just as he arrived, Commander Beal and Zarn joined him.

"Is this a general attack," Beal asked.

Talak felt awkward not being able to advise him of the status of things in his own headquarters' complex. "I don't know yet—I just woke up . . ."

All three went outside, taking in the sounds of gunshots, alarms blaring, and searchlights moving around the inside and outside of the complex.

"There are no operating Wave tech weapons," Zarn pointed out. "All we can hear is human weapons being fired. They must have brought their devices here—we may not have any functional weapons, or working defensive shielding."

Talak swore again.

They discussed human countermeasures since the recent battle, and the development threatening everything the Vicalla built. Being exposed in such a fashion put them at huge risk, negating the means to properly defend themselves from the millions of humans still left on the conquered planet.

Talak called to an officer. "Sub-Commander, are you having trouble with our weapons?"

The frazzled Lizard nodded. "Yes, Sir—for some reason they don't work."

"Forget them—pass the word to use non-Wave tech weapons. Also, bring up the explosive ordnance and mortars—they should work just fine. Start laying down fire on the outside of the wall in case we have an attack in numbers coming. Get going!"

"Yes, Sir!" The officer double-timed it, yelling at troopers as he passed.

"Good choice using the explosive stuff," Beal commented. "They can't affect simpler weapons . . ."

\*\*\*\*

The teams started to pull back when the first of the explosions occurred outside the complex—Team Two, Bodine and Breeze, were already moving when the mortar round landed nearby. Shooting blindly, the Lizards scored a near hit, knocking both of them off of their feet. "Don't move!" Bodine yelled. "There'll be more coming!"

On cue, three more deafening explosions covered them with dirt and debris, both clinging to each other wondering which would be the one to kill them.

\*\*\*\*

Team One—Logan and Drey—pulled out first from the left side of the complex, effectively out of range when the first of the mortar rounds started to land near their former position. Fortunately, they moved just in time, making it back to the rally point.

Team Three drew the short straw.

Devin and Prac were doing their best to dodge through rounds landing around them, both thinking it was surprising the Lizards had so many conventional weapons—clearly, the canceling devices worked since there were no distinctive sounds of the Vicalla's Wave tech weapons. Suddenly, as they ran for their lives, mortar rounds bracketed the two men, engulfing them in smoke and dust—neither made it to the other side.

Team Four struggled to clear the HQ complex's inner courtyard. Like a kicked-over anthill, Vicalla ran amok inside their walls looking for intruders, and the only thing saving the team were shadows created by moving searchlights. If they were caught in one? Well, things could get dicey.

Reese leaned heavily on Tag and Miller, the trio dodging searchlights while trying to get back to the corner of the complex to scale the wall to safety. The ex-Special Forces Recon leader could put little weight on his ankle, rendering him incapable of walking on his own. "Leave me," he suggested through clenched teeth. "I'm slowing you down."

Miller ignored him.

"Like you'd leave one of us if the situation were reversed. Why don't you focus on looking out for Lizards while we get you over to the wall?" Tag knew there was no way in hell he was going to leave Reese to fend for himself.

So, that ended the conversation. Reese figured the kid had a lot of grit and wouldn't put up with any more shit, so he dropped it.

Finally, they made it to the wall—now, to get the injured man up and over. Miller let go, unwinding a coil of rope with a grappling hook on the end from around his shoulders. On the second toss, the hook caught, and he tightened it enough to carry a grown man's weight. "I'll go up first, then Reese. I'll stay on top, and help him from there . . ."

Tag agreed. "Sounds good—I'll handle his butt end from down here."

The scout quickly climbed the rope, disappearing as he reached the top, the outline of his head and one arm extending downward barely visible.

Tag slapped Reese on the shoulder. "Okay—up you go. I'll boost from here."

"Ha! Watch me do this on my own . . ."

"Well, okay—but I'm not catching you, if you fall."

No response. Hand-over-hand, the older man started up the rope, muscling up the wall without putting weight on his injured leg, impressing Tag by the display of raw strength.

Miller signaled Reese made it to the top by yanking on the rope, and Tag started up as one of the searchlights finally succeeded in capturing him in its beam. If Vicalla Wave tech weapons were working, he would have been a large spatter of organic material on the wall. As it was, they went apeshit when they spotted him—another searchlight joined the first, revealing his form highlighted against the wall.

Tag climbed as fast as he could, making it to the top walkway where he joined Miller who had a second rope going over the far side. Reese was in the process of trying to get over the edge of the wall, bad leg and all—as soon as he saw Tag on the way up, he started lowering himself down the other side. On the outside of the wall, it didn't look promising. Searchlights lit up the dark while mortar shells rained down—an apocalyptic sight.

After reaching the top, Tag pulled up the first rope to preclude a Lizard's following him up the line—however, because they knew where they were, he expected them to start appearing along the top of the wall from either direction.

They were in deep trouble.

It was, at least, some comfort when Tag thought about the others. *With their part of the mission requiring them to remain outside the complex, the other teams should've made it back without too much trouble . . .*

At that moment, Logan and Drey of Team One were waiting, wondering.

They stood alone at the jungle rally point.

****

"Something's wrong!"

Claire focused on her friend. "What's up?"

Rose shuddered slightly. "I have a bad feeling there are problems . . ."

"You were dozing off—do you think it was a dream?"

Rose shook her head. "I don't think so—it was vivid. Real. Different from a dream . . ." She tried to make out her friend's features in the dark. "Claire—I'm scared . . ."

Claire hugged her, hoping doing so would be reassuring. "They'll be okay—they're tough, and they can roll with the punches. You'll see . . ."

But, saying it and believing it were two different things.

****

Mortar explosions moved away from their position, allowing for a momentary reprieve to get away. Bodine protected Breeze with his body on top of hers as shells detonated around them—now, however, she wasn't sure if he were dead or alive.

Nudging him, she heard a murmur, but couldn't make out the words. "What?"

"I said, don't rush me, woman. How often will I get a chance to be this close to you?"

Stunned by the comment, it took her a few seconds to comprehend. "You have to be kidding me! We're in the middle of getting our butts blown off, and you're trying to get romantic?"

"It's lame, I know—but I haven't grabbed your attention up until now."

"Well, you certainly have it! Get me the hell out of here and we'll talk about this later!"

"Deal . . ." He stood, pulling her up, and immediately both headed for jungle cover.

Team Two was on the move.

****

Members of Team Four descended the outer side of the southwest corner of the Vicalla's Headquarters Complex, Reese moving slowly as he approached the ground to protect his damaged ankle. Once at the bottom, he pulled his rifle off of his shoulder, covering the area while his companions lowered themselves.

Tag and Miller stood at Reese's sides, supporting some of his weight, and took off at a half run, allowing Reese to make contact with the ground about every eight feet. They made it most of the way to the tree line before a Vicalla searchlight honed in on them—thankfully, they breached the jungle perimeter as the first shells landed short of their position. Even though navigating the thick foliage with three abreast, they didn't pause. The unspoken imperative was to get as deep into the jungle as possible to avoid detection, as well as have a shell land too close.

Team Four made it.

\*\*\*\*

Still at the rally point deep in the jungle, Team One remained in place—more than twenty minutes passed, and no one else showed. "Tag said to wait fifteen minutes," Logan commented. "It's been longer than that—should we go?"

"Hell, no!" Drey didn't care what the order was, someone simply had to show up—all of them couldn't be gone!

"I don't want to leave either—I just thought I'd ask."

"Let's wait to see what happens. We're in pretty good cover, making it hard for the Lizards to find us. With all the crap going on around their headquarters, I really doubt they want to traipse around the jungle in the dark not knowing how many of us are out here."

Logan considered the point. "Smart thinking—I agree."

"Well, I won't forget you said that—I'll remind you of it later . . ."

\*\*\*\*

Explosions increasingly infrequent, Logan and Drey drew their weapons as they heard someone approach.

"Try not to shoot the good guys, okay?"

Logan and Drey relaxed. "Come on in, Tag . . ."

As they approached, a dim outline of three shapes appeared close together, two helping one between them. When they arrived in the small clearing, they eased Reese to the jungle floor.

"The others?" Tag scanned the area as he asked the question.

"You're it so far . . ."

"Aren't you supposed to be gone by now?"

"It's so dark in here," Drey answered, "you can't tell what time it is, and we don't have a watch between us."

Tag looked at her. "That's lame . . ."

"True," she admitted. "But, there it is . . ."

# Chapter Thirty-six

"What do mean you can't find any of them? My headquarters is penetrated. None of our Wave tech weapons work, and you used up nearly forty percent of our mortars and explosives without dead enemies to show for it!"

The Sub-Commander winced slightly at the tongue-lashing, especially because he felt the same way before Commander Talak started in on him.

"Get out! Find me something, or I'll replace you with someone who can!"

When the officer left and Talak was alone pacing his office, he let go of the bluster. Now, he was truly worried—other than a few patrols in the field still equipped with functional weapons, the recent battle and attack that night rendered all of his advanced weaponry useless.

Now, he was desperate.

Not only that, the Vicalla in Talak's and Beal's territories were on a level playing field with the humans.

\*\*\*\*

*C'mon, man—where are you?*

Tag stood a hundred feet away from the others so he could clearly hear the forest sounds. Everything seemed normal—night creatures finished their rounds before the coming daylight broke through into the jungle, and waiting was starting to take its toll.

They'd been through a lot together during the past few months, but, somehow, he always knew Devin would get through—now, Tag wasn't so sure, and serious worry began to nag at him. Other members of the mission were resting, doctoring assorted wounds and, unfortunately, nothing much could be done for Reese's ankle at the moment. *Another five minutes—if he doesn't show up, I'm not standing around any longer, doing nothing.*

Five minutes came and went. Keeping his promise to himself, Tag proceeded along the trail leading to Vicalla headquarters, acutely alert to anything moving. Three-quarters of the way back to the scene of the recent action, he heard someone coming toward him on the trail. At least, he could see a little as light appeared on the jungle floor, affording him a restricted view.

He readied his rifle just in case.

The outline of the form coming toward him wasn't a Lizard. Waiting a few seconds, he slowly pushed forward until he saw what he'd been wishing for—Devin. He could hardly walk, and seemed on the edge of collapse as Tag shouldered his rifle and sprinted toward his friend.

Devin raised his head, trying to focus on who was talking to him. Finally, it registered. "Looks like I made it."

"You sure did—the others are about twenty minutes away. Can you make it that far?" In the increasing light, Tag could see his friend was a mess. Half of his shirt looked as if it had been blown off, blood oozing down his chest and arms from multiple lacerations. Hair covered in dirt and debris, the left side of his face was scorched and cut. One eyebrow was partially gone. Small holes in his pants were bloodstained.

Tag's friend barely survived.

But, survive, he did—Devin was still walking and talking, although, from the sound of it, he was pretty scrambled. Despite all of it, however, he found his way back down the trail heading in the right direction toward the rally point.

Tag figured he knew the answer, but asked anyway. "Hey, Devin . . . what about Prac, your team member?"

Devin stared at him for a bit, and Tag didn't know if he could answer. Finally, he did.

"I tried to bring Prac back, but I couldn't carry all

the pieces, so I left him there. It pisses me off . . ."

He hesitated at Devin's news. "I know—that's okay. When Cletus has his force go back there, they'll take care of Prac for you . . ."

Devin nodded. Tag's suggestion was sufficient . . .

\*\*\*\*

What took five hours from their base to the Vicalla Headquarters at the beginning of the mission, they spent the better part of two days getting home with the wounded. Passing the outer sentries, they entered their home base as everyone rushed to help. Eventually, they were taken for medical care, if needed—for most of them, however, it was a matter of recovering from exhaustion. Satisfied his people would be well cared for, Tag looked for the girls.

He found them down by the river, washing clothes. Rose first caught sight of him and, seeing his condition, she put her hand to her mouth and stood up. Claire saw her move as well as her reaction, then looked behind her to see Tag standing alone. A cold dagger of fear pierced her insides—Devin should be standing beside him.

Stunned, it was an effort for her to stand.

Tag approached them, going to Claire first—he saw how pale she turned. "I brought him back—he's banged up, but he's here. The medical people are checking him over right now."

She clung to him, crying. Rose hugged her from behind, and the three of them stayed that way until Claire recovered.

Tag put a hand under her chin and raised her head up to check if she were really okay. "Would you like us to walk you over there?"

She managed a smile. "No, I'm okay now—you greet Rose properly." With that, she headed toward the medical shelter, but, before she went too far, she stopped, and turned. "Tag?"

"Yeah?"

"Thank you for bringing him back to me, even if he's dinged up..."

"Anytime..."

She continued on, and he turned his full attention back to Rose who had her arms around him. "Sorry—I thought we should get Claire straightened out first..."

"As you should have—you're here, in one piece, and safe. That's all I care about..."

She buried her head on his shoulder and hugged him fiercely.

At the moment, nothing else mattered.

****

"Thank you for leading the mission—it was an important thing to learn."

"You're welcome. It was costly, but I agree it's something you needed to know. Now, you can move forward with confidence."

"Yes—then spread the word as far as we can so others can benefit."

"It's still going to be a long road back . . ."

"True—it was worth fighting for . . ."

Tag and Commander Cletus sat on rocks by the river the morning after the return of surviving members. "Now that the complex has been breached, the Vicalla are vulnerable, and they'll call for help from off-planet. A reinvasion is possible, you know . . ."

The Commander thought about Tag's observation before answering. "I know—I considered it also. Truth is, I'd do the same thing if I were in their position. There have to be millions of us remaining on the planet, and reports from our region indicate not many of them are left to control us."

"The big question is how soon can they get more troops here . . ."

"Agreed . . ."

"And, can they adapt and defeat our Wave tech canceling device, or work around it."

The big man nodded. "Yes—that's the important factor, isn't it? How long can we hold the advantage?"

"You still have Aaron's scientists..."

Cletus looked at him. "I spoke with him while you were away—they're hard at work perfecting the device, and its next generation. Guess what their request was?"

Tag shook his head, having no idea.

"They want us to take out a headquarters, capture Vicalla space-worthy airships, then mount the canceling devices on them. And, they're working hard to extend the effective range to a hundred miles or so—the idea is to zap any arriving Vicalla ships as they get close to Earth, rendering their offensive and defensive technology useless. It's the previous advantage they had which allowed them to roll over us so easily in the first invasion. Take that away, and it's a whole new ballgame..."

"Wow! That'll be awesome!"

Both were quiet for a while considering the prospects of the coming human initiative to free their planet. Eventually, the Commander broke the silence.

"There's another matter..."

Tag studied the older man, recognizing his hesitation.

"While you were away, one of our night patrols discovered something which will be of acute interest to you and your friends—and, as an aside, I'm happy to hear Devin will be okay. The medical people say he's going to be fine. Anyway, back to my original point—the patrol discovered what I think brought you here. The portal..."

Tag immediately perked up!

"I thought that would pique your interest . . ."

"It certainly does! Where?"

"Close by in a little valley a couple of ridgelines over to the southwest . . ."

"When?" Tag's concern was it may already be gone.

"Two nights ago—apparently, it wasn't too hard to find since it was a bright and shimmering beacon. It caught their attention right away . . ."

Cletus noticed the edge of concern on Tag's face. "You'll be pleased to know, it's still there—at least, the last time a patrol swung by. I had them check on it regularly, figuring you'd want to know."

"Thanks, Commander. The others will be excited— at least I think so . . ."

"I know you've been moving from one form of Earth to another—I guess, at some point, you have to wonder where you get off the merry-go-round, and stay put."

"You're right—I've been trying to get back to my home planet, but we keep arriving elsewhere. Let's face it—there's a strong chance it may never take me back. With likely infinite possibilities, why should it?"

"You're welcome to stay with us—you've been an enormous help and, selfishly, I want you to stay. But, you have to do what's best for your group—you've earned that, and more. Just know we support whatever your decision is."

"Thanks, Cletus." Tag paused, thinking about what the Travelers possibly had before them. "I better talk to the others . . ."

"Sure—see you later . . ." As he watched the young man walk away, he saw Nirva coming. She stopped to talk briefly with Tag, giving him a hug before coming over to sit beside Cletus.

"You told him?"

"Yes . . ."

"And, they'll go?"

He looked at her. "I would in his place . . ."

They turned to watch Tag's disappearing figure around a corner of the trees.

"We'll miss him . . ."

\*\*\*\*

"There's a delay, Sir."

"What's that?"

"Off-Planet Command reports they don't presently have anyone they can send to assist. Apparently, they're committed to other planet conquests and stabilizations."

"Then tell them this planet will be lost to us. I request immediate evacuation for me and my staff." As the officer left, the Prime turned to his window. *What a beautiful world, and such a waste to give it up . . .*

****

Two days later they were ready.

The discussion was short—all wanted to go. Yes, they made friends and had been through a lot together, but it was the same on all the previous planet visits, too.

It would be a bit before he was a hundred percent, but Devin recovered enough to feel ready to challenge the portal if it were still there. Cletus had several people sitting on the site and, at last report, it still shimmered within their view.

They said goodbyes to most of their acquaintances, as well as Aaron's group. It looked as if two couples began relationships—Logan and Drey, Bodine and Breeze. Reese said goodbye at the camp since his damaged ankle prevented him from going to see them off.

It was evening by the time those accompanying the Travelers arrived at the portal site. Cletus and Nirva were there, as was Aaron. Kirv, Glade, Millie, and Grub were also there to see them off. Each took a turn saying goodbye and wishing them safe travels.

Then the Travelers faced the Commander.

"Our people," he told them, "can never truly express how grateful we are for your help and friendship. I hope you find your way home, Tag—and, as a going-away present, I thought you might like to take these along." He motioned for two of his fighters to come forward and present Tag and Devin with Wave tech rifles. "These are functional and we included extra charges for them—if the portal allows them through, you may need them wherever you end up."

Tag smiled. "Thanks, Commander—it's been an honor to serve with you. Good luck, and kick some Lizard ass . . ."

Cletus laughed, and heartily shook the offered hand.

In the background, the portal beckoned. The group turned and approached it, watching for a short time its mesmerizing swirl, changing colors, offering the promise of a vast expanse inside the opening.

Tag looked at Rose who took his hand, nodded, and stepped through the opening with him. A burst of light flashed at their entry, its intensity heightened. Within seconds, hand-in-hand, Claire and Devin stepped in. Again, the light intensified with pulsating colors, the air around those remaining charged, causing a tickling sensation on their skin.

Then, suddenly, it was over. The portal flared to its brightest point, then winked out with a loud popping sound. A sudden overpressure in the air swept by those standing close enough, their eyes struggling to overcome the sudden change of intense light to near darkness.

On their way home, most spent the time thinking about the four young people who just left.

****

The portal was as they remembered—incredible speed coupled with being encased in an energy cocoon as they moved through space on an elongated filament protected from the vast cold. It was an experience like none other . . .

Even though the Travelers made the trip multiple times, it never ever ceased to amaze. With more experience in the portal, they could pick out features of the trip which were missed on previous occasions as the newness of the experience overwhelmed the senses. Each was aware of the presence of their partner on the trip, gripping hands, and seeing them beside them. Looking at the face of another experiencing the trip, their faces reflected awe at what was happening.

Then—it was over.

Without warning, each ejected from the portal hovering a few feet off the ground. They landed untidily in bunches—although their dismount was improving slightly—Tag and Rose managing to roll clear when Devin and Claire arrived.

Devin rolled over and groaned. Still recovering from his injuries, he felt the effects more than the others.

"You're getting old, Bro . . ." Tag teased as he helped his friend to his feet. In the darkness, illuminated by the shimmering portal light, Tag could see his friend shake his head and wince. Devin's smile was more like a grimace.

Behind them, the portal flared brightly to twice its previous level, and then winked out with a swish and a popping sound. Each felt a charge in the air, same as before.

Then, darkness.

It was quite warm, similar to the jungle atmosphere they just left, and it took them a few minutes to regain their night vision.

"Well," Claire observed, "here we are again. Somewhere new. Tag—even though it's dark, I take it nothing seems familiar to you?"

Cutting off his answer, the forest reverberated with an unearthly roar of a beast none of them had ever heard. When the noise diminished, Devin looked at Tag, Rose, and Claire. "What the hell was that?"

"I have a very bad feeling about this," Claire responded.

Tag nodded. "I agree. It's no bear, cougar, or wolf, that's for sure . . ."

Again, but closer, the roar shook the surrounding trees.

"We need to get moving," Tag suggested. "I don't know what it is, but I think it's definitely more than we can handle. Everyone stick close, and let's get the hell out of here . . ."

The Travelers moved away from the sound and, for ten minutes, things seemed to be going well. Then, everyone stopped, not daring to move. Something close was panting in the expectation of a kill—then they heard a low growl in a tone and strength shaking everyone to their core. It sounded like pure evil in a living form—and it was hovering close to them in the dark.

By touch alone, Tag and Devin pushed the girls behind them away from where they figured the attack would come. Every sense focused on assessing how to stymie what was surely coming. But, waiting for and expecting it still didn't prepare them for the onslaught of the viscous beast that assaulted them. Shocked momentarily, both men reacted, bringing the Vicalla weapons to bear, opening fire. The whooshing sound of Wave tech weapons discharging matched the roar of the attacking beast, cut off suddenly as the surge hit it. A loud squeal, and then a whimpering and heavy, labored breathing which slowly diminished to silence.

"Quickly—get moving before one of its friends shows up," Tag ordered. "Something tells me they hunt in packs . . ."

It was too dark to actually run, but they made progress as quickly as they could. They hadn't gone far when another beast howled, indicating the hunt was on again.

"This really sucks—who booked tickets here?" That, from Claire.

Devin hurried them along. "Keep moving . . ."

Then, another of the beasts howled from the opposite side—they were trapped between the two. They could hear them approaching, and it wouldn't be long now.

Both men racked their weapons, and the girls made sure safeties were off their hand guns.

There was nothing left to do, but wait.

Each hovered close, seeking protection in numbers—although, from the sounds emanating around them, it wouldn't make much difference.

Then, off to their right, a voice called out. "Over here—quickly!"

They had no idea who was speaking to them, but it didn't matter—a lifeline might be out there. It was foolish not to take it.

They ran toward the voice which triggered the beasts to start hunting. They heard them crashing through the trees and bushes around them.

The voice again. "Here—get in and don't stop."

They made a minor course correction and came to a human backlit from a light source below, holding a trap door open, leading into the ground .

"Get the hell in—it's almost here!"

They didn't climb, but fell into the opening, tumbling down stairs landing in a heap at the bottom.

Above them the trap door slammed shut, followed immediately by the frustrated roar of a beast denied its prey.

Independently, the Travelers verbalized it in their heads differently—however, the thought was the same.

*What the hell did we get ourselves into this time?*

# Epilogue

"Another transition?"

A pause. "Yes—I though it prudent."

"The labors where they were are not done . . ."

"True, but predictable. Others can finish the task."

"Why this place now?"

"It's a layered situation—different, yet again."

"Are they up to the challenge?"

"We shall see. Speaking of challenges . . ."

"Ah—a continuation of the wager?"

"Only if you find the situation to your liking . . ."

"I do—it's been entertaining, so far."

"Then, the purpose is being fulfilled."

"Yes—I, too, am curious."

"About?"

"How far one in his form can be stretched . . ."

"So! You have a favorite!"

"Apparently . . ."

"Is this to be the last step?"

Another pause. "We shall see."

Nothing disturbed the medium around them during their discourse, not even a sound wave. The shimmering forms were elongated, tall, and bipedal, although they didn't use appendages as they floated above the surface.

And, everything was by thought.

Nothing else.

## ACKNOWLEDGMENTS

Writing a book is a solitary experience, but it isn't performed in a vacuum. Those around me provide the framework for allowing the process to unfold—to all of you, thank you.

More specific, an ongoing thank you to Laurie O'Neil for your excellence in editing my work.

To Jen Kramp for all of the great cover designs in the series released, so far. It's fun working with you to achieve the front cover 'feel' for each book. Your efforts won a gold medal for cover design for *Book 1, The Departure*—well done!

To Denton Craig for your outstanding proofreading skills making each book a clean read, thanks.

As always, thanks to Roxanne for keeping my day job duties rolling along smoothly.

Last, to my canine buddies who literally surround me through the writing experience, Boomer, Milo, and Breeze.

## PROFESSIONAL ACKNOWLEDGMENTS

### CHRYSALIS PUBLISHING AUTHOR SERVICES
L.A. O'Neil, Editor
www.chrysalis-pub.com
chrysalispub@gmail.com

### JEN KRAMP STUDIOS
Jen Kramp, Cover Designer
jenkramp@gmail.com

Made in the USA
Charleston, SC
25 October 2016